THE WAR OF THE ROSENS

A novel by

Janice Eidus

Behler
PUBLICATIONS

California
USA

Behler Publications
California

The War of the Rosens
A Behler Publications Book

Copyright © 2007 by Janice Eidus
Cover design by Cathy Scott – www.mbcdesigns.com
Author photograph courtesy of Denise Adler

This is a work of fiction. Names, characters, places, and incidents either are the product of the author's imagination or are used fictitiously. Any resemblance to actual persons, living or dead, events, or locales is entirely coincidental.

Library of Congress Cataloging-in-Publication Data

Eidus, Janice.
    The war of the Rosens : a novel / by Janice Eidus.
        p. cm.
    ISBN 978-1-933016-38-2 (pbk.)
    1. Daughters--Fiction. 2. Bronx (New York, N.Y.)--Fiction. 3. Domestic fiction. I. Title.

PS3555.I38W37 2007
813'.54--dc22

2007005503

FIRST PRINTING

ISBN 978-1-933016-38-2
Published by Behler Publications, LLC
Lake Forest, California
www.behlerpublications.com

Manufactured in the United States of America

Advance Praise for *THE WAR OF THE ROSENS*

"Intensely moving and fiercely intelligent. Eidus eloquently evokes the diverse voices of the adults and children of the colorful, eccentric Rosen family. She vividly captures not only the world of the Bronx in the mid-sixties, but also the world of one Jewish family struggling to survive in a harsh world charged with beauty and possibility."
~**Vivian Gornick**, author, *Fierce Attachments*

"*The War of the Rosens* is as fierce, unflinching and tender as its feisty ten-year-old heroine, Emma Rosen, who carries the weight of the world and the fate of her volatile, unpredictable family on her small shoulders. Eidus explores the timeless world of childhood—raw pain, bitter injustice, dark humor, achingly brilliant flashes of insight—and the elusive promised land of adulthood with clarity and grace."
~**Ruth Knafo Setton**, author, *The Road To Fez*

"*The War Of The Rosens*, with exquisite language and a huge heart, introduces us to Emma, a budding poet seeking answers to questions about the nature of good and evil, while struggling with an alternately brutal and loving father, a meek and "lost" mother, and a spiteful older sister. It is Emma, with a tenacious spirit and an indomitable imagination, who, through the power of love and the force of the written word, instigates her family's salvation. The novel's title is delightful irony, as it becomes clear that this family is a metaphor and microcosm not only of the world's sorrows, but also its joys. Set in the 1960's, Janice Eidus has written a novel of redemption for our time here and now."
~**Sue William Silverman**, author, *Because I Remember Terror, Father, I Remember You*

Praise for Janice Eidus

The Celibacy Club

Balancing humor and depth, [these] 19 short stories reflect the quirky voice, at once cynical and sincere, that has made Eidus a two-time winner of the O. Henry Award....Eidus ultimately turns each story into a well-conceived, finely executed and deeply moving tale.

-Publishers Weekly

Fiction Writer Janice Eidus [is one of] the "Top 10 Young Writers To Watch!"

- The Bloomsbury Review

~

Vito Loves Geraldine

...distinguished by irony, intelligence, and unexpected moments of tenderness.

-Kirkus Reviews

These are stories to mull over, their emotive range rich and their originality magnetic.

-Booklist

~

Urban Bliss

...a ruefully funny, wickedly observant take on urban angst.

-Publishers Weekly

A sharp, sassy love song to New York....

-American Book Review

~

Faithful Rebecca

Janice Eidus...possesses a fierce imagination; the book's surrealistic edge is inventive and darkly amusing...

- The New York Times Book Review

Eidus displays a wonderful ear...

- The Village Voice

For John and Alma

1

It's 1965, and the early August air is surprisingly cool, with a faint breeze; the sky, at dusk, rose-tinted. The air feels charged, defiant, as if it's deliberately flouting summer's expectations. Leo Rosen, age 40, inhales deeply and feels his chest expand. Stunning, crisp air fills his lungs.

Leo holds the hand of his ten-year-old daughter, gawky, blue eyed, freckle-faced Emma, so cute that strangers stop them on the street and say, "She should be on TV." They're waiting to cross the street from the Gun Hill Projects in the northeast Bronx, where they live, to White Plains Road, a major commercial thoroughfare bisecting the Bronx, running beneath an elevated subway line that casts a pervasive, grey shadow below.

Leo and Emma are heading to the local five-and-dime, a few blocks away, a large store nestled among smaller stores: a pet store, candy store, deli, and shoe store, all displaying their wares in slightly soiled windows.

The traffic light on the corner of Gun Hill Road is slow to change, infamous in the neighborhood for its lethargy, and Leo glances for a second behind him, not loosening his grip on Emma's hand. His gaze sweeps the buildings and grounds of the Projects, where he and his family have lived since their older daughter's birth, thirteen years before. Although he's well aware that the Projects are not beautiful, this "lower-middle-income development," built in the early 50's and consisting of six tall, factory-like red brick buildings clustered around an occasional chained-off patch of grass, he loves them, and doesn't mind their institutional look.

The Gun Hill Projects speak to him of hope, of possibility, of a life far better than the one he'd known in the dilapidated Brooklyn tenements and grimy streets of his youth, streets on which he and his sisters walked wearing the cast-off, ill-fitting clothes of neighbors' children, while his volatile parents struggled to keep a roof over all their heads.

Still, Leo is forever shaped by those streets, and proud of this fact, at the same time that he's glad to have left the streets behind. He's long had to fend for himself, and now, fervent is his belief that we're all on our own in this world, that there is no deity, no higher power, to whom we are beholden for the good things that come our way, no deity or higher power to blame or excuse for the bad.

"Individuals shape their own lives," he's fond of saying to his wife and two daughters, in the stirring, theatrical tones he'd perfected as captain of his Brooklyn high school's debating team.

As they continue to wait for the stubborn light to change, he points heavenward and declares, "Remember, Emma, there's no one up there watching out for you."

Emma has heard his No-God soapbox, his Religion-Is-The-Opiate-Of-The-People many times before. Ever so slightly, she grants him a nod, but no more than that, so that she appears neither insolent nor overly enthusiastic about his ideas. She doesn't want to risk his wrath, and she doesn't want to encourage him.

"And that includes a 'God,' who doesn't exist," his fingers describe quotation marks in the air and his voice grows weightier and more somber because he's worried—and he's not prone to worrying about his daughters, he leaves that to his wife—that Emma doesn't fully comprehend how important it is not to be seduced by religion. Whenever he brings up the subject, she's uncharacteristically silent. Usually, she's pretty feisty, not unlike himself as a young boy, always willing to voice an opinion, whether in agreement or disagreement, passionate one way or another, no matter the consequence. Yet, around this subject, so dear to his heart, Emma tends to grow silent, as if weighing words and consequences, as if too unsure, or unwilling, to take a stand.

He feels his eyes narrow and his mouth curl in disgust at her refusal to commit to his way of thinking. 'Wouldn't it be better to reach her ten-year-old intellect, to truly persuade her rather than to bully her? Her eyes are wide and earnest, and there's a hint of a private smile on her lips. Or is it a frown?

After a long moment, Emma looks away into the distance, past the stubborn red traffic light. With her free hand, she tugs at her unevenly cut, dark hair, and pushes it behind her ear. Leo marvels at her beauty, and wishes that her sister, May, was as beautiful.

Still holding Emma's hand tightly as they wait for the interminable light to change, Leo can't resist adding, "Believe me, Emma, atheists are much stronger than those who believe in God, whether they're Jews, Catholics, Muslims, or Hindus."

Tapping his foot, he's acutely aware of how didactic, even pompous, he sounds when at his most emphatic and impassioned. He's also aware of the implicit irony of his stance, touting profound and utter disbelief in a God-like authority figure, while insisting upon his own God-like authority. He can be as self-righteous and self-aggrandizing as any Southern Baptist hail-and-brimstone-evoking preacher. In his bones, he understands the draw of evoking fear to claim power.

Gripping Emma's hand even more tightly, as if passing his wisdom by osmosis into her flesh, he solemnly adds, "What I tell you, Emma, is Truth with a Capital T."

Emma stares off into the distance, mouth and expression ambiguous, giving nothing away. Out of the corner of his eye, on the street below the train tracks, Leo sees a pigeon that had been too slow or stupid to move out of the path of an oncoming train, now bloody and flattened almost beyond recognition. It will remain there for days, perhaps as long as a week, attracting flies and oozing filth, until the Sanitation Department deigns to remove it. The almost-daily sight of these dead birds are, for Leo, wrenching and vivid reminders that, in a random and indifferent universe, death can, and does, strike arbitrarily, sometimes grotesquely, anyone, any time, anywhere. He has already witnessed such deaths of loved ones: his father, his mother, his wife's beautiful young sister, one of his best buddies from college. Too many.

The pigeon is a good object lesson for Emma. "Do you see that bird?" He points emphatically. "Tell me what great and just and fair supreme being—what *deity*," he spits out the word, "would allow such a thing to happen to a dumb, harmless bird?"

Emma stares briefly in the direction of the bird, offers another nod, and another slight, ambiguous smile. Again, he stifles his anger at her as he stares one last time at the pathetic, doomed bird. He forces himself to turn his mind back to the more pressing and immediate matter at hand: Unless the damned light changes pronto, they won't make it to the five-and-dime before it closes at six o'clock. If it weren't for the cars whizzing along Gun Hill Road, one after another, each driver intent on not being the sucker caught when the red finally changes over to green, he would jaywalk and drag Emma along with him.

Earlier that week, Leo had taken Emma to the five-and-dime and promised her that if she wrote three new poems by Friday, he would buy her the diary of her choice from the stack of seductively arranged children's diaries, with their assortment of multi-colored covers and animal-shaped locks and keys. Love of poetry is something he and Emma share. They read Shakespeare aloud to each other, their voices caressing the words in unison, as if they're a father-daughter poetry act. "Poetry," he says to Emma, "is akin to breathing. Without it, we would all die." As for her older sister, May, poetry doesn't move her at all. She leaves the room when Leo and Emma begin their recitations.

In the five-and-dime, without hesitation, Emma pointed at a slim book with a smooth, shimmering pink cover and a gold-colored lock and key in the shape of a butterfly. "I want that one," she said, her voice insistent, yet nervous, as if she couldn't believe he would really allow her to choose on her own.

He'd hoped for something less predictably girlish, he'd had his eye on one with a plaid vinyl cover and a muted brown lock, but the main thing was that, if she loved it, she would be inspired to write. Second only to wanting her to grow up to be a proud and staunch atheist, is Leo's desire that she grow up to become a writer, instead of the owner of a candy store in the Northwest Bronx, on the other side of the borough from the Projects. At too young an age, he'd been forced to earn a living, to provide for a wife and family. With his strong, left-wing political convictions, and the "way with words" his high school English teachers had praised, he could have been—

and aura had been hard to resist. After the failed Bay of Pigs invasion of Cuba, she wished she hadn't. She blames him for the near extinction of the world.

Annette opens the refrigerator door and moves things aside to make room for Emma's beloved Hostess cupcakes, but a tickle erupts suddenly in her throat and she begins to cough. Her hand jerks, knocking over a plastic container filled with the spaghetti-and-meatball dish she'd labored over all morning, for tonight's supper. The linoleum floor is covered with bright red sauce, strands of spaghetti, and squashed fragments of chopped meat. Tears gather in her eyes, and she feels the pain in the back of her neck that's so often a precursor to a migraine.

Clearing her throat and wiping tears from her eyes, she stands in front of the open refrigerator, staring at the food. She had mopped the cracking, chipped green-and-white ("vomit green," May calls it) linoleum floor only yesterday.

Maybe she should just let the damned mess rot where it is. Why not? Instead of doing more back-breaking, mind-numbing housework, she should pay a visit to one of her friends, maybe Henrietta down the hall or Vera in the building next door, with whom she used to occasionally play *mah jongg*, although more and more, she has withdrawn from them. *Yentas*, Leo calls them, his lips curling in his unforgiving way.

It's just become too difficult for her to keep up her end of things with these women, to pretend to be upbeat and cheery, to pretend that she, like they, is relatively content with her life, and that Doom and Gloom isn't just around the corner. *The Truth With A Capital T*, as Leo would put it, is that she's less and less interested in what they have to say about anything. Her world has grown increasingly narrow. Still, on some days, her loneliness is a heavy weight around her neck. But who said that everyone's lives must contain friends? Some lives are meant to be insular, and hers is one of them.

Leo, of course, has his friends at the store, and that's enough for him. The stockboys who work for him, and the customers with whom he dishes about politics and kibbitzes. He requires a constant audience, and he always finds one. And then there's Cookie Coke. Is she more than just a friend? The highly sexual widow who pays weekly—or more—visits to Leo's Candies, or so she gleans from conversations with Leo, who's clearly titillated by Cookie's status as a store regular. Occasionally, Annette runs into Cookie on the grounds of the Projects. "Your husband," Cookie croons, her pearly teeth gleaming, "what a character!" Annette acknowledges to herself that she won't be calling upon her neighbors today—not on the *yentas* with whom she once played *mah jongg*, and certainly not upon Cookie. There's too much to be done around the house, even to *think* about playing hooky. Not that the work she does is valued. She cooks and cooks, catering to everyone's finicky likes and dislikes: May, who wants her steaks so rare they bleed; Emma, who insists her morning glass of chocolate Bosco be strained ten times in front of her to ensure that no slivers of milk container-wax slip in. "Milk container slime," Emma calls them. Leo, who demands pork chops nearly burnt, spaghetti and meatballs drenched in tomato sauce, vegetables tender yet crunchy.

And then May says, "This steak is dry!" and pushes the tender pink meat away. Recently, May's been worse than ever about rejecting food. "It isn't that I'm not hungry," May insists, haughtily, her spine rigid and jaw tight. "I just don't like what you cook." It occurs to Annette that May might have some sort of stomach bug, although in every other way she seems fine—well, maybe she isn't fine. Hasn't there been something else about May lately, now that Annette thinks about it, something off-kilter she can't quite put her finger on . . . But what? Something about the way she looks? As if her insides and outsides no loner mesh, as if her body has become a place of dissonance and discord.

No, that's absurd, May is absolutely fine; rejecting food is just another one of her willful acts. But . . . maybe not. Should she ask Leo if he's noticed anything different about May? No, of course not. He's oblivious to change and nuance in others, just as he is to them in himself. Or, if not exactly oblivious, certainly unwilling to think about such things with any objectivity or calm.

And then there's Emma, as difficult as May in her own way, spoiled and far too clever for her own good, with her huge appetite, especially for sweets, for chocolate cupcakes oozing vanilla cream, and doughy donuts, and multi-colored jelly beans—it's a miracle she's not chubby—shrieking, "I see wax!" after Annette has strained her Bosco the required ten times, so many times that Annette, herself, has developed an aversion to the wax, and imagines slimy-looking slivers where there are none.

And Leo, "the human garbage can," as she sometimes thinks of him during meals, who shovels his food down at breakneck speed, making Annette doubt he has time to distinguish his precious guava jelly from tar. Leo never thanks or compliments her. Just once, he said, "This roast beef is soft," and she assumed it was a compliment, but was never sure.

Then there's the fact that Leo and Emma are both so sloppy, throwing their clothes and papers everywhere, expecting her to pick up after them. Leo's dungarees and his favorite, comfortable, Cuban *Guayabera* shirts, with their highly stylized pockets and embroidery, thrown at the foot of their bed. And Emma, who, like a tornado at the height of its fury, tosses her blouses and skirts every which way, in the room she and May share. "You absolute, disgusting pig," May shouts. "One day you will be punished!"

May, on the other hand, is too much of a neatnick: criticizing Annette for not lining up the sofa pillows exactly right, for not cleaning every single crumb from the toaster.

And now, standing in front of the open refrigerator—something Leo expressly forbids in his presence because "it wastes electricity"—barely noticing its blast of cold air, Annette fantasizes about leaving them all, running away from home like a rebellious teenager, making her youthful dreams come true, traveling around the country organizing non-unionized workers, working for the civil rights movement down south, helping people who would appreciate her, who would remember to say, "Thank you."

But why delude herself? She should know better than to think her dreams will ever come true. Her youthful romance with leftist politics has led her here, to this lonely life in a lower-middle-income Bronx housing project, with no job other than housewifery, a handsome, brilliant, erratic husband, whose fidelity she's begun to question, and two daughters whom she is certain she loves, but not at all certain she likes. And who may, or may not, feel the same way about her. No point in harboring escape fantasies. *Definitely* no point in pretending that Leo won't ever humiliate her again.

On her hands and knees, she begins picking up the wet food from the linoleum kitchen floor and shoving it back into the plastic container. Rising, she walks over to the garbage can in the corner and quickly dumps the stuck-together food, sighing as she does so, knowing that now she'll not only have to mop the floor all over again, but also, from scratch, cook up a whole new batch of spaghetti and meatballs for her family.

4

Hot summer has come and gone, and on the first day of a new school year, 13-year-old May, in her neatly-pleated grey skirt and olive-green blazer, waits for the elevator in her building to take her down to the third floor, where Bonita Taranto lives. She and Bonita will walk together to their new junior high school, passing empty lots and nondescript one-and-two-story homes, some run-down, others better maintained, but all with an air of loneliness, May had thought, when, by herself, she'd taken a rehearsal walk to the school a few weeks before.

May feels the slightest twinge of pain in her forehead, which moves quickly to her left eye, the lazy eye. But then in an instant, the pain is gone, barely registering. Instead of worrying about it, May deliberately thinks about the fact that Bonita is merely her *current* favorite friend. May is proud that she's fickle when it comes to friendships, because it shows that she covets new people and experiences. She'll never get stuck, never be trapped. The wide world awaits her, in all its glory.

So what if last year, frizzy-haired Susan Gartner was her favorite friend, and the year before that, a girl named Bethie Zimmerman, whom she stopped liking when Bethie began writing poetry and wearing black tights, too bohemian for May's taste. If anyone in the Rosen family is destined for the beatnik lifestyle, it's Emma. Hanging around musky, smelly bars with unwashed folk singers and bad poets will never be May's scene.

May knows exactly whom she is, and what she is destined for, and there is one area in which she has not been fickle, and never will be. Where romance is concerned, she has loved Marvin Ludwig, and only Marvin, for absolutely forever, starting back in fourth grade, when Marvin earned a gold star as "Best Math Student" from Mrs. O'Reilly, scoring one hundred percent on four tests in a row.

May, who'd won second place, a red star, wasn't even jealous, because Marvin truly deserved the gold. He's so handsome, with his high forehead, full, round cheeks, and overall earnestness and sincerity. One day she overheard him telling Mrs. O'Reilly that he was hoping to go to medical school and become a doctor, and that was the exact moment she knew she would become his wife, and that his love for her, like a hand placed firmly on the small of her back, would hold her steady in a rocky world. Although they have no relationship yet, aren't even close friends, they will be united before too long.

Marvin is a good boy, a religious boy. His parents smile politely when they see May, and his younger brother, Charlie, who's Emma's age, is well-mannered and polite, nothing like the obnoxious "E-Bomb," who bursts into rooms, loudly reciting her juvenile, mawkish poetry, causing a commotion, spilling and breaking things, stealing everyone's attention, as destructive and toxic as the hydrogen bomb May learned about in sixth grade.

A few afternoons a week Marvin attends Hebrew School on Allerton Avenue in the basement of a synagogue. On Jewish holidays he dresses up in a dark suit and tie, with a golden silk *yarmulke* bobby-pinned to his equally silky blond hair. It's not clear to May, when she catches him in certain lights, where the *yamulke* ends and his hair begins.

May is certain that she and Marvin will live happily ever after in a beautiful house decorated with chandeliers and velvet sofas and chairs. In the back of the house, there'll be a lush garden that she, Marvin, and their three children, two boys and a girl, will tend together, and a dazzling turquoise swimming pool where they'll all swim on summer nights beneath a gleaming sliver of moon.

At bedtime, she'll wear a transparent, lacey nightgown, looking like her idol, the platinum blonde movie star Kim Novak, who'd starred in a bunch of wonderful movies back in the fifties. May had seen some of those movies with her parents when she was a little girl, while Grandma Thelma babysat the E-Bomb, and she's never forgotten them: *Pal Joey; Bell, Book, and Candle;* and *Vertigo*. Kim, with her sparkling, blonde hair and cool manner, was so absolutely, exquisitely regal, much more appealing than the current crop of immature, giggling, Gidget-y actresses. Kim was pure grace, elegance, and class, all with sensual undertones, and it's Kim whom she emulates, and Marvin, unable to resist, will one day soon fling himself into her arms. This, she believes, is God's plan.

Despite her parents' fervent atheism, May has believed in God ever since the Saturday afternoon when she was in fifth grade and happened upon an abandoned copy of the Bible beneath a bench in the playground across the street from the Projects. Alone on the bench, she ran her hand along the book's smooth leather cover for a long moment before gathering up the courage to open it.

Then, in the pink afternoon light, ignoring the sounds of the kids all around her playing handball and ping-pong and nok-hockey, she pored over *Genesis* and *Exodus* and *Leviticus*. She whispered aloud: *"In the beginning, God created the heaven and the earth . . . I will harden Pharaoh's heart . . . if ye will not hearken unto Me . . . I will appoint terror over you . . . ."*

She, who usually preferred numbers to books, was utterly enthralled. The words of the Old Testament spoke to her in a way no other words ever had. Grandma Thelma had been right all along, not her mother and father. Her father reviled her grandmother, calling her a "foolish, foolish woman with oral diarrhea." If only she had paid more attention to Grandma Thelma before she died. If only she had spoken privately with her, away from everyone else, about God and Jewish law — of which she now knows so very little.

Once married, she and Marvin will figure out all the rules together — what you could and couldn't eat, how to separate your dishes, what you could and couldn't do on *Shabbos*. In the meantime, she understood enough to know that this was the way the world really worked. The world, and that included the Bronx and the Gun Hill Projects, was ruled by a righteous God, a God who recognized how righteous and fair May herself was — a God, therefore, who would have no problem smiting May's enemies if she asked him to.

Ever since that day on the park bench, May has been totally bored and restless, sometimes even angry, although she doesn't dare show it, whenever her father reads aloud to her and Emma from *The*

Atheist Manifesto. If he weren't such a maniac about the subject, she would tell him so. Not that she needs to confide in him, or anyone else, about her special relationship to God. Or about how when no one else is around, she reads the Bible she took home that day from the playground, which she keeps wrapped up in a towel and pushed way back in one of her bureau drawers, safely hidden from the prying eyes of her family. Possessing such a great secret makes her feel mature and mysterious, the kind of woman men yearn to possess, like Cookie Coke, her father's friend, who carries a Bible with her sometimes and who is, in a way, a brown-skinned, bounteous version of Kim, her voice and gestures flowing and enticing.

May's favorite section of the Bible is *Exodus.* She loves the way God has Moses kill Pharaoh's cattle and turn Pharaoh's rivers to flowing red blood. She completely understands God's motive in seeking such dramatic revenge upon the evil Pharaoh, but what she doesn't understand is why, since *she,* although focused and driven, is not an evil person, God has chosen to punish her by not making her as attractive as she deserves to be. For reasons only He knows, she was born with a severely crossed left eye. Surgery years before didn't fully correct it, so now it's a so-called "lazy" eye, frequently drifting inward, toward the bridge of her nose.

She sniffs loudly, pursing her lips. This elevator, inching toward Bonita's floor, smells really bad, as though someone has been smoking a cigar in it, and there's a foul puddle of urine in the corner, which luckily isn't spreading: a perfect little oval-shaped pond that May carefully avoids stepping in.

With a loud groan, the elevator stops. May steps out into the dimly lit, third floor hallway, and she feels that pain behind her eye again, flickering, on-off-on-off—and once more wills herself to ignore it, to pretend it isn't real.

Fire-haired Mrs. Taranto, Bonita's mother, one of the few divorced women in the Projects, opens the door, nodding her head sleepily toward Bonita's bedroom. Mrs. Taranto works as a secretary in Manhattan, and today she's dressed in a fitted, ever-so-slightly-low-cut, polka-dot dress so clingy and classy it's worthy of the great

Kim Novak herself.

How much more exciting Mrs. Taranto is than May's own mother in her boxy, waistless, *schmata* housedresses, with her mousy brown hair streaked with old-lady white across one temple. Sometimes, when May is out with her mother, conscious of the stares of her peers, she's mortified by her mother's dowdiness and misery, both of which cling to her like scents she'll never be rid of.

Bonita, chronically lazy, hasn't begun getting dressed for school. May sits on her wide bed and watches with envy as Bonita rummages through her overflowing closet for an outfit. It's difficult for May to stifle her envy as she eyes Bonita's expensive clothes. Mrs. Taranto, no wealthier than the Rosens, never bargain hunts the way May's mother does. May believes that her mother would be happy if May dressed in old-lady *schmatas* as cheap and unflattering as her own.

May, sitting against the pearl-white headboard of Bonita's bed, watches as Bonita carefully rolls a pair of nylon stockings along her shapely, naturally bronze-colored legs. Bonita is a Sephardic Jew. Leo has explained to May that Sephardic Jews come from the Middle East and North Africa, unlike the Rosens and the other Jews in the Projects, who are Ashkenazi, from Eastern Europe. "They speak Ladino," he told her, "not Yiddish." May could tell that he was drawn to the Sephardim, the way he's always drawn to those he perceives as exotic and unlike himself and his family.

Bonita is incredibly lucky: Not only is she beautiful, and the only Sephardic girl in school, but she's also an only child, with no snake-in-the-grass sister coming onto the scene to betray her and steal her parents' love. Bonita fastens a gold, heart-shaped locket around her neck, then brushes her fiery hair with a bejeweled, tortoise-shell hairbrush.

"How's Marvin?" Bonita asks, her voice too syrupy-sweet for May's taste. May shrugs, since Bonita knows perfectly well that, although May adores Marvin, he doesn't pay any special attention to her—although that will change one day very soon.

May straightens her cat's-eye glasses and wishes that, like Bonita, she had twenty-twenty vision, and that her left eye wasn't weak and sluggish. Bonita claims to like Joey Maestre, but, more than once, May has caught Bonita staring at Marvin with way too much intensity, her dark brown eyes predatory.

At last, Bonita finishes dressing. Now, like May, she wears a pleated skirt and conservative blazer. "Look, we're almost twins today," she says, seemingly pleased, although May wonders. May forces a smile: What if Marvin prefers Bonita, whose eyes are flawless, to May?

May had her one and only special moment with Marvin Ludwig shortly after she graduated from sixth grade, on a sweltering afternoon in July, in the Project's windowless basement laundry room.

May has always liked doing laundry because it gets her out of the apartment and away from her family. She savors the strong, crisp smells of bleach and detergent. She enjoys separating colored clothes from white, measuring detergent and bleach, folding sheets and pillowcases. Doing laundry makes her feel the way she imagines all-powerful God felt as he created the universe, sculpting order from chaos.

Another good thing about doing laundry is that sometimes she deliberately "loses" an item or two of Emma's. She loves seeing Emma's face when she realizes that she's missing one of her favorite pair of flowered anklets, or one of her stained, oversized tomboy-ish polo shirts. In order to make it seem accidental, May also occasionally loses one of the white cotton handkerchiefs her mother buys for herself by the batch at Woolworth's.

Usually, the laundry room is crowded with women her mother's age, accompanied by crying little children. But that day, possibly because of the heat, there was nobody else around. Ordinarily, there weren't any decorations on the chipped, peeling walls, but that day there was an art exhibit by Mr. Roshansky, one of the dozen or so survivors of the concentration camps who live in the projects. May and her friends call the heavily bearded, wrinkle-faced, Mr. Roshansky "Mr. Dirty Old Man," because he's constantly trying to fondle young girls, including her. He reaches for their breasts as if he's a drowning man and their breasts will pull him to safety. She avoids him as much as possible, and she averted her eyes from his pitiful watercolors of scraggly trees and lopsided rose bushes.

And just as she was carrying her sopping wet clothes over from the washer to one of the tall dryers in the center of the room, who should enter but Marvin Ludwig? May held her breath for a long minute, certain that God had conjured Marvin up especially for her, a vision formed by the hot steam.

Marvin, wearing a tan polo shirt and a pair of Bermuda shorts the exact shade of creamy butter, looked so handsome, so perfect, so much older, she thought, than 12 and a half. His shopping cart overflowed with three bulging nylon bags of laundry, and May's heart soared at the sight of those bags. He'd be in the laundry room for quite a while.

"Hi, Marvin," she said casually and bravely, while her heart raced. Barely nodding at her, he turned around and studied the crookedly hung watercolors.

She stood there stupidly, racking her brain for what to say. He began tossing clothes into one of the washing machines, and she caught sight of some wrinkled brassieres and ladies' underpants, as well as some boys' tee shirts and socks. Seeing his family's dirty clothes made May feel very close to him. Until then, their relationship had been no more than cordial. They'd spoken briefly a few times after school, when they happened to exit the building at the same time. "After you," he said, holding the heavy school door open for her. "Why, thank you," she replied, her cheeks burning.

But that day all that would change. Being alone with Marvin in this hot, windowless room—which suddenly felt like the most romantic spot on Earth—was a dream come true. How to take advantage of the situation? Should she just come out and inform him that God intended for them to be married one day? Should she tell him how much she loved him?

"Math is my favorite subject," she said, finally. "Remember, I got the red star?"

"Umm," he muttered, his back still to her. Then, without a word, he turned around abruptly and walked right over to her, dramatically taking her in his arms. His skin felt damp and soft, and he smelled of ketchup. He was so passionate that he nearly knocked her eyeglasses off. She leaned backward, feeling faint in the steamy room as his washer and her dryer whirred together in the background like musical instruments. He smothered her mouth with the kind of grownup, hungry kisses she'd seen only in movies.

And then he stopped. He turned and walked slowly back to his washing machine and stood facing it as though it was the most fascinating thing he'd ever seen. His back, in the tan shirt, was an impenetrable wall.

May, mortified, opened the dryer door and pulled out her hot clothes. Haphazardly, she threw them into her mother's nylon laundry bags. "Marvin," she finally said, looking up when she was finished, forcing herself to speak to his broad back, "what happened?"

Not moving a muscle, he didn't answer.

"Marvin?" she tried again. Instead of continuing to look at his back, she stared at one of Mr. Roshanksy's paintings: a forlorn sparrow with strange, buggy eyes who appeared stuck in a tree. She grabbed her laundry and ran outside, tripping over her feet, into a day so hot her throat immediately felt parched.

5

Leo, awakening at nine o'clock, very late for him, is coming out of a familiar nightmare, his muscles tight all over, a familiar feeling, calves, arms, backs . . . Slowly, rhythmically, his father beats him with his cat o' nine tails. Arnold, the cruel, demented musician, lashes Leo, his instrument, over and over on his bare buttocks, raising ugly, fierce welts. So many times this happened in life, and now in dreams, a performance to be replayed for all eternity.

Breathing heavily, inhaling the room's stale air, opening his reluctant eyes, Leo throws his rumpled covers off and sits up in bed, rubbing the dark, curly hair on his bare chest, then smoothing his cool seersucker pajama bottoms. He allows himself a wide yawn — "hippo mouth" — Emma calls it when she sees him yawn like that, and the sound of the yawn makes him start to feel more in control, no longer a helpless child.

Out of the blue, he wonders how Cookie Coke would feel if she knew the truth of his childhood. Would she be moved to pity? Would all of her do-gooder, Church-going instincts be aroused, those instincts which, in anyone else, would nauseate him, but which, in Cookie, intrigue him? Since the last thing he wants from Cookie is pity, he vows never to tell her the truth of his childhood. Better to shroud his past in mystery. But why should what Cookie thinks matter? His relationship with her is light and easy, and will never develop into more. He takes his marriage and his responsibilities to his family seriously, and is proud of this fact.

He yawns again, another full-fledged hippo yawn. Every now and then, he allows himself a late morning like this, and his stockboys, Jorge and Pocho, open up the store for him. "We can handle it," they tell Leo repeatedly and proudly, in their tough Puerto Rican street accents. Jorge, who's 18, attends community college in the evenings, and has worked part-time at the store for the past two years. Pocho, his cousin, a few years older and a high school dropout, is sharp as a whip. "Leo," Pocho says, "I'm proud to work for such a political *hombre* as yourself." Leo believes that Pocho means what he says, and that he's not just flattering the boss. Sometimes, in the back room of the store, while Pocho rips open boxes with a sharp box cutter, and then climbs up and down a ladder, stacking candy neatly and carefully on the shelves, Leo tells him about Karl Marx and the pitfalls of capitalism. "*Viva* Marxism," Pocho says, smiling yet serious, taking a break and stuffing a Milky Way in his mouth. Once, Pocho said, "So, Leo, *hombre*, how can you, a Marxist, justify being the boss man?" "Because," Leo said, helping Pocho open a particularly well-sealed box, glad that Pocho had asked, "in my heart, I remain the worker." As he and Pocho together lined up Snickers Bars and Chunkies in neat rows, he conceded to himself that there was irony in his statement. And yet, despite the irony, it was *The Truth With A Capital T.*

Now, as Leo lingers in bed, muted light seeps through the slats of the venetian blinds in his bedroom. Tentatively, with eyes closed, he feels for the comfort of Annette beside him, but she's already gone, undoubtedly in the kitchen preparing his breakfast. The girls are starting school today, he remembers, and Annette must have been up very early, getting them ready, feeding them, making sure they had their books and supplies.

Despite the distance that's so often between himself and Annette, the distance he knows he creates with his temper and sarcasm, the distance that's been exacerbated recently by his thoughts about Cookie, he loves Annette and appreciates, more than he could ever express, her steadfastness, endless hard work, and selflessness.

Coming to life, stretching and sitting up, he remembers that this is the morning he's supposed to call Brenda and Evie, his sisters, who rent a small house together across the country, in Santa Monica, not far from the beach, where the sun hasn't yet risen, and where, together, they're raising Brenda's son, who's the same age as Emma.

For some reason, Brenda and Evie are proud that they never

get a full night's sleep. "Insomnia's our middle name," says Evie, the youngest, in her affectless voice, her Brooklyn accent still the strongest of the three of them.

It's hard for Leo to believe that he's now 40, Brenda 38, and Evie 36. His throat feels dry, and he leans heavily against the headboard of the bed, as he realizes that they're all well into middle age, although his body is still lean and firm, attractive enough to kindle a light in Cookie Coke's eyes. Back when they were kids, he had been especially proud of Evie, the way she belted out show tunes á la Ethel Merman, danced as gracefully as Ginger Rogers. Smart, too—that girl could discuss Tolstoy's novels and Babel's stories, not merely parroting critics, but offering her own quirky insights. "Babel," she'd say, clearly proud of herself, grinning at Leo, and doing a little soft shoe, "said the most with the least." Now, frail and dazed-looking, unmarried, Evie works as a file clerk in a real estate office, none of her promise realized.

Like him, his sisters had once believed in the universal good intrinsic to Communism. Now, they refuse to discuss what they call "political ideas" with Leo, so that he has no idea what they believe in and who they vote for.

Brenda, too, had appeared destined for a life better than the one she's ended up with. Never outgoing and ebullient like Evie, she was pretty and shy. Leo was as protective of her back then as he believes he is of his daughters now. How happy Brenda had been, marrying a handsome young probation officer, a good, steady man with a good, steady job, who called her "Brennie," and held her hand in public like a lovesick teen, right up until the day he left her alone with their two-month-old son, never to be heard from again, like a con-artist wraith who'd walked briefly among the living, getting away with whatever he could.

Together, in their middle age, Leo's sisters live insular, unimaginative lives. He wonders for the first time if nightmares similar to his own are what keep them awake. Do they also dream of Arnold's beatings with the whip-like cat o' nine tails? Of Arnold's heavily whiskered, unshaven face and cruel hands? Of their mother's endless litanies about all the men who desired her, and how, if it weren't for her three pitiful and ungrateful children—*nebechl*, she called each of them in Yiddish, *harpe*—she could leave their father?

Do they dream about the way their parents cursed each other in Yiddish and English both, like a long-running vaudeville act? "You *shmuck*," his mother spat. "You shit," his father responded.

Do they dream, as he sometimes does, about the time he and they ran away together from their parents and their Brooklyn tenement and slept in Prospect Park for two nights, beneath a black sky dotted with faint stars? They huddled together, cold and hungry, trying to stay warm, until, after being propositioned by a lunatic with six months worth of food stuck in his wild beard, they rose as one and ran home through the dark streets. Better to face the known enemy, they agreed, than the unknown.

Sitting on the edge of the bed, he dials the phone on the nightstand. Brenda answers. Her voice is a zombie's, disembodied and unengaged, as always, except when bragging about her son. Leo pictures her as she looks now in photographs, her once beautiful face swollen and red like a florid moon, her obese body draped in tent-like muu-muus.

All Leo knows about Brenda's son, his nephew, is that he's supposedly some kind of "genius," attending junior high rather than elementary school, who eats only baby food, the strained peas and applesauce May and Emma gave up before they were walking. In public, Freddie won't eat at all, since he doesn't want to be seen eating baby food, yet nothing—not even the specter of public shame—will induce him to eat anything else. According to Brenda and Evie, this is because "Freddie is sensitive." And maybe they're right. Isn't he himself the first to insist that being different from the mainstream is a good thing? Maybe the boy isn't crazy. Maybe Freddie is an iconoclast, separate from the herd, by choice and birth.

Sometimes, right before he falls asleep, Leo pictures obese Brenda mashing Freddie's pitiful food and dropping it from her mouth into his, like a bird. The image nauseates, and shames him— these people are his blood. Brenda, he thinks, must have inherited his parents' craziness, although she's not brutal, the way they were. He is, in fact, the brutal one, the one like his parents who uses fists to make a point and get his way. Could he be wrong though about Brenda and Evie not being brutal? Perhaps a cat o'nine tails is kept hidden in Brenda and Evie's home, to keep the brilliant Freddie in line. Leo prides himself on the fact that he will never touch his girls with a cat o' nine tails. He remembers too well the pain, and it's a proud distinction he makes between himself and Arnold.

When Freddie was a toddler, Brenda and Evie came back east to visit Brenda's husband's parents. "I'll show my son he at least has grandparents," Brenda huffed, "if not a father." With Freddie in tow, they stopped by the candy store. Leo remembers a gap-toothed, wiry child with copper-colored hair who scowled at his uncle and evinced no interest in the candies on the shelves. That alone had been disconcerting. Little kids who came into the store coveted, and lunged at, every single piece of candy they saw.

Brenda, chewing on the sugary gumdrop Leo had offered her, had looked vaguely around at Leo's merchandise and said, "We're too busy to take the bus over to the Projects. Say hello to Annette for us, and we'll meet your girls next time." But there never was a next time. And he never went to Santa Monica to visit them. The prospect, he admitted to himself, was too unappealing—frightening, even. Now over the phone, Brenda launches into a recitation of her woes, the same ones she recites to him every month when he calls: Her back aches, her feet swell, her sinuses clog. Her roof leaks, her landlord is a thief, her neighbors are stupid *buttinskis*.

Leo feels conflicted, as he does whenever he speaks with either of them. As children, they pricked their fingers and swore eternal allegiance to one another. Brenda and Evie alone bear witness to his childhood and he to theirs; they are bound together, connected in a way he will never be to his wife and children, despite his fierce love for them. In a crisis, they would do anything for him, and he for them. But is that true? Would they? He has met Freddie just once. They've never met his daughters. How is this familial love? How can he not acknowledge to himself how self-pitying and insular they've become? How can he not acknowledge that they never ask about him, or Annette, or the girls? Do they care whether he and his family live or die?

Yet, he, who ordinarily insists on being the center of attention, and who will do whatever it takes to be so—play the clown, the intellect, the wild-eyed radical, the ham, the provocateur—is reserved and measured with his sisters, never intruding. Isn't that the least he can do for them?

His life, after all, has turned out so much better than theirs. His marriage is stable, he owns his own store, and although his daughters may not be so-called wunderkinds like Freddie, they damned well know how to behave in public, and they damned well know how to eat.

"Put Annette on," Brenda says, as she usually does at some point, ready to move on to her next victim, to repeat her exact set of woes to Annette. "I want to talk to her."

Annette, in the kitchen, is feeling relatively contented: relieved that the girls went off to their respective schools without any arguments erupting between them. They'd been sober-faced and serious about their morning ablutions, readying themselves for the big day. She savors the peace and quiet like the chocolate she loves best from Leo's store, the most expensive candy he carries, a creamy, milk-chocolate bar imported from Britain, which only his most discerning customers—and even among those, only the ones with a little extra pocket money—can afford to buy. Usually, adults buy it for themselves, Leo tells her, not wanting to waste it on children who are happy enough with Milk Duds and Raisinettes. He frequently brings it home for her, and she recognizes this as a great gesture of love. She forcefully beats eggs for Leo's breakfast in a large metal bowl while listening to sultry-voiced Patti Page on the radio, singing irresistibly about romance and hard times.

This is the morning of Leo's monthly call to his sisters, and by now he's on the phone with them, listening to them whine and *kvetch*. Careful to pour just a half-spoonful of milk into the eggs, the way he likes it, she resumes beating the mixture, and wishes she liked Brenda and Evie just a little bit. But she can't help herself, she dislikes how self-centered and intolerant they've become, nothing like the delightful young girls she'd met back in Brooklyn. She remembers Evie best, in her floral-patterned blouse, her voice like music when she'd stopped Annette on the street and introduced herself. Remembering that day, Annette yearns for her *own* sister, her dead sister, *her* May, her best friend, gone so young, gone too many years. What would May be like today if she had lived? Kind, smart, beautiful. A socialist, like Annette. A schoolteacher or social worker, happily married, with children who would be loving cousins to her girls . . . .

Last month she'd told Leo that she didn't want him to put her on the phone with Brenda and Evie any more. "What's the point?" she asked. "They repeat themselves endlessly and never listen to a word I say."

But here's Leo, heading directly toward her in his pajama bottoms, yawning widely, scratching his bare chest, then regarding her with such a mischievous, impish smile she immediately knows he's disregarding her wishes. "Pick up the foyer phone," he says, arching his dark eyebrows.

Annette's eyelids tremble with anger she doesn't know how to express any other way. "No, please," she says, wishing she didn't have to endure the sound of her own pleading, "I told you . . . ."

"Brenda's waiting," Leo says, smiling even wider, eyes crinkling.

How he relishes her discomfort, her inability to stand up to him. Blinking back tears, her mood totally ruined, she wipes her hands on her faded flowered apron, then slowly moves toward the phone on the wall in the foyer. She hears Leo opening the refrigerator, undoubtedly looking for something to nosh on before breakfast, one of his irritating habits.

"Brenda, hello," she says, frowning, forcing herself to sound cordial.

"Freddie's I.Q.," Brenda announces, already growing strident, as though she expects Annette to protest, "is the highest for his age in the whole state of California."

Annette says, "That's wonderful," making no attempt to sound sincere. She stops listening. She's thinking instead about how betrayed she feels by Leo this morning. How *especially* betrayed, because last night they had made love for the first time in about a month. Twice recently he had wanted to, but once she had a migraine, and once was the evening he had exploded at Emma for accidentally knocking the glass of soda from his hand, and she simply hadn't been able to bring herself to touch him. "I can't," she'd said that night, more insistent than she usually dares to be around Leo, "not after what just happened."

"Bitch," he'd called her and her heart froze. He had never before called her such a vile thing. Was this some new page that he'd turned, some marker that he no longer cared for her at all? No more had been said. He'd fallen asleep, and eventually, so had she.

But last night had been . . . What was the word?—*lovely*. No, more than that. *Rapturous*. Not a word she often associates with her sex life. More often, sex for her is uneventful at best, a painful chore, at worst, even though she continues to love Leo with all her heart, hotheaded and cruel though he sometimes can be. On nights when he falls asleep before she does, she luxuriates in watching him, the way his long eyelashes flutter and his full lips part slightly, the way he wheezes ever so slightly at first, before settling in to sleep. When she's the first to awaken, she finds herself comforted by the sight of him, despite the fact that she never knows whether he'll be in a decent mood when he wakes up.

But sex has always been a different story, even during the most romantic days of their marriage, before the children were born. She feels too vulnerable, too exposed, when making love. Woodenly, she goes through the motions, not comprehending why Leo grows so passionate, why he craves, time after time, being inside her, how he's able to lose himself so completely in the act.

But last night she had felt herself relaxing, expanding. Her head had felt light and airy, her body, svelte and limber, not stiff and resistant. She wasn't sure why, wasn't sure what was different . . . maybe because he'd approached her more slowly than usual, his expression more dreamy than intense. For an instant, she feared that he was thinking of someone else, of another woman, Cookie Coke, perhaps, who so often becomes the repository of her jealous imaginings, despite the fact that she has absolutely no reason to think anything is going on between Cookie and Leo. Well, there is the fact that Leo mentions Cookie's visits to the store more and more frequently. In truth, when Annette runs into Cookie in the Projects, she likes her seemingly irrepressible optimism, something she herself knows nothing about, and the way Cookie never fails to ask after Emma and May.

But then in bed last night, Leo had softly whispered her name and she knew it was only herself, no other woman, reflected in his eyes. She kissed him without waiting for him to kiss her first, held him tightly around the waist as he climbed on top of her. Her hips moved in tune with his, she heard herself sighing and murmuring, making sounds she barely recognized as coming from her own lips. And, when she awoke this morning from a dreamless sleep, she'd felt so close to him, and had decided to go all out for his breakfast, the whole shebang, a he-man-sized meal, perfect for the King of his Castle, eggs, bacon, toast spread with his precious guava jelly, oatmeal, and his favorite fruits, strawberries and blueberries . . . .

But now, grasping the phone tightly while continuing to blot out the sound of Brenda, who's droning on about the pains in her legs, she changes her plan: no crisp bacon, no fresh strawberries, no cinnamon-laced oatmeal. Two eggs, a bit overdone, not soft and runny the way he likes them, and one slice of burnt toast—that will be all he gets. Let him complain, let him rant and rave, she doesn't care. She'll just play dumb, which is what he thinks she is, anyway, isn't it? The woman who didn't go to college, the woman who didn't remember Ma Joad. Not that giving him a less-than-glorious breakfast is much of a victory, she knows. In fact, it's no victory at all. But it's the best she can do at the moment.

6

The following day, Leo sits in the wobbly, narrow folding chair he keeps behind the counter at his store. Jorge and Pocho are off for the day. Outside, the fall rain beats steadily in concert with a relentless wind. Things have been quiet at the store all afternoon, and he's enjoying himself, re-reading *Tortilla Flat*, a book he loves because, in bittersweet, comic prose, Steinbeck speaks clearly and succinctly of the plight of the common man. It's not Steinbeck's masterpiece, doesn't have the scope and ferocity of *The Grapes of Wrath*, but, in its deceptively simple way, it packs a punch.

Time to relax and read is a rare pleasure—time to forget financial and familial problems, to allow himself, even as he reads about the trials and tribulations of Steinbeck's comic heroes, to indulge in fantasies about Cookie Coke and her lush lips, round face, and full breasts . . . to imagine how good it would feel to embrace her, to pull her close to his chest, to hold her tight. Fantasy is fine, he tells himself. It's like writing fiction, and neither fantasy nor fiction should ever be legislated away.

Still, the reality is that it's never good when a whole afternoon goes by with so few customers. Where are the rambunctious kids who should be packing the store at the end of their school day, elbowing each other, counting their change, lisping and shouting and mumbling their needs? Are they all at Sweets Brothers? Maybe, but he's confident that any lost customers, kids and adults alike, will return, because Leo's Candies is alive and authentic. He is not a fat-cat bossman. He keeps up with the times, with what people like. His customers are drawn to him because he relates to them as individuals, not as mindless consumers with open wallets. They linger to schmooze and kibbitz, to ask his opinion on politics and books.

One of the neighborhood kids, Terrance Riley, copper-colored with beautiful lips like a girl's, has been reading Marx at Leo's urging. Just the other day, Terrance's father, copper-colored like his son, but without the lips, stopped by to ask Leo's advice. "Listen to me, Leo, my buddy," he said, in hushed tones, "my woman won't put out any more. What do you have to cure that?" A non-drinker himself, not caring for the taste, Leo smiled: "Candy won't fix what she's got. Go next door — liquor is quicker."

The door opens and he puts down the novel, not needing to mark his place because he knows it so well, and rises from the precarious metal chair.

"Leo," Cookie cries, her accent like an island breeze, shaking out a large, canary-yellow umbrella, then tucking a tendril of her ebony hair behind her ear, "I've been visiting Khenan and the kids, and it is mighty wet out there."

Slowly, she unbuttons her raincoat, her fingers deft and swift, and then places a metal bowl on the counter. It's covered with foil, and smells of exotic spices Leo can't identify. "For you," leaning forward in a clingy dress the same bright yellow as her umbrella, elbows on the counter, so that he can see her cleavage, her powdery perfumed breasts.

This isn't the first time she's brought him lunch, although he doesn't tell Annette about this, and he already knows how her food will look and taste: a rich, thick, dark stew overflowing with tender chunks of meat, onions, and peppers. Like Cookie herself, the meal appears ripe with possibilities.

But what of the lunch Annette has dutifully made for him today, just as she does every day, the heaping roast beef or steak sandwich, unspiced, no relish, pickle on the side, not exotic, not exciting? He'll save it for a late afternoon snack.

He imagines himself once more in bed with Cookie, a woman clearly in love with her own body, adventurous in ways that Annette, with her migraines, timidity in the bedroom, and Doom-and-Gloom scenarios, will never be. Cookie would touch him in new ways, re-kindling an exotic spark he once had but has somehow lost, although married love is about much more than sex. He loves Annette's quiet strength, and he appreciates things she'd be

astonished he cares about—her willingness to strain Emma's
damned, sickeningly-sweet Bosco ten times every morning and even
her misguided integrity in clinging to Socialist rhetoric. He especially
loves her for bringing his daughters into the world.

Cookie, perhaps sensing his thoughts drifting away from her,
begins to hum a pop tune which he half-recognizes—something
about shrimp boats and dancing —and, lured in by her dark eyes
and moving hips, he imagines a line of white boats, sails aloft,
swaying together on navy-blue water, and Cookie on the shore, her
dancing body in sync with the movements of the boats, sipping from
a cool, fruity, colorful drink.

Listening to her sing, watching her sway her hips so lightly and
gracefully, he marvels at how upbeat and cheerful Cookie remains,
despite her many hardships: widowed and living alone since her
early 20s, working the nurse's night shift at Jacobi Hospital, riding
home on the city bus in the dark early morning, day after day. Yet,
there's nothing sad or beleaguered about her—she's more alive and
vibrant than any woman he's ever known.

"How are your lovely daughters?" Her interest seems genuine.
Another part of her allure is that her sincerity and coquettishness are
complementary, not dissonant. Sometimes when he's out walking
with the girls in the neighborhood, they run into Cookie. "Pretty
blue-eyed one," she says, bending down to pat Emma's dark head, at
the same time affording Leo, as usual, a glimpse of her ample
cleavage, so that, even with the girls in tow, he can't help but imagine
her barely-hidden aureoles like dark, ripe plums.

Once, to May, she declared, "How charming and grown up
you are!" Then, with a radiant smile, she removed a tiny bottle of
perfume from her pocketbook and sprayed both of May's wrists,
as May grinned from ear to ear, a rare and transforming sight.
"Now you're a lily of the valley," she'd whispered *sotto* voice to
May, whose grin grew more expansive.

"My kids are fine," he answers Cookie, although this is true
only of Emma, not of May, who isn't fine, not really. he feels that
in his bones, and he knows that Annette feels it, too, although she
doesn't speak of it to him because he won't give her any opening

to do so. He cannot accept any more illness or grief in his life.

As for Emma, there he can rest easy, and there he speaks the truth to Cookie. Emma is more than fine, she's superb—his truest daughter.

The air in the store grows increasingly electric, as Cookie ceases her dance and, uninvited, comes behind the counter and stands beside him with no self-consciousness at all. Leo feels her presence like a sharp bolt of lightning, and it's he who grows self conscious, unsure what to say next, since he never talks politics or religion with her, the way he does with most everyone else, passionately sharing his left-of-center views with those who agree with him, and arguing with those who don't, not caring if he loses their business. Cookie, religious, God-fearing, and on the politically conservative side, despite her low-cut dresses and provocative manner, is the kind of person who usually enrages him. Yet, it's lust, not anger, that consumes him as they stand so close together.

As Cookie, moving closer to him, resumes her song about the shrimp boats, Bertie Franklin, a skinny twelve-year-old black kid from the neighborhood, flings open the front door, racing inside as if he's being pursued by the cops. Not sure if he's disappointed or relieved by Bertie's sudden presence, Leo exhales loudly.

Bertie is sopping wet from the rainstorm outside, his tight curly hair matted to his skull. Leo knows the bare-bone facts of Bertie's life, not so different from the lives of lots of the kids who frequent the store. Bertie's father skipped out right after Bertie's birth, and his mother, rarely home for him, works two jobs, as a home aide and a cleaning woman. Bertie comes by the store a few times a week, to shoot the breeze with Leo. "My teacher," he likes to complain, fiercely popping his bubble gum, "she don't know crap." Leo regales him with tales of his own problems with authority as a youngster. "But," Leo adds, "school's important. So put up, for now, with their crap." Bertie listens hungrily and nods sagely. Leo loves the idea of himself single-handedly turning Bertie's life around.

Bertie, eyes bulging, stares at Cookie, clearly very impressed by her presence behind the counter, no matter what the reason—and this fact pleases Leo, despite himself.

After a moment, Bertie says, "Hey, Sugar, lookin' good," trying to sound slick and grownup.

"I'll 'Sugar' you, young man," Cookie laughs, placing her hand briefly on Leo's arm.

Leo, also laughing, is reminded, by Bertie's arrogance and bravado, of himself at that age. He nods in the direction of the raisin-and-nut-filled Chunkies, Bertie's favorites, stacked together on a shelf below the counter. Bertie helps himself to a greedy handful, mumbling a sweet thank you, seeming his age again. Leo feels what he knows is a real rush of love for the boy, more vivid, perhaps, than the love he feels for his own girls, because there's so little he can really do for Bertie. He reaches below the counter, pulls out his only umbrella, a clunky black one he's had for years. "Take this," he says, and Bertie, like the slick song-and-dance man from *Porgy and Bess*, retrieves it with a swift dance kick.

As soon as Bertie's gone, racing out the door, in hobbles aggravating old Mrs. Gottlieb, imperiously tapping her ornately-handled cane on the floor. Leo's stomach turns over at the sight of her.

"Mr. Rosen," she says, right on cue, barely seeming to notice Cookie beside him, so intent is she upon her mission, although Cookie self-consciously moves away from Leo at the sight of the old woman, "you owe me a nickel for the licorice I bought from you yesterday. The new store sells it for five cents less."

Leo feels the cold white heat that often envelops him when he grows angry, an icy-hot breath of air. Inhaling deeply, he focuses all his rage on Hilda Gottlieb: whiney voice, gaudy jewelry, brightly rouged face, constantly needling him for not going to *shul*, just like his late, prune-faced mother-in-law, Thelma Baum, constantly trying to nickel and dime him. She makes his flesh crawl. Like clockwork, once a week, she's in his store to drive him mad with her whining and bitching. "*Mr. Rosen, your chewing gum is old. Your cough drops are broken. Your M & Ms melt. I want my money back.*" She's a living, walking, breathing Nazi stereotype of a stingy Jew, and this thought is so disturbing, he wants to vomit, despite the delicious perfumed scent of Cookie beside him.

"Then shop at the new store, you cheap biddy," he roars, his neck bulging so much he wonders if his collar will burst, "and never come back!"

Cookie shakes her head. "Leo, Leo," she says, sounding more bemused than disapproving, slowly moving her body from behind the counter, a sight which Leo, even in the midst of his rage, finds arousing, "temper, temper."

Mrs. Gottleib storms out of the store, snorting and spitting like a mad horse, tapping the floor furiously, her cane her weapon. "I'll write a letter about you!" she threatens nonsensically, as she does every week, slamming shut the door.

Leo smiles, pleased with himself for putting on such a good show for Cookie, his anger melting into an ooze of desire for her.

"Leo," Cookie speaks musically, as she gracefully slips out from behind the counter, buttons up her raincoat, swoops up her yellow umbrella, "surely, your bark is worse than your bite." Her lips curve invitingly. "*Ooh la la*," she says, in her island accent, "*la la*."

He watches her go, her smile making him feel like an endearingly naughty child, his skin still vibrating from her touch.

7

At the front of Emma's classroom, Miss Harper puts down the book of poetry she's been reading from. Her eyes generously sweep the room, including Emma, who marvels at her luck in landing such a warm, upbeat, poetry-loving teacher this year.

"What does the narrator of this poem mean," Miss Harper asks, "when he says he has 'miles to go before he sleeps?'"

Miss Harper, pretty, young, and tall, with glittering, heavily lashed, hazel eyes, is a huge relief after fourth grade and stoop-shouldered, math-obsessed Mrs. O'Reilly, who, in her brittle voice, used to repeatedly single Emma out. "*This* girl cannot do math any third grader could do in her sleep!" *This girl, this girl* . . . Mrs. O'Reilly never bothered to learn her name.

Emma is convinced that she knows the correct answer to today's question about Frost's narrator. Like Pandora, whose myth Emma's father has recounted to her numerous times, the narrator still believes in "change and revolution," and thus in an "infinity of possibilities," as her father puts it.

Just as Emma is about to raise her hand, she glances over at Rosemary Mammano sitting beside her. Emma genuinely admires Rosemary for chewing gum so surreptitiously in class that teachers never catch her. Rosemary is the only girl in class whose mother allows her to wear earrings and lip gloss—today, plastic red hoops dangle provocatively from her ears, and her lips are shiny and moist, as if she's been eating a juicy peach.

On the other hand, Emma doesn't admire everything about Rosemary. Once, she'd said to Emma, "God likes Catholics best, which is why I'm glad I wasn't born Jewish like you. You all killed Christ."

Emma had allowed herself to glower at Rosemary in response, but, oblivious—or not, Emma wasn't sure—Rosemary continued.

"I'm even gladder I wasn't born black," she said, "because then I would have killed myself."

Remembering Rosemary's bigotry, which, she hopes, doesn't reflect the beliefs of all Catholics, Emma forgets all about Frost's narrator, and starts to worry instead about the Virgin Mary. Ever since the day she spoke to her in the Church's courtyard, she's been promising herself that she will soon find the courage to attend a real Catholic Mass, in order to learn more deeply about Catholic rituals and secrets—and how they really feel about Jews. This coming Sunday she will do it, she decides, *come Hell or high water*, an expression her father sometimes uses when he's at his most emphatic, although, of course, he adds, "Hell is a metaphor, no more."

Emma yearns to dip her fingers into the basin of holy water, and she yearns to sit on a wooden bench, eyes shut and lips parted, humbly tasting the flesh of God. Most of all, she yearns to kneel inside a dark, shadowy booth, confessing her most shameful thoughts to a handsome Italian priest with hooded eyes, who looks like Bobby Gaglione.

But what if the Catholics spot her as an imposter? They'll call her a Christ-killer and a dirty Jew. They'll drag her home by her ear. Her father will beat her black and blue. He and her mother will never forgive her. In their eyes, she will have betrayed them for all eternity. But . . . she takes a deep breath—she will not be stopped in her mission.

It occurs to her that she needs an accomplice to watch her back, someone trustworthy and Jewish, someone who loves and understands her. Only Shelley fits the bill, of course, the best friend whom Emma loves as she cannot love her sister. Shelley lives on the first floor of Emma's building, and, according to their mothers, who are cordial to one another, but no more, Shelley and Emma became friends while still in baby carriages. Shelley likes to say, "One day I'll live in Paris and be a famous actress, and you'll be a famous poet in Greenwich Village, and we'll write letters to each other every day."

Emma turns her attention back to Miss Harper, and, at last, she raises her hand. But Miss Harper is already calling on Charlie

Ludwig, Bobby Gaglione's best friend. Charlie gulps ever so slightly, and Emma notices how much he resembles his older brother, Marvin, the boy with glittery blonde hair, the one May has such a crazy crush on.

"It's about death." Charlie Ludwig speaks shyly, his eyes downcast. "About not wanting it. Ever."

Miss Harper smiles with delight. Her pearly teeth shine. "Excellent answer, Charlie."

Emma is disappointed. Her answer, referring to the beautiful and timeless myth of Pandora, was much more interesting and poetic than Charlie's. The bell rings, signaling the end of the school day. Emma gathers up her books and joins Shelley for the walk home. Slowly, they walk up Magenta Street hill to the Projects, Emma's calves feeling tight and knotted, although they haven't even made it past the schoolyard yet, with its intimidating, tall fence that some of the boldest older kids scale on weekends.

Shelley quietly hums to herself as they walk, and Emma decides to plunge right in. "Come to Catholic Mass with me on Sunday."

"Are you nuts? Why in the world?" Shelley frowns and tosses her thick, jet-black hair with irritation, as they make room for a grandmother in orthopedic shoes to pass. "You're too damned bossy."

Shelley's accusation stuns Emma. Her calves knot more tightly, and she stops in her tracks. Is there truth to Shelley's accusation? Well, there *was* the time Emma had insisted that Shelley walk with her all the way to the Coops housing development on Allerton Avenue, two subway stops away from the Projects, farther than either of them is allowed to walk without an adult. Emma had heard a rumor that "secret Communist cells" met regularly in the Coops, and how could she resist seeing those cells for herself, since her father had once been a "card-carrying Communist," and since he says that, in his heart, he will always be one. But this fantasy of Emma's hadn't inspired Shelley, whose parents are "at best, mildly liberal," according to Emma's mother, which might be one of the reasons her mother and Shelley's don't click.

Nevertheless, Emma had forcefully dragged the sulky Shelley

along, and they'd just made it past the Burke Avenue subway station, when who should appear but Shelley's mother, Tessa Gould, wearing a madras shift and rollers in her hair, and lugging a shopping wagon filled with bags of groceries. Just their luck, she'd decided to shop that day at the Burke Avenue supermarket, rather than at the A & P near the Projects.

She'd asked no questions. "You are grounded for a week," she'd said to Shelley, her words sounding like the cries of an enraged bird.

Emma wonders now if Shelley still hasn't forgiven her for that. They're almost home, and as they cross the street to the Projects, Emma tries again. "Idjut," she says, calling Shelley by the pet name they have for each other, "I bet no Jewish kids have ever gone to Mass before. We'll be Jewish outlaws. Like the James boys, Jesse and Frank, because . . . ." She's at a loss to say more, but hopes that Shelley will be hooked by the chance to be so dramatic and outrageous.

Immediately, Shelley wrinkles her small nose with pleasure. "Jesse and Frank. Shelley and Emma. Jewish outlaw girls on the loose, making history."

How wonderful to know someone so well, that you can turn their desires into mirror images of your own, Emma thinks. Perhaps even more wonderful, is having her needs come first, so unlike the way things are at home, where her father and May's needs are paramount. Unable to stop herself, she waves her fist in the air, a gesture of victory that Shelley, luckily, doesn't catch.

8

On the same day that Emma, in her classroom, ponders the desires of Frost's narrator, May, in her own classroom, struggles to ignore the slight headache, the building pressure she feels as she works on the algebra problems that Mrs. Press, her first period math teacher, has assigned. May admires Mrs. Press, whose hair is cut short in a kind of sophisticated pixie, and who dresses elegantly in pearls and muted greys and soft blues, so unlike the teachers back in P.S. 41, or "Babyville," as she now thinks of her former school, which Emma still attends, with their falling-down skirt hems and flyaway hair raining bobby pins.

May genuinely likes her new school, with its imposing brick facade and labyrinth-like hallways, even though it's known throughout the Bronx mostly for its gang fights. She simply ignores the pompadoured-and-leather-jacketed "hooligans," as her mother calls them, and their trampy girlfriends. They exist in a world apart from hers. Her class, 7-1, is filled with kids like herself, kids who listen to their teachers, do their homework, raise their hands, study hard for tests, and achieve high grades.

Marvin, across the room from May, stands out from the other students in a shirt the color of a brilliant emerald. At the sight of his pink cheeks, broad shoulders, and golden hair, particularly wispy and fine today, floating like a whimsical cloud above his head, she feels her cheeks growing warm. The blood in her face pulses along with her throbbing headache, as if they're partners in a fierce dance.

As usual, Marvin is busily engaged, writing down answers in his workbook, not glancing up at her. What went wrong that day in the laundry room, she asks herself for the zillionth time? Was her breath foul? Did she slobber all over him? No, she never forgets to brush her teeth, and she's been told by the few other boys she's kissed at make-out parties, that she's a good kisser. Once, Mike Schecter, whose family has since moved to the more affluent neighborhood of Forest Hills, Queens, held her in his arms, and huskily mumbled, "May, you've got the touch," as his curled-up tongue swirled inside her mouth.

The reason for Marvin's betrayal must be the simple, most obvious one. She's just not pretty enough for him, and she never will be, because of her damned left eye—God's cruel and sadistic joke on her. If someone in the Rosen family had to be punished with a weak eye muscle, why couldn't it have been Emma?

Self-consciously straightening her eyeglasses, May resumes her work. Her head throbs insistently. Maybe when she gets home from school, she should tell her mother about this sudden, intermittent, but persistent, pain. As soon as she thinks that, the pain abruptly dissolves, and as she twirls her pencil in her fingers, she decides not to say a word about this to anyone, especially her mother, who'll just panic and take her to the doctor. And May, who has hated and feared doctors since she was three years old, will not allow that to happen.

9

When Annette was 29 years old and pregnant with Emma, the doctor who'd been monitoring three-year-old May's left eye, the one that was severely crossed since birth, decided that the time was right for an operation. "We can fix that eye," he told Annette, who was sitting across from him in his tweedy, low-ceilinged Manhattan office. The mustached doctor's thin, nearly lipless mouth was as fixed as a ruler. "There's no time to waste."

But as on so many days since this pregnancy began, Annette wasn't paying full attention to what was going on around her — she felt drowsy and slow, only half-present in the doctor's office, focused on the baby kicking inside her. She was hoping for a boy, hoping that having a child of his own sex would calm Leo down. Maybe he'd identify so strongly with this child that some of the hurt from his own *meshugane* childhood would go away.

"Can't you wait," she asked, "just a little bit longer to do an operation, until six months or so after this one is born?" She stared self-consciously at her stomach, hoping that the doctor would understand her predicament and be sympathetic, even if he was a man.

"No," he insisted, scowling, reminding her so much of Leo at that moment her heart sank and bile instantly rose to her throat, "it has to be now. In case it's not completely successful the first time around, we may need to do more surgeries." He placed his beefy hands on his cluttered desk, knocking over a notebook, which he didn't bother to pick up, probably confident that some underling would do so later.

With much effort, Annette looked down past her large belly at her scuffed, sensible shoes. They pinched her swollen, difficult-to-fit feet. She was horrified at the thought that her child might need to go under a surgeon's knife more than just this once. If only she'd found a kinder doctor, someone less brusque and officious. There was still time, she could ask around, try to find a doctor who cared about *her*, who saw *her* suffering. But she knew she wouldn't. She was too exhausted. This doctor would have to be the one.

Besides, she was ashamed of herself. How could she possibly expect her own daughter to live six more months with a crossed eye just because it would be more convenient for her? This doctor was right, May's needs trumped her own. Even with her swollen feet, aching back, piercing migraines, and wrenching vomiting spells, she would make certain that May's eye was taken care of.

I'm a terrible mother, she thought, avoiding the doctor's eye, the worst mother in the world. She touched the long, lightning-shaped, white streak in her hair, which she'd had since she turned twenty, and felt unattractive, like a skunk. She vowed to herself that she would do everything possible to hide her deficiencies from May, and also from the baby boy on the way. She nodded at the doctor. His eyes looked suddenly wolfish and cruel, and she acknowledged defeat. Her body sagged.

That evening, after May had fallen asleep in her room, Annette sat beside Leo on the sofa. She told him what the doctor had said, keeping her voice and expression as neutral as possible. She never knew what would set him off.

Leo turned away, staring out the window at a black, starless sky. Loudly, slowly, one by one, he cracked his knuckles. He couldn't stand the pleading look in Annette's eyes. No more talking, no more thinking, about illness, doctors, hospitals . . . He was young, still, but already he'd had enough. His mouth tasted metallic, as though he were growing ill himself.

And now his own daughter . . . He remembered how, in the hospital, the first time he beheld May in Annette's arms, her tiny, beet red body, bald head, wrinkled, pruney mouth, he'd turned away. His child was supposed to be a dazzling beauty, the kind of baby whose face melted hearts and sold jars of baby food and infant formula. But even as an infant, May's expression was dour and inward, and soon it became clear that her eye wasn't normal.

"Fine," he said to Annette, experiencing anger so intense toward her that even he knew he was irrational. "Schedule the operation. Just don't bother me about it. No more details."

That night, in bed, he stared at Annette's belly as she slept, as far away from him on the bed as possible, a deliberate act, and he wished for a boy.

Even at three, May hated her crossed eye, hated seeing herself in mirrors, the way the eye behaved as if it were separate from the rest of her, hated being asked by other kids, "What's wrong with you? Your eye is crooked." She especially hated hearing the mothers of the kids say, "Shush! That's not polite," as if she were a leper. But, she still didn't want to go to the hospital.

"No!" she had screamed when her mother told her that she needed an operation. "Not fair!" She kicked out and her foot crashed into her mother's shin. She kicked again, heady at the contact, narrowly missing her anguished mother's stomach, where another child already lived.

May was terrified of the pain, terrified of being left alone in the hospital, a place she envisioned as dark and maze-like, filled with rotting corpses that the doctors hadn't saved. She screamed and kicked nonstop in the airless taxicab en route. She screamed and kicked when she was taken to her room, which she was forced to share with a girl with dried snot on the rims of her nostrils who "has something wrong with her heart," according to the girl's teary-eyed mother. She screamed when her mother, sitting by her bedside for hours holding her hand, let go to wipe her own brow.

The operation was deemed a success. May wore a black eyepatch that was scheduled to come off in a few weeks. The very best news, according to the thin-lipped, mustached doctor, whom May despised as much as her mother did, was that, "beneath the patch, her eye was no longer crossed, but merely lazy." There would be no need for any more surgery. He added, "She'll never look better than this."

On the day that Annette and Leo brought her home from the hospital, they carried red and yellow balloons and boxes of candy. May, disoriented by the eyepatch, turned her head away from them, ignoring the balloons and refusing to taste the candy, even though they'd brought her favorites, sticky Ju-Jubes and crunchy Malted Milk Balls. "Take me home," she said coldly, feeling a new kind of pleasure as she saw the stricken look that passed across her mother's face.

Once the patch was removed, much of the time May's left eye seemed normal. But then at other times, for no reason that anyone could fathom, the muscle grew weary and the eye drifted inward, like an unmoored ship. "I'm not healed," she screamed at her mother, who insisted, "This is healing, May. It has healed."

May had nightmares about falling, about going blind, about dying. She woke up screaming. Annette, with her sore feet, huge belly and red-rimmed eyes, came to her, comforted her, whispered, "There, there," and "Go to sleep now," counting the minutes with dread until she would return to her own bed.

Then, Annette, back in bed, lying beside the obliviously snoring Leo, her hands resting lightly across her swollen stomach, was unable to fall back to sleep herself. She was haunted by images of herself as an old, haggard woman, never getting a night's sleep, never again at peace. She tried to speak to Leo about May's nightmares. "I told you," Leo said, "no details."

A few weeks later, Emma was born. She was so beautiful that neither Annette nor Leo cared that she wasn't a boy, and that they wouldn't be naming her Joe, after Joe Hill, the singer of labor ballads, as they'd planned. Instead, they named her Emma, for Emma Goldman, the fiery Russian anarchist.

On the day that Annette and Leo brought Emma home, May saw her father look into the pink-skinned baby's barely open, sky-blue eyes with a kind of rapt adoration she'd never before seen on his face. Even the usually sober Annette cooed and burbled over the infant in a way that made May's blood boil.

May stared hard at the wrinkled, squalling, squashed-faced baby lying in her crib—the same crib May had slept in. "You are not my real sister," she said just loud enough for her mother, standing slightly behind her, to hear, "and you never will be. So just go away."

Annette told herself that surely she has misheard. No child would ever say such a thing to her beautiful newborn sister.

10

Alone in the store, Leo's tired and ready to lock up. On Friday nights he keeps the store open until eight thirty, a half hour later than the rest of the week, since the first night of the weekend inspires strong cravings for sweets in many of his customers.

His last customer has left, the wife of the liquor storeowner next door, after buying six large bags of potato chips. The cash register is closed and the floor swept, when the front door quietly swings open. Cookie, motionless, stands framed in the doorway, reminding Leo of an old-fashioned cameo necklace. Her hair is swept up into some kind of tight bun, and a small lavender flower is pinned above her ear.

For a moment, Leo's lungs can't find air, but then he's able to breathe again, and he waves her in. She closes the door behind her. A sudden urge overcomes him to dim the lights, but he resists. She removes her bright green coat, and lays it on the counter, revealing that she's dressed gypsy-style, in a ruffled peasant blouse and layers of sheer skirts. Her eyes are large and secretive, the curve of her round face soft and inviting.

A mist forms on his upper lip. He's not sure how it happens, and will never be sure, even years later, when he looks back at this day, how the line is first crossed. All he's certain of is that he walks over to the front door and locks it. And that, seconds later, she's in his arms, and their bodies and mouths are intent upon each other and nothing else. He grows hard and presses against her, feeling her hips move to accommodate his presence, and the movement of her body is both fierce and delicate, and then he knows that he must stop, must retreat back to the line of safety, the line which he can never cross again.

Drawing upon strength he's startled to discover he has, he pulls himself away, and is about to say something awkward and foolish, something from a trashy, Grade B movie, like, "We mustn't do this," but she's already buttoning up her coat, her fingers nimble and swift, her expression remarkably peaceful and unfazed, and she's walking toward the door, opening the lock with no struggle, closing the door soundlessly behind her, and exiting into the cool night.

He shakes his head, half-convinced—and fully wanting it to be so—that he's fallen asleep and dreamed what has just happened.

11

Sunday has arrived, the day that Shelley has agreed to attend Catholic Mass with Emma. In her excitement, Emma wakes up earlier than usual. Luckily, May is already gone, probably out visiting her bigheaded, snooty friend Bonita, with whom she often spends weekend mornings. Emma removes her pastel-pink diary from its hiding place in her underwear drawer. *Dear Diary,* she writes, carefully drawing hearts for dots, *today I will learn what makes the Catholics tick.*

She closes the book, running her fingers along its creamy pages and soft pink cover, before returning it to her drawer, carefully burying it beneath a stack of identical white, cotton panties, inexpensive and utilitarian, purchased by her mother at Alexander's Bargain Basement on Fordham Road.

Emma opens her sticky bedroom window and breathes deeply of the crisp October air. She inhales the fragrance of freshly baked bread from the Bond Bread Factory, a few blocks away. Her stomach growls, and she suddenly craves not bread but a freshly baked sugar donut. She can already taste the white powdery sugar and the doughy flesh. Of course, her mother considers donuts "dessert," and not breakfast, so that's one craving she won't be able to indulge this morning, unlike her craving to experience the very essence of Catholicism.

In her brightly-striped, loose-fitting pajamas, she walks into the kitchen, taking slow, deliberate steps, trying not to reveal her excitement. Greetings are considered unnecessary much of the time in the Rosen household, so she and Annette don't even acknowledge each other. Emma seats herself at the oilcloth-covered table in the plastic chair that tilts slightly to one side. As she often does, she props up a Wonder Woman comic book in front of her, but, too excited to read, she only pretends to do so as she chews a dry slice of rye toast and sips her full glass of blessedly wax-free Bosco.

Annette, in the kitchen, cleans and defrosts the refrigerator, listening to the radio. Dreamy-voiced Perry Como's music appeals to her in a way she can't justify to herself, since he's a lightweight, seemingly apolitical, crooner, whose songs carry no message. Yet, despite herself, she hums along with "Catch a Falling Star," his frothy homage to dewy-eyed romance, as she stacks containers of milk, cans of applesauce, and jars of store-bought gefilte fish on the already cluttered countertop.

Emma deliberately chews, swallows, sips, and turns the unread pages of her comic book, trying not to appear rushed, or out of control in any way.

In the kitchen, Annette scrubs the shelves of the refrigerator, frustrated by an especially resistant, sticky stain. Softly, she sings along with another embarrassingly silly song: *How much is that doggie in the window* . . . .

Breakfast finished, Emma leaves her plate and glass on the table for her mother to clean, as is the Rosen ritual. Walking slowly, she returns to her room, still concealing her excitement beneath a blasé surface. Once in her room, however, with the door shut, she allows herself a gleeful chuckle, as she lays out her Friday morning school assembly outfit on her bed: knee-length, A-line navy blue skirt and starched white man-tailored blouse. Her heart leaps slightly as she stares at the clothes. From now on, they will be reminders of this day — a day that will, inevitably, change her life.

She's relieved that May isn't there to bombard her with antagonistic questions about why she's putting on her best school clothes on a Sunday. Usually, on weekends, Emma wears what May calls "stereotypical sloppy kid clothes," jeans with drawstring ties and striped tee shirts two sizes too big, also plucked from Alexanders' Bargain Basement sales bins by Annette.

With May out, Annette so busy with her endless domestic chores in the kitchen, and Leo already gone for the day, doing inventory at his store, it's easy for Emma to slip unnoticed out the front door. Her mother won't worry, since Emma and Shelley spend most Sunday mornings together.

Shelley is waiting for her on the corner of Holland Avenue, directly across the street from the church, wearing a yellow-and-white flowered skirt falling demurely to her knees, and a long-sleeved blouse buttoned to her collarbone. Shelley's eyes are luminous. With her black hair shining as always, and her dark eyes huge in her olive-toned face, Shelley could easily pass for an Italian-Catholic girl, someone savvy about the Church's rules and regulations. Emma desperately hopes that with her own fair skin, blue eyes, and freckles she can squeak by as an Irish lass.

"We're true outlaws," Shelley says, in greeting, "going where no Jewish girls have gone before."

"We're bold," Emma says. "Fearless. Untouchable." Did Frank and Jesse James eventually get caught? She can't remember for sure, but a voice inside her says they were not only caught, but killed.

The air feels suddenly moist as they cross the street. With brief hesitation, drawing courage from each other, they join the line of families entering the church, as if they do this all the time, as if they truly belong and aren't trespassers.

Emma is relieved and pleased that she doesn't see anyone she knows—at least she won't be recognized. In her fantasies, she'd never allowed the possibility that Rosemary Mammano or Bobby Gaglione might be at church, so she has no script to follow if she runs into them.

She's less pleased, however, that all the Catholic women and girls are dressed in much fancier clothes than she and Shelley, decked out in light-catching satin dresses and gloves and the most feminine hats she's ever seen—hats with silver pins and jewels and intricately woven, lace veils that semi-cover their eyes and reach almost to their lips, cloaking them in mystery.

She and Shelley seem dowdy in comparison, perhaps disrespectfully so. What they had thought of as modest and proper attire might be viewed as rebellious and improper. Should she and Shelley have worn hats? Is it a Catholic law? She glances at Shelley, who looks as worried as she feels, her eyes wide and her jaw tense. In unison, they pinch each other's arms for reassurance, one of their special, best-friend gestures. "Idjut," they whisper to each other, offering comfort. Shelley pinches so hard that Emma's skin hurts, but she's grateful that at least together they can find the courage to slip inside the church.

The instant Emma steps inside, she feels queasy. The stained glass windows, so beautiful and inviting when glimpsed from afar, overwhelm her with glowing religious scenes she can't make sense of and that seem vaguely threatening. Her pulse beats in her wrist. Her mouth rapidly opens and shuts, opens and shuts, like those of the slinky little guppies her father keeps in a tank in the living room. She can't take in enough air, can't breathe.

Emma is terrified: If she remains inside, something very, very bad will happen to her, just as she has feared. *Oy vey*, she thinks, mimicking Grandma Thelma, *I've made a terrible mistake*. She is no outlaw, she admits to herself, no Jesse James. She's just a bad Jew, a snotty kid, a Doom-and-Gloom Rosen, desperately trying to become something she's not.

Emma looks at Shelley for help, but Shelley's dark eyes are cast down, her expression demure and untroubled, as she dips her dainty hand into the basin of holy water, then raises her eyes to meet Emma's, waiting for Emma to take her turn. But Emma is too frightened even to look down at the precious, sacred Holy water, the water she has dreamed of and yearned to feel so many times.

"Go on," Shelley stage whispers, "it's your turn. What are you waiting for?"

Violently, going for broke, Emma plunges both of her hands into the Holy Water. Immediately, they turn so numb that she can't feel the water at all. Is it warm?   Cool?   Is it really water at all? Perhaps the touch of her Jewish hands has transformed it into molten lava or filthy, stinking, maggot-infested garbage.

In terror, she steps off the line and stares up at the bloody, emaciated figure of Christ on the wall, hammered to the Cross, a torturous crown of thorns atop his beautiful head with its tousle of long, wavy hair. He seems to recognize her as a trespasser, a heathen, a pagan—His Killer. His accusatory, sorrowful eyes show no forgiveness.

To escape his gaze, she looks down at her hands, expecting

them, then and there, to turn bright orange and scarlet, the colors of Hell. For a moment, she thinks she sees two black crosses, one on each palm, burning into her flesh, scorching her, scarring her for life. Ignoring both the puzzled stares of the others on line, and Shelley's sharp, outraged cry of protest, she grabs Shelley's hand and pulls her out the door, then drags her down the church steps, causing the sleeve of Shelley's lovely blouse to stretch past her wrist and lose its shape. Outside, Emma continues to tremble, gasping for air. The air no longer smells like a delicious sugar donut, but instead like the stench of charred flesh.

"Idjut, what's wrong with you!" With a burst of real and surprising violence, Shelley shakes loose of Emma's grip and brushes herself off.

"We're Catholic now, don't you see? The holy water did it! Look at my hands! Look at yours! Emma's voice is loud and screechy, like chalk on a blackboard, a horrible sound, but she doesn't care.

Sullenly, Shelley looks down at Emma's hands, which Emma is usually embarrassed by because of their bitten, nubby fingernails and wild-growing cuticles, although right now she's too upset to care about that. Then, slowly, Shelley's gaze lights upon her own hands. She examines the lovely moon-shaped cuticle on her own thumb. "I don't see anything." Her voice is brittle enough to snap.

"Idjut," Emma says, made more panicky by Shelley's stubborn and stupid refusal to face the Truth With A Capital T. She lets out an exasperated, steamy breath. "We have to go home and bathe in our own water, in Jewish water, for at least an hour! This is the only path to cleansing themselves, Emma is sure. Clean, Jewish water will slowly erase the taint of Catholicism from their bodies and souls.

As if she's seen the light, Shelley's eyes grow wide and her upper lip quivers. "Okay, okay, Jewish water!" Shelley once again seems as frightened as Emma, her voice also loud and screechy. Her mysterious courage and calm have vanished, and Emma is vindicated. She is in the right. In this situation, she must be the boss, and Shelley must obey her commands.

Hand in hand, their perspiration intermingling, their heavy

breathing in sync, they race the few blocks back to the projects, ignoring traffic lights and dodging cars. Shelley races up the stairwell to her apartment on the first floor, without even a goodbye or one last best-friend pinch, and Emma jumps into the elevator, relieved that she's finally all alone, safe from the probing, disappointed eyes of Catholics, safe from Shelley's shifting moods.

The elevator, as it so often does, smells of rank, sour urine, but she doesn't hold her nose. For once, she relishes the distasteful odor which symbolizes her escape back to her home turf, free from the clutches of the Church. Inside the apartment, she rushes past the kitchen doorway. Annette is bent over the stove cooking something that smells slightly burnt—and given the fact that Emma is bound to burn in Hell, this seems horribly ominous. Luckily, May still isn't home, and Emma quickly pulls off her church-going, neat-as-a-pin, assembly clothes, now sullied forever, and dashes into the bathroom.

Feeling dazed, she watches the clear water flow from the bath faucets in an urgent rush, and she understands that this water, this Jewish water, is the only water her body must ever come in contact with. She must never again go to Mass, or discuss Catholicism with Rosemary Mammano, or sneak into the church courtyard to ask the beautiful Virgin Mary for advice. She has done a terrible thing. Although she has escaped with her Judaism intact, she will not be given another chance.

The water grows so cold that Emma's skin sprouts goose bumps, and she promises herself that when she is finally cleansed enough to depart the bath, when she is certain that she is free and clear and one hundred percent Jewish once more, she will write in her diary: *Dear Diary, I must learn to be a good Jew.*

12

Unaware that her youngest daughter has just taken the most frightening bath of her short life, and that her husband has recently been in the arms of another woman, Annette watches as May, carrying her nightgown and a change of clothes in a vinyl overnight bag, flouncing and preening like a caricature of a movie star, closes the apartment's front door behind her, on her way downstairs to Bonita Taranto's pajama party. Something still troubles Annette a great deal about May. If only she could put her finger on exactly what it is . . . Is what she's feeling pure and unadulterated "mother's intuition?" Unlikely, since she doesn't trust her own intuition, and isn't entirely convinced she has any. She's certainly not like those mothers one hears about who wake up in the middle of the night, sensing that their child, 3000 miles away from home, is in danger. Her gut feelings are never so clear. Leo's constant belittling of her and her daughters' defiance have eroded whatever confidence she may have once had. Not that she had much to begin with, thanks to the critical, overbearing Thelma Baum.

Annette locks the door behind May, double bolting the top lock, sliding the police bar into place, wondering if what she's really so bothered by these days has nothing to do with May. Maybe it's her other worries: money, for one. She and Leo are a long way from paying off the loans he took out in order to open Leo's Candies, and now the store appears to be on the brink of going under, as some of his most loyal customers—children and adults both—desert him for Sweets Brothers, "foolishly seduced," according to Leo, by "glitz and glamour." Not to mention the two brothers who run it, who sound calm and sober—without Leo's charm, true, but also without his volatile, unpredictable temper.

Annette returns to the kitchen and puts up water on the stove. She needs a large cup of strong coffee, even though sometimes too much caffeine leads her straight to a severe migraine. She'll take the risk, however, in order to have five minutes to sip the dark, bitter brew, and to shut out all thoughts of her difficult, headstrong daughter.

Downstairs at Bonita's pajama party, May sits on Bonita's wide bed next to Bonita and directly across from Susan Gartner and Francine Goldlust. In the center of the bed, in neat lines, Bonita spreads some boxy, black-and-white photos that she's recently taken of the boys in their crowd with her new Brownie camera. "Okay," she nearly chirps with excitement, "who do you think is the absolute cutest, the one who makes you weak in the knees, the one you'd take a bullet for?"

May leans forward to look more closely, to study the boys' photos, their crew cuts, acned jaws, and awkward smiles, and she's struck by a thrust of sharp pain in her forehead and eye. She smothers a cry. Gritting her teeth, she stares intensely at the photos, her gaze drawn to the one of round-cheeked Marvin Ludwig. The pain immediately vanishes. Just the sight of him is healing; her love for him is more powerful than any medicine could be.

She smoothes the nylon fabric of her lavender-colored, shortie nightie, a slinky number á la Kim Novak, boasting complicated, swirling ruffles at the neck and hem. Slightly winded, she leans back and tells herself that the pain was merely a sign that she shouldn't be wasting her time thinking about boys other than Marvin Ludwig, for whom she would take a million bullets, not just one. "He," she points to Marvin's photo, "is the cutest."

Francine is so overcome with giggles that spittle gathers at the corners of her mouth, and May worries that Francine's notoriously weak bladder will give out right there on the bed. "Marvin *is* cute," Francine is finally able to eke out through her convulsive giggles. May is unthreatened by Francine's comment, since Marvin, the boy with the golden future, would never be interested in Francine, who's nice enough, but devoid of class and grace.

Breath caught in her throat, May nods, and waits to see what Bonita will say about Marvin. Despite the fact that Bonita is her current best friend, May doesn't trust her. Bonita, gazing across the room, seems distracted. May follows her friend's gaze and her eyes alight on Bonita's prized doll collection. Bonita's rich aunt in Great Neck orders these dolls in their wonderful costumes from all over the world. May loves Bonita's ultra-feminine dolls, these porcelain, fragile, vividly painted flamenco dancers, ballerinas, English governesses, Dutch maids . . . casually propped up on bureaus, lined up on the floor, peeking out from the closet. May knows that her own parents would label such an excessive number of dolls "offensive," and "blatantly materialistic," and she envies Bonita a mother and aunt who encourage indulgence and excess.

"I love Joey," Bonita says, finally tearing herself away from the sight of the dolls, still not addressing the Marvin issue, which makes May suspicious, as she so often is, about Bonita's supposed lack of romantic interest in Marvin.

Bonita lifts up the photograph of Joey Maestre, one of the few Puerto Rican boys in their class, and presses her lips to it, making an exaggerated smooching sound. Over the photograph her eyes seek out May's with an expression that May can't read, not that it matters. Marvin is May's destiny and she is his, and Bonita cannot interfere with what is preordained.

May accepts one of the flower-shaped, chocolate-cherry candies that Bonita has begun passing around, even though recently she hasn't had much of an appetite. Lately, her stomach is often bloated and painful, even when she hasn't eaten a thing. She refuses to tell her parents about this, just as she won't tell them about the intermittent throbbing in her skull and behind her eye. Why should she, when on so many days, she feels perfectly fine? And she is . . . perfectly fine. She chews the candy slowly, noting how different it is from the chocolate candies her father sells in his store, the Nestles Crunches, Hershey's Kisses, and peanut-and chocolate-filled M & M's. It's exotic, like something Bonita's dolls would eat, if they came to life.

May surprises herself by asking for a second piece. *You see,* she assures some imaginary listener—God, perhaps, or her parents—*my appetite is fine. I am fine.*

Just at that moment, May feels a twinge of nausea, and, as if there's been an eclipse, her world grows dark. She's gone blind, and she's barely able to stop herself from gasping aloud in terror. Then she can see again. In fact, everything around her is clearer and brighter than before: Bonita's red hair so bright it's blinding; the dolls—grinning mouths and startled eyes—seem alive, with genuine crimson blood pulsing beneath their painted skin. May tells herself that none of this is real, not those earlier lightning-quick flashes of pain, not the blackness, and not this exaggerated, heightened, colorful reality all around her. She's imagining things, that's all. Living with the Rosens, especially with Emma, the destructive, poisonous interloper whose legitimacy in her family May will never accept, is truly driving her mad.

13

On Rosh Hashanah morning, a crisp fall day, colorful leaves gather at the feet of the Projects' trees, and Leo, unseasonably dressed in a mid-thigh bathing suit and flip flops, is in a wondrously jolly and magnanimous mood, due partially to the weather, and partially to the memory of his embrace with Cookie Coke, replete with its ecstasy and guilt. Cookie hasn't been back to the store since, nor has he run into her in the Projects, and, despite a strong desire to see her, he's relieved. Better to remove the temptation than to give in to desire. He assumes she's come to the same decision. Anyone can make a mistake, can slip up once.

His flip flops slap the floor noisily as he pads along the narrow foyer towards his daughters' bedroom, and opens their door without knocking. In the doorway, voice singsong, he calls out, "Up and at 'em, both of you. We're going to the beach. Put your suits on."

Leo pats his slight paunch, imagining himself an atheist Santa Claus spreading cheer on the Jewish holiday, an image he relishes for its absurdity, going so far as to cry, "Ho Ho Ho! Comrades, it's off to the beach we go!" Thoughts of the beach never fail to bring out this boyish, irreverent side in him—his best childhood memories revolve around sun and sand. Arnold and Myrtle Rosen, both strong, serious swimmers, took Leo and his sisters to Coney Island every weekend, all summer long, into the early fall. Just the sight of the ocean calmed his mother and father, who spoke in sensible, soothing voices rather than their usual manic, raw shouts. "Come here, Leo-kin," his mother called gently, using her rarely offered pet name for him, holding out her jiggling, loose arms, standing at the water's edge in her dark-skirted bathing suit. His forbidding, bald-domed father, typically sour and resentful of the demands of family life, playfully splashed water at him, smiling and laughing good-naturedly when Leo splashed back.

Emma, sitting up in bed in her striped pajamas, rubs her crusty eyes, pleased by her father's upbeat mood, but surprised that he wants to go to the beach today. She knows enough about the Jewish High Holy Days to know that this is definitely not a day for beachgoing. This will mean more trouble for the Rosens, if God is spying on them from Heaven, but of course there is no-God, so there's nothing to worry about.

If only she could return to the Virgin Mary, to ask her opinion about the options available to good Jews . . . beach-going or not . . . but she cannot return. She sighs with the enormity of the knowledge that Mary is forever off limits to her, mutters *oy vey* under her breath, and is startled by how much she sounds like Grandma Thelma. Although these days it's not Grandma's Thelma's *Yiddishisms* Emma remembers most vividly, but her terrible hands, each missing two fingers, with crooked stumps where fingers once were. Grandma Thelma had an illness that, according to Annette, had forced the doctors "back in the old country," to cut off four of Grandma Thelma's fingers. "So you see," her mother says, "Grandma is an example of the curse our family carries, far and near, the Baums and Rosens, both."

"Cursed by whom?" Emma once asked her mother. "We don't believe in God, right? So who can curse us?"

Annette had sighed, looked into the distance and said, "Who do you think?" Which explained absolutely nothing.

Now, in the doorway, Leo taps his foot loudly, his good mood clearly evaporating, and this concerns Emma, who's still in bed, blanket up to her chin, unable to stop thinking about Grandma Thelma, worrying about the curse. If Thelma had been right, if there is a God, then Grandma Thelma herself must have done something so horrible that God had punished her by giving her that dreadful disease. Had she been, despite her synagogue-attendance and candle lighting, a bad Jew? Will Emma's fingers one day be chopped off and replaced by gnarled stumps? Will she spend the rest of her life paying for the sin of not believing in Him, the sin passed down to her by her parents?

Or maybe, Emma thinks, Grandma Thelma was punished by

God because He disapproves of Socialists, which is what Grandma Thelma once was, before she became so deeply and devoutly religious. If that's true, then won't her mother, who still votes Socialist, also be punished in some terrible way? And what about her father, who was once a proud member of a young Communist group, like the ones that supposedly meet in the Coops, whom she'd been so eager to see on the day of her ill-fated walk with Shelley? What will God do to her father? Surely, God disapproves of Leo's commitment to the idea that even violence is "justified as the means to an end." Leo's hands and feet might be chopped off in their entirety.

"Get a move on," Leo says, hovering impatiently over her bed in his cotton bathing suit. She stares at his hairy, strong chest, and feels overwhelmed, nauseated by his power over her. *Not fair*, she wants to scream into his face.

Leo is beginning to glower, and now there's no mirth, no musical playfulness, in his voice. Why aren't his daughters grateful for the pleasure he's offering them? They should be squealing with almost kittenish joy, the way he and his sisters did on beach-going days.

He leaves, slamming the door emphatically behind him, and Emma notices that May, on the other side of the room, is out of bed and stepping into a pink bikini the exact shade of Pepto Bismol.

Finally Emma rises from her own bed and rummages in her crammed bureau for the dowdy green tank suit that some second cousin of her mother's, whom they've never met and who lives way out in the suburbs, sent as a birthday gift. Emma quickly pulls her hair into a ponytail. In her rush, she pulls so tightly, her forehead stings.

When she and May are washed and dressed, they join Leo at the front door. He's scowling and holding the door open in his impatience to leave. Emma assumes that their mother is coming with them. But Annette, who's wearing one of the flowered housedresses that May, behind her back, calls a *schmata*, shakes her head no. "I'm as opposed to organized religion as you," she tells Leo, her voice strained. She hands him the large blue plastic picnic bag she's packed with sandwiches. "But you don't have to rub everyone's faces in your beliefs."

Annette tries to catch Leo's eye, hoping that he'll change his mind and stay home today, reading, or watching TV with the girls. But it's useless, he always does exactly what he wants, while she ends up sounding like an ineffectual nag, a *yenta*, a whiney *kvetch*, the kind of woman no one, including herself, likes. Annette hates what she has become, and would understand if Leo is drawn elsewhere, to other women, like the seductive Cookie Coke, although she would not ever truly understand, not in her heart. She would never forgive Leo if she were to find out he'd been with someone else.

"Oh yes, I do have to rub their faces in it," Leo insists, happily, meeting her eyes. Mischievous music has returned to his voice, the scowl transforming, like a miracle, into a crooked but wide grin. "I have to show these so-called good Jews a thing or two!"

Emma, witnessing the drama between her parents, wonders at her mother's stony face. She has heard her father use this phrase before — *these so-called good Jews* — and she wonders what makes these particular Jews only "*so-called.*" What would it take for them to be the real thing? Why is there so much attention paid to this Good Jew-Bad Jew stuff? Was Grandma Thelma, who went from not believing in God to passionately and fervently believing in Him, a good Jew or a "so-called?"

Are there so-called Good Catholics? Is Rosemary Mammano, with her prejudiced comments against blacks and Jews, a good one or a so-called one?

And what about so-called good Protestants? Not that there are a lot of them in the Projects. Some of the black kids are, but they don't talk about their religion nearly as much or with the same intensity as the Catholic kids. Protestantism seems sober and unextravagant, without the passion and mystery of Catholicism. Only one white Protestant family lives in the Projects, the blond, blue eyed Crowells, who say "Oh gosh," and who come from Sioux City, Iowa, a place that Emma has heard them describe as "flat, green, and Godly."

Emma tags behind May, who like her, has thrown a light

cardigan sweater over her bathing suit. The elevator, as if to appease impatient Leo, moves swiftly and is urine-free, and as they walk to their car through the Projects, Leo hums one of his old labor songs. His voice is so flat and off-key Emma can't figure out which one, but she vaguely recognizes it, and guesses it's the one about the union maid who's not afraid of "goons and ginks and company finks."

The Projects are deserted at this early hour, other than for a young Puerto Rican mother, whose root beer-colored hair is pinned up in fist-sized rollers. She's wheeling a baby carriage and, like Leo, humming to herself. Her voice is beautiful and Emma instantly recognizes the song as one her mother often sings: *Catch a falling star . . .*

Emma and May follow their father into the secondhand black Oldsmobile scarred by bullet holes in two of the windows, a great source of pride for him. "I got this baby for a song," he likes to say, "from a guy who hangs around the store." The way he says, *a guy who hangs around the store*, seems like a code for someone criminal and unsavory, and Emma knows that this is why Annette hates this car.

Today, Emma is allowed to sit in the front seat beside her father because that way she's less likely to get carsick. May narrows her eyes, but Emma decides not to care, since she's the one who's always vomiting her guts out into the large plastic "puke bucket" that her mother and father insist she keep balanced between her knees whenever they take a car trip, no matter how short. Luckily, it's only a twenty-minute drive to the beach, and this time, Emma doesn't get sick, which pleases her immensely, and she wonders if this is God's gift to her on Rosh-Hashanah, her reward for keeping her promise not to visit the Virgin Mary again.

On this October day the sky is slate blue, the air is nippy, and the beach desolate, but Emma has to admit that the fine white sand is cleaner and more lovely than in the summer when the beach is crowded with people and cluttered with blankets and umbrellas and cans of soda and beer. Nevertheless, it's during the summer, not now, that she loves the beach. She loves the way the hot sun makes her sleepy and lazy, and the way the wave-crested water cools her off.

In their cardigans, she and May sit silently together on the thin woolen blanket Leo spreads out for them. "Don't do anything I wouldn't do," he grins and starts the long walk to the water's edge, leaving them alone.

Emma regards May closely, marveling at how little they have to say to each other, despite sharing the same blood and having both been on the receiving end of so many of their mother's Doom and Gloom predictions and their father's violent outbursts. Emma usually thinks that May is pretty, despite her cruelty, with her dirty-blonde hair and her cats'-eye eyeglasses, but right now she's scrunching her face up as though she's the one who's going to vomit. For a moment, Emma worries that May is really sick—and if this were the case, she worries what her own response would be. It might not be sorrow. It might, in fact, be happiness, and this realization simultaneously saddens and pleases her. In any case, May is fine. She's deliberately making an ugly face, in order to frighten Emma. But Emma's not about to fall for a stupid trick like that.

Tired of May's petty cruelties, she turns her attention to her father, studying him as he walks slowly down to the edge of the dark, choppy water, a lone figure against the landscape of sea and sky, never looking back at his daughters. She doesn't ease her concentration as he begins to swim, his movements through the water strong and fierce, his head turning smoothly and rapidly from side to side as he takes in air.

Only when she loses sight of him, does she feel she can relax enough to turn her concentration back to herself. She wraps her suddenly chilled body in a large, brightly colored beach towel. Curling herself up as tightly as she can, she begins composing a poem in her head about water and sand, using the words "aqua" and "ivory," words she loves because they sound as beautiful as the colors they represent. *The aqua water is like sky*, she thinks. *The ivory sand is bright and fair. Good lines,* she thinks, and she repeats them silently twice more. As soon as she gets home, she'll write them down so she won't forget.

Waiting for Leo to finish his long, solitary swim, she grows hungry. She reaches into the large plastic picnic bag, removing one of the two sticky peanut butter-and-jelly sandwiches that her mother had packed.

May, who's been lying face down on her stomach, sits up, and for a long minute watches Emma as she begins to eat. Self-consciously, Emma chews carefully with her mouth closed. She licks crumbs delicately from her lips, unable to shake the oppressive feeling that May is judging her, finding her even more lacking than usual in grace and elegance, the two things May is always saying that she, herself, "like Kim Novak," possesses. Despite her self-consciousness, Emma consumes the sandwich in record time, and is struck by her own large appetite, so much like her father's, and so different from her sister's.

Like a weapon, May's silence is aimed directly at Emma. May reaches into the bag and pulls out the second sandwich, but not before removing a paper napkin and placing it daintily on her knees. With a disgusted expression, pursing her lips, she shakes her head at Emma.

Emma is reminded of awful Mrs. O'Reilly who pursed her lips in class and called Emma "This Girl." *You don't rule over me*, Emma thinks, *you petty tyrant*.

May eats very slowly, making a deliberate and big show of constantly dabbing her mouth with her napkin, not with her tongue, obviously to distinguish herself from Emma, whom she has called, in the past, "boorish and vulgar." Yet, after all that, May doesn't finish her sandwich, carefully re-wrapping the untouched half. Of course, Emma thinks—truly feminine girls who exude what May calls "class," would never reveal too hearty an appetite.

A gull flying overhead swoops surprisingly close to them, then soars far away. A new poem begins to take shape in Emma's mind. The gull, as narrator, revealing his urgent need to flee. But the poem remains vague and intangible, and soon the words are as far away as the gull itself, which has disappeared in the sky, in the same way Leo seems to have disappeared into the ocean.

Finally, after what seems like forever, so long that Emma is truly beginning to worry that Leo has been sucked down into a wicked dervish of a whirlpool, she spots him on the sand, walking toward them. In the distance, he looks so small and harmless. Emma wishes this moment could be frozen, rendering him that way forever.

A moment later, Leo, full-sized once more, rejoins the girls on the blanket, breathing deeply and drying off his dripping body with two oversized beach towels. "Up and at 'em," he says again, his voice happy once more. "Time to go home."

As Emma fumbles with the buttons on her cardigan, Leo says, "Come on, come on, get a move on." Emma can tell that he's serious, not fooling around. This time he will not be kept waiting. There will be hell to pay—a beating, perhaps more than one—if he doesn't get his way. May, too, is obediently readying herself, quietly buttoning her own cardigan.

Dripping water, Leo is now in such a hurry to get home that he keeps his wet bathing suit on, not even slipping on his zippered windbreaker to warm himself. He rushes them to the parking lot where once again May sullenly slithers into the back seat, and Emma climbs quickly, monkey-style, into the front.

Leo accelerates so fast that both girls gasp, and he crosses lanes, cutting off the Number 12 bus, which in the summer is packed sardine can-tight with beachgoers but today is nearly empty. With a wild screech, he steers across the busy intersection of Pelham Parkway and White Plains Road. Trying to quell her lurching stomach, Emma looks out the bullet-scarred car window, and sees a Jewish family, a father and three sons, all dressed up in dark suits, crossing the street. She knows they're Jewish because they're wearing *yamulkes*, although she doesn't understand the significance of the skullcaps, another sign of her bad-Jewishness. No point in asking her father; he'd just say, "Pure superstition. No more."

Intently, Emma watches as the fair-skinned, chubby family walks together almost dreamily, as if in slow motion. Are they truly good Jews, or just *so-called*? They must be on their way home from synagogue, where they've celebrated Rosh-Hashanah, however it's done. With music and prayer, she guesses, and special foods. She's heard of *davening*, has witnessed her father's comic renditions of it, in which he lurches back and forth and wails as if he has to urgently go to the bathroom.

Is she the only Jew in the world who's never set foot in a Jewish temple? Even May attended the *barmitzvah* of George Zimmerman, Bethie Zimmerman's older brother, during the brief period that Bethie was May's best friend, before May dumped her, as she eventually dumps anyone close to her.

Leo parks the car on the far side of the Projects, and Emma immediately understands that he has done this deliberately, so that they'll have to walk past all five of the other buildings, in order to reach their own. This has been the real reason for the entire excursion, this parading around in their bathing suits on Rosh Hashanah. By now, the Project benches will have filled up with Jews, home from synagogue, chatting and sharing news of God, or whatever it is that religious Jews discuss on the High Holy Days. This must be what her mother meant when she'd said to Emma's father, "You don't have to rub everyone's faces in your beliefs."

Like two little ducklings, May and Emma trail behind their father, the three of them in their bathing suits. Their rubber flips flops slap the sidewalk in drum-like rhythm. Emma's toes and fingers are freezing, and, beside her, May also shivers, although she won't meet Emma's eye to commiserate.

Of course, Leo doesn't appear to be cold at all, and it's crystal-clear to Emma how proud he is of the figure he cuts as he walks through the Projects, his back straight, head high, a strong man who can withstand cold water and cold weather, a muscular man with his two obedient and unquestioning daughters in tow.

It's also clear to Emma how much her father relishes the shocked and disapproving stares from the Jews, who, as Emma predicted, are now sitting in clusters of three and four, on the slatted wooden benches outside their buildings. They wear their nicest wool coats, the men wear *yarmulkes*, and the women wear cloche hats and lots of gold jewelry, which may or may not be real. All she knows for sure is that the few gold pieces her mother has, and which she rarely wears, are all fake, something her mother seems proud of. "We

Rosens don't care for material things," she insists. "Fakes are good enough for us. Fakes are not really fake at all," she adds, enigmatically.

As the Rosens pass, the Jews on the benches shake their heads, whisper, frown, roll their eyes and click their tongues, reminding Emma of Looney Tunes' cartoon characters.

Leo, grinning ear to ear, stage whispers, "We're stronger than they are. That's Truth with a capital T."

Emma hopes that Mr. and Mrs. Freedman, sitting on the bench closest to them, haven't heard him. The Freedmans have a black-haired daughter named Rachel whom Emma and Shelley sometimes spend time with, and whom Emma likes a great deal, because Rachel writes poetry, and has, a few times, shared her poems with Emma. Emma remembers the beginning of one of Rachel's poems: *Horses inhabit my dreams* . . . . It had surprised Emma, because there were no horses in the Projects, and, as far as she knew, Rachel had never ridden one.

Emma also hopes that Mrs. Zelig, sitting next to the Freedmans, hasn't heard Leo. Mrs. Zelig and her branded arm, with her kind, inclusive smile—even if her teeth are grey and chipped, who says *oy vey* just like Grandma Thelma used to.

But next to her, filling out the bench, is the rheumy-eyed, bearded widower Mr. Roshansky, wrinkled head bobbing. Emma hates him because he likes to touch the breasts of young girls—hers, Shelley's, Rachel Freedman's, even May's—under the pretense of being nice and friendly, slipping his bony, hairy hand beneath their undershirts. "Everyone's Jewish Uncle," he calls himself. His touch makes Emma cringe, makes her want to vomit all over him, and all over herself, as well, wherever his hands have landed. Sometimes he tries to go even lower than their breasts, below the waistbands of their pants, and even lower still, all the way down to their privates, what she and Shelley like to call their *vajakas* because it's their own special word, more musical, more esoteric, than the basic, clumsy, *vaginas*.

Once, back when Emma was nine, she found herself alone in the lobby with Mr. Roshansky waiting for the elevator. She stood all the way over by the mailboxes, trying to keep out of his sight. Fearful of his roving, spidery, hands, she felt tiny and breakable. When the elevator arrived, he got in first and held the door open for her. "Little Emma Rosen," he called softly, "I'm waiting for you."

Trying not to show fear, she pressed the button for her floor and as the door closed, she backed into the corner and held her hands over her breasts, unable, alone with him in such a small, closed space, to pretend any longer that she wasn't fearful.

He amazed her by remaining in his corner, not making a move toward her. Instead, he spoke even more softly, as if sensing her fear and wanting to reassure her. "I've been watching your sister," he half-whispered. "She's got the inner devil. She's not right in the head." He touched his own head with his thin, old man's finger. "She's *teched.* So don't worry, Emma Rosen. I know the truth."

Emma had held her breath before allowing herself to nod, letting her hands fall to her sides. "Yes," she said, in amazement, as softly as he.

The elevator stopped on his floor, and he got off. "Remember," he whispered, "we both know." The doors closed.

Emma hasn't known what to think since then: Is he right? Is May *teched*? Sometimes she thinks so, and it gives her comfort. Just the other day she wrote in her diary, *May is teched and evil, a flesh-and-blood version of the cackling, cruel Wicked Witch of the West from The Wizard of Oz. I am Glinda, the Good. If there is a God, he loves me.*

Still, it's difficult to fully believe what Mr. Roshansky says, considering the fact that he's so clearly *teched* in the head himself, a lecherous *alta caca.* Even May calls him "Mr. Dirty Old Man." But none of the girls ever tell their parents about the way Mr. Roshansky touches them, not Emma or Shelley or Rachel, not even May. It's an unspoken agreement among them to protect him because of what Hitler did to him, because of that rigid line of pale blue numbers lining his arm.

In a book of her father's about Adolph Eichmann, Emma had seen photographs of concentration camp survivors on the day they were freed, barely-alive wraiths, with hollow eyes and shaved skulls.

Mr. Roshansky had been among them, had looked like them. She doesn't ever want to add to Mr. Roshansky's suffering. Maybe, she tells herself, Mr. Roshansky wasn't like this before Hitler came to power. Maybe he was once a gentle man who played nice games with little girls, who never thought about touching their breasts.

And now, on Rosh Hashanah, as she walks past him, she's more confused than ever. Is Mr. Roshansky, whose *yamulke* sits atop his head at an almost rakish, hoodlum's angle, a good Jew, or a *so-called*? Mr. Roshansky, with his branded arm, thick, ragged beard, and phony, flat smile, has suffered in ways that Emma knows she can't even begin to understand, and now he dresses up in his suit and tie and goes to synagogue and prays. But as soon as he can, he'll be sidling up to Emma, putting his bony arm around her, trying to stroke her nipples, beneath her blouse. Just because Emma hasn't set foot in a synagogue, hasn't suffered at Hitler's hands, isn't even sure of God's existence, does that make her a worse Jew than he?

Hannah Zelig suffered just as much as he did during the war, and she behaves kindly toward all the children in the Projects. Nothing excuses what he does, and as Emma trails along behind her father, she meets the full-bearded Mr. Roshansky's bespectacled, watery eyes, and she shivers again. Then she feels glad that she's wearing a bathing suit and walking beside her father and sister on Rosh Hashanah instead of sitting beside Mr. Roshansky on the bench. *Try to touch me now,* she thinks, *you dirty old man, you so-called Good Jew.*

May, however, isn't at all glad, since Marvin's parents, Mr. and Mrs. Ludwig, are among the religious Jews sitting outside. And the *zaftig*, double-chinned Mrs. Ludwig, whose wrinkled, soiled brassieres and panties May had glimpsed the day Marvin kissed her in the laundry room, is glaring directly at her.

And there's no mirth at all in the eyes of the fair-skinned Mr. Ludwig, a salesman of lighting fixtures in a small store on the Lower East Side, who loves to perform magic tricks for the kids in the Projects. On a few occasions, May and her friends have joined Marvin and some others, and watched Mr. Ludwig make coins disappear and appear, and playing card numbers recur at his will.

But now, as he stares at the Rosens walking past in their provocative and shameful bathing suits, his *yamulke* sits stiffly and rigidly atop his head, his eyes are grim, and there's no magic in the air around him.

Even if she threw herself to the ground and begged her father to apologize to everyone on the bench, even if she told him that he's ruining her life and destroying her chance for happiness and a golden future, May knows that he wouldn't care. And she's right. Because at that moment, not only do his needs come first, but Leo believes that his needs are his daughters' needs. He recognizes no separation between their flesh and thoughts and feelings and his own. Leo runs the Rosen family; thus, he is the Rosen family.

Nor does he perceive the Jews sitting on the benches as distinct individuals, as ghostly, long-suffering widow Mrs. Zelig, for instance, or Hyman and Bella Freedman whose daughter Rachel has dined at his table, or loudmouthed Aaron Ludwig, who clumsily performs magic tricks that any six-year-old boy can do better, and his smug wife, Judith, and her floppy, unappealing bosoms, the size of a small country.

Right now, all Leo sees is a huddled group of nameless, faceless men and women who, frightened of pain, death, and sorrow—as are we all—foolishly and desperately turn to the supernatural, wrong-headedly calling their fears "faith," despite all the empirical evidence to the contrary, too weak to acknowledge their own frailties.

It suddenly occurs to Leo, however, that Cookie might see him too, parading around in his bathing suit, but he has a feeling that his mischievous ways will titillate her more than disappoint her. He admits to himself that he likes the idea of her seeing him in his bathing suit, and he allows himself a fantasy of the two of them, side by side on a beach on her island, Cookie in a white bathing suit that sets off her nutmeg skin, the sky overhead violet and magenta, the water a swirling turquoise mist. What if he ran away with her to a tropical paradise and lived a life of pure freedom, no loans to pay off, no whining children, no *kvetching* wife? Once, a month or so ago, while visiting the store, she had smiled at him and said, "Leo, you are boy and man together, and what's not appealing to a woman about that?" But now isn't the time to think about Cookie and to want things he'll never be able to have—now is the time to delight in the present, in the here and now, on this High Holy Day when he will show the world what he thinks of the very concept of holiness.

May, sensing her father's feelings, tries to affect an impassive expression that shows her lack of agreement with him. She pulls down her too-short cardigan in order to hide her pink bikini, but the gesture seems obscene, and she feels vulgar and trampy. At least, she thinks, Marvin isn't on the bench with his parents to witness her sacrilege and shame. But even so, she wants never to have to show her face again in public, she wants to die. She wants all records of Leo Rosen's firstborn wiped from the books. After today, Mr. and Mrs. Ludwig will order Marvin to keep as far away as possible from the daughter of the *meshuge* Leo Rosen, and how can she blame them? In their place, she would do the same.

A gust of wind knifes through her, but May resists shivering. She keeps her head down, not wanting to see for another second the icy disapproval in the Ludwigs' eyes. As she follows her father into the building, she feels that pain again, first in her forehead and then behind her eye. Much worse than it's been. Quick. Stabbing. A message of some sort. Like Morse Code. *Rat a tat tat. Roger and out.*

Two overhead lights in the lobby are out, and the semi-darkness mirrors May's dark mood. Leo, grinning from ear to ear, like a crazed circus clown, rings for the elevator. Emma, in her ugly, vomit-green bathing suit, grins back at him. Sickened by their mutual-admiration society, May forces her features to remain calm.

The elevator arrives, and out spills the Williams family, who are black. Her father greets them far more warmly than he ever greets any of the Jewish families. May is sure that he likes blacks and Puerto Ricans better than he likes anyone else. He never says "so-called blacks," or "so-called Puerto Ricans," as if there's no way someone could be black or Puerto Rican and not be authentic. This, despite the fact that most blacks and Puerto Ricans, from what she can tell, attend Church regularly and believe fiercely in God. She's not sure why he's so tolerant of the same "weaknesses" he's so repelled by in Jews, but she imagines it's somehow connected to his own "*meshuge*" parents, and his Communist youth, of which he's so proud, because it proves his solidarity with "the little man."

Around Cookie Coke, who smells of vanilla and lavender, he's positively gaga, and she's amazed her mother lets him get away with it, if her mother even allows herself to acknowledge what is so obvious. Not that her mother, who can be so pathetic at times, ever stands up to him about anything. May promises herself that she will be strong on her future children's behalf, although, because Marvin will never do anything to make her jealous, sad, or angry, she'll never be tested.

Leo affectionately pats the heads of the Williams twins, two small boys with enormous eyes and close-cropped hair who grin up at him with admiration and awe, neither of which May, at the moment, feels toward him.

Mrs. Williams says, "Hello there. Have you all been for a swim in this weather?" Her smile reveals one dazzling gold front tooth. May wonders what Mrs. Williams really thinks of the three of them. The Williams are Protestants, and May has seen Mrs. Williams all dolled up in her Sunday church-going clothes, wide-brimmed hats, stiff dresses, and white stretchy gloves. Does she, like the Jews on the benches, perceive the Rosens as absolutely crazy and disgraceful?

Mr. Williams slaps her father on the back as though they're old friends, and as though seeing a family in their bathing suits on a cool October day is nothing unusual. "Leo Rosen," he smiles, "How goes it?"

Leo nods, says, "Can't complain. Can't complain."

Mr. Williams holds the elevator open with an almost formal, gentlemanly bow. Leo and Emma step inside. Emma bats her eyelashes at Mr. Williams and says, "Why, thank you very much," probably imitating some trashy movie actress like Jayne Mansfield, nobody as classy as Kim Novak. Emma will grow up to be a slut, May is certain, the kind of desperate female out to please men at all costs, choosing her men foolishly, going for the ones who cheat and drink and gamble. No golden future for Emma. But, after today, perhaps May won't have a golden future, either.

Wishing she were invisible, May glumly follows Leo and Emma

into the elevator. Losing her balance, she briefly stumbles. But nobody seems to notice, and she figures she's just so distracted over seeing Marvin's parents that she's not her usual, graceful self. At least the pain behind her eye has completely subsided, and she rests her back against the elevator wall, narrowly missing leaning against a wad of chewing gum that might very well have been Emma's, since Emma chews a lot of Juicy Fruit, which Leo brings home for her from the store five, six packages at a time. Yes, the E-Bomb is definitely inconsiderate and piggish enough to discard her gum in such a disgusting, childish way.

Emma, meanwhile, is reciting a new poem to Leo, some hooey about sand and sky. *Pretentious*, May thinks, proud to use a word that Bonita often uses. "Miss Kitty on *Gunsmoke* is pretentious," Bonita says, or, "Beatniks are pretentious." *Pretentious*, for May, has come to mean everything that she and Marvin Ludwig, as real and authentic as two human beings can be, are not, and will never be, everything that Emma embodies.

Just then May's stomach turns over, and everything around her goes black. For a second time, the world is suddenly devoid of light, and she hears her father's disembodied, boisterous voice saying, "Emma, kiddo, you're gonna win a Pulitzer!" and Emma, in response, giggling like the moron she is.

May stands still. Her back against the wall is frozen and rigid. She must reveal nothing; if they suspect, they'll tell her mother. And then her mother will send her to a doctor. Inevitably an operation will follow, and she will never be the same. Her life will be as good as over.

An explosion bursts inside her head, and she can see again: Emma's goofy, proud smile; Leo's equally proud, nauseating grin. The elevator stops at the eleventh floor. May steps out first, keeping her back to them. In the grey-wallpapered hallway, she walks quickly to their corner apartment, fearful that she might lose her balance and stumble again. Her flesh feels moist behind her knees, her mouth is sour, and she grits her teeth, thinking: *careful, careful, one foot in front of the other, give nothing away.*

She rings the doorbell even before her father has his key out, and then completely ignores her mother who comes to the door to greet them.

"So, Leo," Annette says, tensely, a vein on her temple visibly throbbing, stepping aside to let them in, running her hand through her embarrassingly premature white streak of hair, "now are you satisfied? Are you proud of yourself?"

May, pushing past her mother, heads quickly to the bathroom, not waiting to hear her father's reply, not even giving him first dibs on the toilet, the way she usually does, since, according to her mother, he sometimes has "bathroom problems."

She closes, then locks, the bathroom door, and stares at herself in the mirror above the sink, blaming Emma for the ugly smears of toothpaste on the glass. Piggish Emma, who stole their parents' love, who defaces and destroys everything and everyone she touches.

In the mirror, May's dirty blonde hair looks messy, her skin unnaturally pale. Her rebellious lazy eye is acting up, shifting inward. She doesn't look real to herself: a shadow girl whose sight comes and goes.

Closing the toilet lid, she sits down heavily, her head in her hands. She feels her shoulders rising and falling as though she's sobbing, but there are no tears in her eyes. The pains she's having aren't just headaches; she's certain of that. They're nothing, for instance, like Annette's migraines, which come on every couple of weeks, sending her into the bathroom where, like Emma during car trips, she loudly pukes and pukes, sometimes for hours on end, while May grows angry and queasy just listening to her. Afterward, her eyes rimmed by dark circles and her skin like chalk, Annette returns to the land of the living, wearily announcing to May and Emma, "I inherited Grandma Thelma's migraines, and one day, wait and see, you'll get them, too."

Despite Annette's prediction, May knows that what's happening to her has nothing to do with migraines. Or with the headaches shown on TV commercials in which an aspirin or two solves all problems. What she has is unreal, alien, too intense for this planet, like something from *The Twilight Zone*.

No, that's not it either, she thinks, *I am not otherworldly. I'm just a sick girl, plain and simple.* Something is seriously wrong, deep inside her bones, her marrow. She splashes cold water on her face, feeling at last the full-blown panic she hadn't allowed herself to feel in front of her father and Emma.

Why me, she whispers, squeezing some peppermint toothpaste onto her toothbrush. *Why not Emma?* Up and down, side-to-side, she vigorously moves her toothbrush as she was taught by the crisp and efficient nurse from Montefiore Hospital who'd visited her first grade class. "Be sure to brush your back teeth," the nurse had said, as May admired her form-fitting, pristine uniform and glossy smile. If Kim Novak ever played a nurse, this would be the one. She was a Hollywood fantasy come to life.

Now, May carefully follows her tooth-cleansing regimen, with more ferocity even than usual. If she cleanses her mouth, maybe she'll be able to rid her body of all germs and contaminants. But it's no use: God has chosen her, and she must accept it. It is He who's sending the nausea, the clumsiness, the blindness, the strange clarity that follows. The fact that she has a lazy eye, a toxic sister, a chronically sad mother, and a madman for a father, clearly isn't enough to satisfy Him. He wants her to endure yet another trial in order to prove that she's worthy of Marvin's love. It's not a punishment, it's a test.

She will not question His plan. Nor will she tell anyone about it. She rinses her mouth, spits, wipes her face, re-folds the towel before hanging it on the rack, and opens the bathroom door to a scowling, red-faced Leo, who was just about to begin pounding on the door, yelling "Get the hell out!" which is what he does to her and Emma and even to their mother, when he really, *really* needs to go.

14

The Friday after Rosh Hashanah, Leo's last customers have gone, a gaggle of teenage boys off to a neighborhood party. "No parents, man," he hears one say, excitedly, "and lots of chicks!"

Leo has shut down the register, wiped the counter, tidied the shelves, and is about to close the store, when, like *déjà vu*, the front door swings open, and Cookie, once again a dream-apparition, stands framed in the doorway, her hands hanging loosely at her sides, her posture perfect, surely aware of the sensational effect she creates, her curtain of black hair loose and unfettered, her full figure in her bright green coat emphatic and intense.

Behind the counter, Leo puts down the dust rag he was using to clean up, and takes an involuntary step forward, toward her, although he immediately steps back, embarrassing himself. He realizes that all along he'd known that she would return. He takes yet another step back—any more, and he'll disappear into the stock room. He forces himself to try to behave more casually, and is about to wave her in, but she's already closed the door and is walking slowly and deliberately toward him, quickly covering the breadth of the small store, not looking left or right at any candies or sweets that might distract or tempt her, perfectly balanced and poised on a pair of precarious, high-heeled, bright green shoes that exactly match her coat. The silence between them is threatening, although Leo knows that what's unspoken is even more so. "Leo," she finally says, breathlessly, coming behind the counter to join him, now so close that his entire body pulses with want.

"About what happened the other day. I must explain—I am not an easy woman." She speaks urgently, with passion, and yet there's something else in her voice, something he can't quite place—is she amused by what's taking place between them? Or is the trace of amusement he senses her way of protecting herself? He can't be sure.

She's so different from Annette, whom he believes he can read like an open book.

With one hand on the counter to steady himself, he raises his other to interrupt, intending to assure her that he doesn't think of her as "easy," whatever she really means by that. But she's quicker than he, and she places one of her be-ringed hands atop his on the counter, and holds up the other to silence him.

"I," she says, still breathlessly, "should have stopped myself before it happened, but . . ." She hesitates, her dark eyes grazing his, their intensity stunning.

The pressure of her warm hand upon his is more than he can take, and he lifts his away, amazed that he is the pursued, not the pursuer, for the first time in his life. He reaches down in front of the counter and grabs a bag of M & Ms, as if for ballast.

"You remind me of someone," she says, softly, not taking her eyes off him, as he puts back the unopened bag of candy, knowing he has no appetite. "Of someone from before. Someone I loved very much."

Before, he assumes, means back in Jamaica. He nods, aware that he still hasn't said a word, he who loves to talk, loves language and wordplay. He has completely turned over control of the situation to her. She begins stroking his hand, and he tries to remember what he's put together from her comments and from things her brother, Khenan, and others have said . . . that she and her young husband, a doctor in Jamaica, had come here to start a new life, to begin a family. Khenan had said, "Cookie's man was good to her. Educated, and kind. Murdered in a botched robbery." Leo tries to remember where in the Bronx it had happened—not in the Projects, but definitely nearby. He can't remember the rest of the story, if he ever knew it.

As if reading his mind, Cookie says, stroking his hand more forcefully, pursing her scarlet lips, "That man . . . the man I loved, still love . . . He was struck down. In cold blood." Her black eyes glow like embers of coal.

Leo takes a step closer to her, so that nothing but a wisp of a breath separates their bodies. "I'm sorry," he says, stumbling over the words, like a blind man on unfamiliar, rocky terrain.

Okay, he thinks, *okay, I am not a married father, I am someone else, a dead man, a ghost, a guiltless man, and Cookie is not an adulteress, she's a young, innocent woman far from home, filled with hope and optimism* . . . .

And then the front door opens, not silently this time, but with an explosive creak, and he silently curses himself for not locking it, and a teenage girl in skintight pants and a short jacket comes inside and looks around the store with a bewildered expression, and before he can blink, Cookie has grabbed her coat, and is gone, out the door, as if she had never been there, like a whisper that only he has heard, and, in a daze, he says to the girl, "Can I help you?" and she sniffles and asks too loudly if he carries Dentine chewing gum.

15

"Show me the dress that you're going to wear to Bonita's Halloween party," Annette says grimly to May, looking up from the sink full of dirty dishes she's washing. She wants to get a look at this so-called "Kim Novak outfit" that May keeps talking about, and that she'll be wearing later this afternoon at Bonita's party.

At the table, May swings her legs, sips a glass of root beer, and licks the foam mustache that's forming on her upper lip. She's feeling pretty good about things for a change. For one thing, she's felt absolutely fine all day: no pain at all. She'd hungrily eaten an entire hamburger, the bun, the meat, the relish, even the slightly runny, gravy-soaked mashed potato on the side.

She's also excited about Bonita's party, which will provide her not only with an opportunity to wear the wonderful dress she borrowed from Mrs. Taranto, but also to spend time with Marvin. Ever since Rosh Hashanah, she's been convinced that he's been avoiding her, looking away when she enters the classroom, rushing out the door like a bullet when the bell rings. His parents must have told him of her family's outrageous, *meshuge* behavior, of their *pretentiousness*, she thinks, fondly remembering that word and its power to label and demean.

The other day, May had gathered up all her courage and approached Marvin at three o'clock outside the school building. Her entire body on pins and needles, trying to sound both casual and sexy, something Kim Novak excelled at, she pushed her sliding eyeglasses up, and, so softly she could barely hear herself, whispered, "Marvin, do you like algebra?"

He frowned, shook his head, and quickly turned away.

Biting her lower lip to keep from crying, she half-walked, half-ran the whole way home, not bothering to push up her eyeglasses as they slid further and further down her nose, wishing that, like Kim, she had perfect sight and sparkling, deep eyes. It was difficult not to curse God for making her this way, but she refrained.

Now, taking a final slurp of the bittersweet soda, May rises and stretches. "Okay," she says to her mother, although she knows it's probably not a great idea, "I'll try on the dress for you." Her mother, the world's biggest fuddy-duddy and party-pooper, the least sensual woman on the planet, will undoubtedly disapprove of the black, slightly low-cut sheath dress. On a number of occasions, her mother has already made it very clear that she doesn't approve of redheaded Mrs. Taranto, who wears form-fitting dresses, has boyfriends, and allows 13-year-old Bonita to throw boy-girl parties. "I don't trust that woman," Annette says. "She's motivated by I-don't-know-what."

Nevertheless, May allows herself to stand proudly in costume before her mother, who's still busy washing dishes. May's spine is straight and her feet are perfectly balanced in the pair of glowing, ebony, high heeled, pointy-toe shoes she purchased at Alexander's—and not from the sales bin—with her own allowance money on the same day Mrs. Taranto loaned her the dress. A vinyl, sequined purse, also from Alexander's, dangles elegantly from her wrist. Around her neck she wears a strand of fake, pink-white colored pearls, inherited from Grandma Thelma. She pirouettes, feeling just like a beauty pageant contestant parading before the judges, like Miss America, or better yet, Miss Universe, who conquers and is unsurpassed in the entire solar system.

But Annette, whose hands are encased in a pair of ripped yellow rubber gloves and immersed in a sink full of heavily scented soap bubbles, feels nothing like a beauty pageant judge. She feels exhausted and beleaguered and sick of washing dishes three times a day and sometimes more for her ungrateful family. Although she knows very little about the Bible, she knows enough to think: *I am the real Job.*

This has been a particularly rough week for Annette: two migraines already, one not too bad, the other was among the worst she's had in years—and then to top it off, on the night of the killer migraine, May refused to eat a single bite of her dinner, claiming her lamb chops were "rubbery," and making Annette wonder again whether she was being spiteful, or whether she had some kind of recurrent stomach upset. Was it possible for a 13 year old to have inherited Leo's stomach problems, the colitis, the ulcer? She's definitely inherited his stubborn and cruel streaks, so why not his medical ailments?

Annette sighs and wonders, yet again, whether she should take May to see a doctor, but she knows how much May hates doctors. Just going for a checkup is agonizing for her, and she still throws full-blown temper tantrums, like a spoiled toddler.

Annette stops in the midst of scouring an egg-encrusted pan with a Brillo soap pad. She stares at her daughter who's so clearly proud of herself, and she finds her unbearably pathetic, a child trying to be a sultry *femme fatale*. Had this girl truly emerged from her loins?

"It's not right to borrow Mrs. Taranto's dress just for a silly party." Annette's own harsh, unforgiving words are startling. She's ashamed of herself, since she knows that what she's really so worked up about isn't that May borrowed the dress, but that May is so desperate to be attractive to boys. *You're ridiculous*, she wants to say to her daughter, *like Narcissus, lost in your own reflection*.

But Annette knows that, no matter what she says, May will do exactly what she wants, even though no teenager in her right mind dresses up on Halloween as Kim Novak, a flash-in-the-pan Hollywood nobody, a vacuous bimbo with dyed blonde hair and a pushup bra. May will suffer at the party, dressed like this. The other kids won't get it, they'll mock her, if not to her face, then behind her back.

Annette suspects that, as with so many things, May's desire to wear this dress has something to do with Marvin Ludwig. She's known for months about May's infatuation, ever since she'd overheard her one night on the phone talking about him to one of her friends—probably to Bonita who, like her mother, is a terrible influence. There's no question that Mrs. Taranto's values are nothing like Annette's: not as liberal politically, not as conservative sexually. Like Cookie Coke, Mrs. Taranto strikes Annette as a woman desperate for male attention.

At her daughter's age, Annette wasn't even aware that boys

existed. May is growing up way too fast. Mrs. Taranto has probably been coaching May on how to win boys. Hence, the loan of this improper, absurd dress. If only May would go back to being best friends with Susan Gartner or Bethie Zimmerman, such nice, smart girls. Even silly Francine Goldlust would be preferable to the dangerous Bonita.

"You're too young to dress like this," Annette continues, turning back to the sink and picking up the bristly soap pad. "Besides, Kim Novak is a . . ." she pauses, then decides to say the word aloud ". . . *slut.*" Annette scrubs the crusty pan even harder than before, so hard she feels tension forming at the base of her skull. She's stunned by her deliberate use of this loaded, ugly word in front of her daughter, even though May has used it plenty of times in front of her.

Annette feels herself blushing, imagines her cheeks as pink as the soap bubbles erupting in the water. Without thinking, she rubs a wet, rubber-encased finger through her white streak of hair, and then, embarrassed, realizes what she's doing, remembering how May has begged her to dye that streak, so she won't look "so much older than the other mothers," as May puts it. May must compare her constantly to Mrs. Taranto, and must find her lacking in every way.

Annette almost apologizes to May for calling her beloved "goddess," Kim, a slut, but stops herself in the nick of time, since she believes that mothers must never, under any circumstances, apologize to their children. Children mustn't see their mothers as weak. Besides, all she did was speak the truth. Those so-called "Hollywood bombshells," Kim Novak, Marilyn Monroe, Jayne Mansfield—it's no secret they're all desperate women who've slept their way to the top.

May has stopped pirouetting. Her skin feels hot as she watches Annette attacking the frying pan with such vengeance. Her mother never uses vulgar language. How would Annette like it if this time it was May who threatened to wash *her* mouth out with soap, instead of the other way around? The nerve of her frumpy, rubber-gloved mother criticizing gorgeous Kim. Kim has class, sophistication, and style.

May simply will not stand for this. Like the God of Exodus, she will not be denied her revenge. And so, right there in the kitchen, poised on her high heels, she opens her mouth and begins to scream. The sound is wonderful and satisfying, as loud and bloodcurdling as a scream in a horror movie, the pure, unadulterated sound of rage and terror, and she hopes that all of their neighbors hear her, so they'll know exactly how much her mother has provoked her.

Annette refuses to turn around. She bends over the sink. Tears fill her eyes. Salty and bitter, they run into her nose and mouth, since she can't wipe them away with her rubber gloves on. She wants to scream herself, as loudly as May, to have a screaming match, to prove to the world that it is she who suffers, she who gives and gives of herself until there is nothing left, gives to this crazy daughter whom she birthed and now harbors beneath her roof, gives endlessly, without thanks, or reward, to her crazy, cursed family.

She also wants to smack May hard across the face, to shut her up, to silence her cruelty, her pain. But she doesn't believe in using violence to discipline the girls; doing so would only backfire. That's what Leo's *meshuge* parents did to him, and surely that's why he's the way he is. Like father and mother, like son, like daughter. She will not lower herself to become what he is at such moments, despite the fact that May's scream has reached an unearthly, glass-shattering crescendo. She will not allow herself to become what Leo is at his worst, the thing she despises, no matter how crazy May is driving her. Trying to ignore the taste of her acrid tears, she takes a deep breath and scours the pan so hard, soap bubbles foam and gush, and her forearm aches.

May stops screaming, not to appease her mother, and not because she is satisfied, but because she feels that shooting pain in her forehead. In her high heels, nearly stumbling but then regaining her balance, she walks as haughtily as possible back to her room, praying to God that her mother doesn't see the pain beneath the bravado.

She slams the door to her room, hoping that the sound gives her mother the worst migraine of her life. Sitting on the edge of her bed, she takes a deep breath, then another, and another—until the pain dissipates, and in her slinky Kim Novak dress, she rises and begins to pace back and forth, past her bed and the closet, past Emma's unmade, sloppy bed, and each of their squat, unpainted wooden bureaus, which their father had built himself in order to save money. As she paces, rather than feeling calm, as she'd hoped, she grows increasingly worried that, despite all her planning and hard work, Marvin will pay no attention to her at Bonita's party.

What if he ignores her the way he did when she'd tried to talk to him after school? Back and forth she paces. Her steps are careful and measured. One, two, three four five steps forward, then one, two, three four five back. Six steps forward, six back. Ten forward, ten back.

Then she starts all over again; pacing calms her down. Sometimes she does it the night before a math test, or when her lazy eye is acting up. But only when there's nobody else around to see her. Pacing is a meticulous, precise act, one that sloppy, impulsive Emma could never perform well, no matter how hard she might try.

Because so much is at stake with Marvin, pacing doesn't calm her as it usually does. She's never been to a costume party before, the sort of party wealthy girls in elite private schools must take for granted, girls who've never set foot in a Bronx housing project and never will. Kim Novak, in her sprawling, lavish Hollywood home, must throw such events all the time for her glamorous guests, women with upswept hair, men smelling of leathery colognes, drinking an endless parade of highballs, frolicking and ending up fully clothed and laughing in the swimming pool. Perhaps she and Marvin will become part of that world some day—*Marvin Ludwig, Doctor to the Stars; Mrs. Marvin Ludwig, devoted wife to the Doctor to the Stars, loving mother of his children.*

She paces and paces, noting Emma's filthy fingerprints on the wall above Emma's bureau, and grimaces in distaste, willing herself neither to dwell on Emma's disgusting habits nor the pains that keep recurring smack-dab in the middle of her forehead, that gradually find their way right behind her eye, causing sight fuzziness in her vision. And the nausea. *Back and forth she paces; back and forth.*

At the party, she'll be ravishing in her midnight-black dress, and Marvin won't be able to resist. He'll fall into her arms and kiss her just as he had in the laundry room, and this time, their kiss will be absolutely perfect. A force like gravity will bring them together, and he'll discover what she's known all along: that he loves her with all his heart. He will be her prisoner of love, and she will be his warden. She'll throw away the lock and key.

May smoothes the shiny fabric along the dress's entire length, which ends above her knees. She loves this dress, and she doesn't care one bit that her mother hates it. Back and forth she paces, thinking about the way the dress shows off her legs, which are slim and long, with delicate ankles, as good looking as Kim's, legs that most definitely belong in the Hollywood Hills, not in a dumpy Bronx housing project.

Pain behind her eye again. Missing a step, she nearly falls. Her breath catches in her throat. Placing her hand against her chest, she feels the rapid, hysterical beating of her heart. Abruptly, the pain stops. She is still, working hard to calm herself down. A pain that comes and goes so suddenly and inexplicably is nothing to worry about. She needs no hateful doctor to interfere.

Her hand against her chest feels hot; she stares down at her breasts and suddenly has a brand new worry, something much more immediate: What if she looks foolish in such a low-cut dress? This hasn't occurred to her before, but Mrs. Taranto and Bonita are both perfect 34Bs, the "ideal bra size," according to the teen magazines that May reads in order to learn how to dress and act and win her man. May is not a 34B—she's a ruler-flat double A. Another act of betrayal by God.

But she will not stuff her bra like Francine Goldlust, who's as flat as she, but who possesses no class. May is no slut-in-the-making, despite what her mother just said. She'll stick to her double A, and maybe this dress will help her to look more like a "firm and perky 34-B." Swinging the sequined purse from her wrist, she resumes pacing. With the pain gone, she has no trouble walking in the high-heeled, pointy toe shoes, which click-clack reassuringly and solidly on the wooden floor as she takes her small, measured steps. Back and forth in the small room, from

Emma's bed to her own, from Emma's bureau to her own.

Her armpits are wet, although she rarely perspires, unlike Emma, who sweats like a hairy construction worker on a hot day. May hopes that the dampness won't ruin the dress. Not stopping, she sighs and straightens her eyeglasses. Kim doesn't wear eyeglasses and never will.

May can tell, without even looking at herself in a mirror, that her glasses are crooked. It's bad enough being so nearsighted that when she's not wearing her glasses the world around her becomes sketchy and vague, but what's worse is that her glasses never fit or look quite right. That's because every year her father takes her for a checkup at the small, run-down Harlem shop of mustached, booming-voiced Henry Watkins, his black optometrist buddy. Henry is nice enough—when she was little he gave her lollipops, and now every year, seeming genuinely embarrassed, he apologizes for having "so few frames for girls your age." Henry must know that she belongs elsewhere, in a store catering to a fashionable clientele, to girls who wear the kind of eyeglasses—cat's eye, with rhinestones and glitter—featured in glossy magazines. But her father, selfish and oblivious, receives a discount from Henry, whose prices are already dirt cheap. He also gets the chance to *schmooze* with one of his black buddies from his "political days." Her father sacrifices her, once again, for himself. He'll be sorry, she thinks, when she and Marvin get married and move to California, three thousand miles away from the Bronx.

Every year, she tries on the pitiful frames while Henry and her father animatedly discuss "the WPA, the Rosenbergs, and McCarthyism." May doesn't know much about the WPA or the Rosenbergs or Senator McCarthy, but she does know that nothing about the way that Leo and the other Rosens view the world sits right with her. She often wonders if she was adopted, if the parents who conceived her live somewhere else, a religious Jewish father with gentle hands and a benign manner, a mother like Kim, blonde, dazzling, and full of life.

Last year at Henry's, she ended up with unstylish round frames, but at least they were an attractive violet color. This year, her nearsightedness once again worse, the only pair that fits comfortably, and which she will consent to wear, is a dull, lusterless brown, although its angular cat's-eye shape is okay, stylish, even. She poses in front of the full-length, unframed mirror, which hangs a bit crookedly on the wall between her bureau and Emma's. Her lazy eye appears to be drooping a bit, almost as though she's been in an accident or a fight. Better to concentrate on her hair, to admire the way, earlier, she had gathered the fine, delicate strands together, and, upsweeping with a glorious rush, pinned them into a movie-star's French twist.

Her gaze lingers on her long, fully exposed neck. A swan's, she thinks. *My best feature.* From now on she'll wear a French twist every single day, in order to show off her slender lines. It will become her *signature.* Perhaps, over time, she'll develop some other styles, other signatures, for which she'll be known and envied: glittering eyeglasses that bedazzle; dagger-sharp high heels; exotic pocketbooks layered with seashells and pearls, like Cookie Coke's.

If only, May thinks, pacing once again, stumbling but then righting herself and carefully stepping over a pair of Emma's dirty underpants, she didn't have to share her room with Emma, whose half of the room today is as messy and chaotic as a nuclear disaster area. Emma, the selfish, uninvited guest, has dumped her clothes, papers, crayons, pencils and books everywhere. Sometimes Annette orders Emma to clean up, but Emma just shrugs, at most deigning to hang up a blouse or two in the crowded closet that she and May share. Their father is the only one who could make Emma clean up her half of the room, but he doesn't care, since, like Emma, he doesn't value order and cleanliness, and expects his slave, Annette, to pick up after him.

Everything Emma does is fine with him. True, May has seen him hit Emma plenty of times, but never for her sloppiness. And anyway so what? Emma is still his favorite, the one he worships and adores, his "great Semitic beauty." Emma and he behave as if they've lived a thousand previous lives together, from Biblical times to now.

Lately, Emma has been trying May's patience even more than usual, by illustrating her stupid poems on colored construction paper, then sloppily scotch taping them to the fingerprint-splattered wall above her bed, as if her scrawled poems and doodles are works of great significance, as if the bedroom is her personal art gallery. May loathes Emma's poems and art, loathes how her father favors Emma, loathes Emma, loathes her own lazy eye and flat chest and crooked eyeglasses, loathes her desperation over Marvin, loathes herself, her life, the world.

She steps away from the mirror, and she can't help herself, she can't stop herself from doing what must be done. She, like a righteous God, is fully entitled to do this. At this moment, justice equals vengeance, and it will be hers. She rips the poems from the wall, every single one of them. And then she rips the thick colored paper into tiny pieces, and then into even tinier pieces. She sprinkles the pieces like ashes over Emma's badly made bed with its rumpled, crumb-filled sheets and blanket.

Emma is outside with Shelley, in the playground across the street from the Projects, chewing gum and playing "A, my name is Alice," with a brand-new, high-bouncing, pink Spalding ball. The weather is unseasonably warm, and she wears a light jacket, bright red with a narrow metal zipper that she enjoys sliding up and down. Doing so makes her feel graceful and coordinated, not like the klutz May declares her to be.

On the slatted wooden bench, Shelly patiently sits, awaiting her turn while Emma sings happily, turning her leg to the right over the ball, and then to the left, in rhythm with her words: "A, my name is Arlene, and my husband's name is Alfred, we come from Alabama, and we sell aardvarks. B, my name is Belinda, and my husband's name is Brad, we come from Brooklyn, and we sell bracelets. C, my name is Carol-Ann ... " She's all the way to "L, my name is Lynette," when the ball suddenly develops a mind of its own and rolls away from her.

The thrill of getting all the way to "Z, my name is Zelda," has eluded her. She chases the ball into the bushes where it's landed, retrieves it, and then squints from the sun and wipes her slightly runny nose with the white handkerchief her mother shoved into the pocket of her jacket before she went out.

"Idjut, now it's my turn," Shelley says, dark eyes glowing, rising from the bench and grabbing the ball. Emma sits quietly on the bench while Shelley turns her leg over the bouncing ball and sings out, "R, my name is Rosetta." Shelley has not yet stumbled on a name or missed the ball, bypassing Emma.

Bored, Emma glances at her watch. "Idjut," she cries out urgently, "it's almost time for Trick or Treat. Let's go. We can play more tomorrow."

Shelley frowns and contemplates her leg-turn over the ball. "Do not," she explodes, her anger like a sudden storm front, "tell me what to do. I cannot *stand* your bossiness!" She completes her leg turn and pockets the ball.

Startled, Emma lets out a noise a little like a burp. Such an outburst, such anger on Shelley's part, is uncalled for. Before she has a chance to say a word in her own defense, Shelley, whose moods seem lately to shift on a dime, shrugs and says, "Okay. Because it's Halloween. Just don't get bossy with me ever again."

Relieved, Emma promises herself that when the impulse next strikes, she'll take a deep breath and think of other things. She does not want to turn into a human bulldozer, like her father and May.

There are no cars coming, and Emma and Shelley race happily across Magenta Street, pinkies linked tightly, and then into the lobby of their building, lightly pinching each other's arms for good luck. Shelley disappears into the stairwell, while Emma waits for one of the perennially crotchety elevators, which reeks today of someone's foul and contraband cigar. She imagines the hairy, bony Mr. Roshansky, with his watery eyes and furrowed face, puffing away. Even breathing through her mouth, the odor is penetrating.

Her mother is in the kitchen, wiping the counter and cabinets with what smells like an ammonia-soaked sponge. She nods at Emma, gives her a half smile, wrinkles her nose as if in reference to the ammonia, but doesn't say hello.

Doing a half-skip, Emma opens her bedroom door, and then stands abruptly still. Something is wrong, but she's not sure what. The air in the room feels charged, and the walls seem to be closing in on her. May, dolled up in a tight, way-too-grown-up, black dress, is standing over Emma's bed, which is covered with tiny scraps of colored paper. She's smiling right at her, one of the craziest smiles Emma has ever seen, a *satanic* smile, Emma thinks, the opposite of what a smile is truly meant to be.

And then like one of those grinning women on the TV quiz shows Grandma Thelma used to watch, those women who dramatically point to the prizes of washing machines and cars, May points to the wall above Emma's bed. The wall is completely bare. Emma's fingers and toes turn to ice. She looks again at May's smiling face, and then at the scraps of paper on her bed. How could she have been so dumb, so innocent, not to have seen this coming? Why did she ever hang her poems and art on the wall in the first place? Why didn't she have enough sense to hide them, the way she hides her diary? Anything she loves, anything precious to her, must be kept away from this foul creature that is her sister by blood but by nothing else.

Frozen in the doorway, she stares at May, who's still smiling, her teeth as brittle-looking as the fake pearls around her neck. Emma looks again at the naked wall, and at her bed covered with the fragments of construction paper that were once her poems, her drawings, her heart, her soul. She hates May, with her crooked, sharp-edged, shit-brown eyeglasses and her ridiculously "fancy-schmancy" hairdo, as Grandma Thelma would have contemptuously described it.

If only, Emma thinks, still immobile in the doorway, and terrified of May's power, despite herself, she were the same size as May. If only someone from outside the Doom-and-Gloom Rosen family were around to help her, someone bigger than she who would take her side. Someone who would understand how badly she has been violated. If either the Virgin Mary or Glinda the Good were here, they wouldn't hesitate to help. Or even *teched*-in-the-head Mr. Dirty Old Man Roshansky, sick as he is himself, because he knows the truth about May, about her twisted and warped mind, her inability to love her own sister.

Emma watches as May, still grinning with evil intent, walks

across the small room to her own bed. It is, as always, neatly made: The vanilla-colored blanket is perfectly smooth, and the matching pillow is puffed out like a proud bird. Sitting on the edge, she crosses her pretty legs and sighs loudly. "You think you're so special." Her voice, an imitation of a sultry Hollywood purr, makes Emma's skin crawl. "But you're not special at all." May swings her feet back and forth in her high-heeled shoes.

Emma, rigid in the doorway, wants to hurt her sister as much as she's been hurt. Or even more. "You'll never, ever be anything like Kim Novak!" she shouts. "You'll never be one tenth as glamorous or famous because ..." Can she go further, and speak the unspeakable? May will never be a star, a knockout, a woman desired by millions of men, because one of her eyes is *off*. Emma wants to go even further than that, wants to tell May that Marvin Ludwig will never give her the time of day because she's far too crazy and cruel, and Marvin is a nice boy who's not out to make waves. And because she saw him one afternoon not long ago holding hands with Bonita Taranto outside the laundry room. Emma knows all about May's crush on Marvin, even though May doesn't know that she knows. Emma knows because May's friend, Francine Goldlust, told her about it one day when they found themselves playing potsy together in the playground, each of them waiting for one of their "real" friends to come downstairs.

As furious as she is, Emma can't bring herself to say any of this to May. The words form but her throat closes. She's fearful that by speaking the *Truth With a Capital T* aloud, she will set all of May's demons free at last, rendering her even more powerful than she already is.

Instead, Emma gathers enough strength to walk slowly to her bed. Not bothering to remove her jacket, she sits heavily, sinking down into what feels like a sea of paper confetti. She pulls her wrinkled blanket to her and clutches it tightly. Her eyes flood, she's hiccupping and gasping, nearly choking on her chewing gum. A stream of watery snot drips from her nose. She lets it run and drip. "You're just a fucking bitch!" She has heard Rosemary Mammano curse like this. "*Fucking bitch*," Rosemary says when she fails a test, and once when Valerie Colucci turned her in to the teacher for chewing gum in class, and sometimes for no reason at all that Emma can see. But this is the first time that Emma has spoken these words aloud. "*Fucking bitch*," she repeats.

Although Emma sees it coming, she's too slow to react, and May is up like a flash and towering over her, her face oversized and distorted. With a tsunami's force, she slaps Emma.

Emma's cheeks sting, then burn, and she imagines each of May's fingers leaving a bright red imprint on her flesh: five bloody scars that will never fade, so that she will be branded forever, like Mr. Roshansky and Mrs. Zelig. She cannot allow May to get away with this, she cannot give her life over to this person who despises her. With what feels to her like lightning speed, amazing herself by her agility and grace under fire, her leg moves swiftly, and she retaliates, aiming to kick May right in the stomach.

But May is nimble enough to move out of the way, especially since Emma's kick isn't nearly as glorious as she wants it to be. In fact, it's weak and random. She's crying much too hard to be strong or accurate. *But at least I'm trying*, she tells herself. *I will not go down without a fight.*

May stands above her, slightly to the side, gloating and smiling. Her lazy eye begins to float inward. "I don't ever want to see or hear another one of your poems!" she says, still speaking with that fake Hollywood purr. "Do you understand me? Because next time I won't let you off so easy. Next time I'll kill you. I'll pierce your heart and cut it out and hang it out to dry."

Their mother, looking crazed, is standing in the doorway. Her eyes are huge, her hair, wild and messy, and she rubs her forehead, ferociously scrunching up her eyes and mouth. Her face is knotted with worry and rage. She grasps the doorway frame with both hands, and her knuckles turn red, then white. "You two are no better than wild animals. How could you do this to me?" Her voice, shrill and on the verge of hysteria, is a voice Emma knows all too well.

"Emma deserved it," May says calmly, flouncing back to her

own bed, offering no further explanation.

Emma can't resist. "May is a *fucking bitch*," she says through her tears, deliberately resuming chewing her gum, proud of her own defiance, because, for the moment, it's all she has left.

16

Annette storms out of her daughters' room. In the foyer, she sits at the small table beneath the black wall phone. *Monsters. Ingrates.* Growing up, she and her sister had never laid a hand on each other, never even argued, and certainly never dreamed of cursing like sailors in front of their parents. She and May were each other's greatest fans and supporters. She tenses, listening for sounds from the girls' room: At least they're quiet . . . for now.

Near tears, she reaches for the phone and dials Leo's number at the store. She's sure that May's the one who started the fight. True, Emma can be . . . what's the word . . . *insouciant* . . . but she's never the one who instigates these violent outbursts. May's feelings toward Emma aren't normal, whatever normal is, and Annette knows it, knows that her firstborn child harbors something within her that's like poison rotting her soul.

She has to speak with Leo, even though she never calls him at work unless it's for what he deems an "acceptable reason," as opposed to "foolishness." "Acceptable" includes her calling to remind him that he has a dentist's appointment or an appointment to take the car in for repair. "Foolishness" includes her calling to tell him that Emma's been sent home from school with a fever, or that May has a toothache.

One afternoon back when they were first married, when he was working at a penny-candy store on the Lower East Side, she called him just to say hello, to hear the sound of his deep, rich voice, to feel that much more connected to her beloved. "This is foolishness," he declared, and hung up.

Now she's the one who hangs up the phone, before it rings. That call from a young wife to her young husband seems like a million years ago. These days she sometimes wishes to be less connected to him, not more, and she thinks about leaving him, despite the fact that she still loves him, cares about his well being and happiness, wants him to love her and be faithful and true. Yet, when he humiliates her in front of the girls, or when he's violent toward them, or when she must acknowledge to herself—like now—how little real intimacy is left between them, the fantasy of leaving him blooms anew.

But how would she survive, with two young children? Maybe she could find work using her old bookkeeping skills, but on such a small salary, she wouldn't even be able to afford an apartment in the Projects. Besides, she'd be miserable without him—after all this time, and all the disappointments, she still loves listening to him discuss politics and Steinbeck and Hemingway and Sinclair Lewis . . . She secretly studies him, his nose aquiline and heroic, his body increasingly firm and masculine as the years go by. She's never cared that he didn't write The Great American Novel. More important is that he's never complained about going to work, keeping his family fed and clothed.

She listens again for sounds of turmoil from the girls' room. So far, so good. According to her watch, only five minutes have passed, although it seems so much longer. Perhaps they've managed to make up and apologize to each other, and have promised to be good and kind to each other for the rest of their lives. Perhaps May has once and for all transcended her ongoing, relentless rage toward Emma, and will gather her younger sister her arms and declare a lifelong truce. More likely, May is silently regrouping, plotting some new twist of revenge. And it's all Annette's fault, isn't it? Aren't mothers always the ones to blame because they love not enough or too much or badly?

She will call Leo, she decides, and risk his wrath. She'll jump out of her skin if she doesn't talk to him right now, not later when he comes home from work and is too tired and irritable to listen to her. "It can wait," he always says, unsmiling, waving her off as if she's an annoying fly, no matter what "it" is.

Steeling herself for Leo's anger, taking a deep breath, Annette dials his number. The phone rings only once before someone picks up. This is unusual: Leo tends to let the phone in the back room of the store ring at least ten times before he or one of the two part-time stockboys picks up.

"Allo?" a gruff woman answers, voice raspy and harsh.

"Is Leo there?" Annette's suspicion is tangible and corporeal—a sharp object within her chest. Whose voice is this? Is Cookie in the back room with Leo, cozying up to him, so comfortable she answers his phone?

"No!" Slam goes the phone.

Annette's head hangs heavily in her hands. She's so rattled, she's gone and dialed the wrong number, and now, worse than that, she's allowing herself to grow paranoid. Of course the woman who picked up the phone wasn't Cookie. The woman's voice over the phone was rough and raw, while Cookie's voice is like romantic Calypso music, evoking hot sun, temperate breezes, and tropical scents. Back when she and Leo first met, he used to say, "One day we'll all be the same earth-brown color, and that will be the end of bigotry." Well, Cookie's skin is the earthiest, most vibrant brown Annette has ever seen. She presses her trembling fingers tightly together, hurting herself, the tips turning white.

Should she call again? No. Yes. Definitely yes. This time, she dials carefully and listens as the phone rings fifteen times, longer than usual. Since the store is in financial trouble, she hopes this means that Leo's busy out front with customers—not with Cookie, of course. Other customers, like William Laster, the liquor store owner, a "fellow traveler," one of Leo's favorites, who buys jelly beans and gumdrops every day to put in a bowl for his customers. It's no surprise that Leo's Candie's isn't doing well, despite his long hours and devotion. Too arrogant, too childish, too volatile, Leo is not a good businessman. He won't woo new customers or try to hold on to the ones he has. Just a few days ago, he'd bragged that he'd tangled, for the umpteenth time, with Mrs. Gottleib, a longstanding customer, for daring to complain about his prices. Sure, Mrs. Gottlieb is whiney and cheap, Leo has spoken of her enough times that Annette can fully picture the cross, embittered old woman. But if Mrs. Gottlieb wasn't Jewish, if she were black or Puerto Rican, he would have just teased her, flirted a bit, maybe even given her the nickel she demanded, or at least some free licorice. He idealizes those unlike himself, while Mrs. Gottlieb and her ilk bear the brunt of his anger. Deep down he's ashamed of being a Jew, just as her mother always insisted he was. Nevertheless, let some non-Jew make a remark he perceives as anti-Semitic, and he's up in arms. Once, some drunken fool on a bus said something about "dirty kikes," and Leo stood and socked him in the eye. The other passengers, black and white, applauded. But then again, fighting is a source of pleasure for him, hardly a sacrifice he's making for the honor of his people.

Jorge, one of the two stockboys, finally picks up the phone and says hello.

Annette stiffens as she announces herself.

"Leo," Jorge shouts, "*su esposa!*"

Annette attempts no small talk with Jorge. She's met him a few times, a wholesome-looking boy with a faint mustache. She's convinced that Leo gives him, and his cousin Pocho, a lot more attention than he gives his own daughters, remembering their birthdays and favorite songs and foods, things he needs Annette to remind him about for Emma and May. "Jorge loves baseball," he tells her, and the next thing she knows, he's taking him to a Yankees game. It's not the boys' fault, of course. But she can't change the way she feels.

Leo comes to the phone. "What's up?"

As she expected, he's abrupt and uninviting. She pictures the way he must look, his cheeks beginning to turn red, his blue eyes blinking rapidly the way they do when he's annoyed but hasn't yet crossed over into real anger.

She takes another deep breath. Gravity is weighing her down. Slowly, in an unfamiliar, reedy voice that she can't turn off, she describes what has happened between the girls. Furtively, she looks around the foyer to make sure that neither of the girls has snuck out and is listening to her. Guilty again, like a criminal.

Her heart wrenches inside her chest. What a mistake calling Leo was. He'll want to give the girls beatings, which is after all, the way he disciplines them. He's never interested in *why* the girls behave as they do. She should have thought of this before she called him.

"Don't hit them," she pleads. "That's not what I'm asking for." She pauses, feeling frantic. "May needs help, Leo. Help we can't give her. She needs to see a . . . psychiatrist." Has she really said this? Why not—it's the truth, isn't it? May is deeply troubled. Annette has always known this: a young girl so consumed with envy, choking with rage toward her sister, her parents, her friends, herself. Although she's not crying, Annette's cheeks feel slick and wet.

Leo, standing in the stock room, his feet hurting in a pair of new shoes that offer no support for his arches, has moved from his initial state of annoyance into full-blown anger. An electric fire inside him has suddenly been turned on full force. He doesn't want to hear this. Especially now, on Halloween, one of his busiest days of the year, and right now, he's got not one, but three good customers out front— Billy Lenahan, a neighborhood cop, a blond, snub-nosed kid really, still in his early twenties, with three kids already, one more than Leo, with whom he likes to swap off-color and rabbi-priest jokes. And Mr. and Mrs. Nemiroff, a deeply religious couple around Leo's age, who, for some reason he also likes, maybe because, despite their piety, they care about the working man, and they love to talk politics with him.

He can't stand Annette when she's like this. A hysteric. A doomsayer. Just like her mother. He refuses to believe that his daughter is *mentally ill*, which is what she's implying, even if she's not saying it outright. The very words are revolting. He's sure that she's blaming him, as though his genes are at fault for his daughter's so-called craziness. Yes, *The Truth With A Capital T* is that his family, parents, sisters, himself, are all different—eccentric, iconoclastic. He's proud as hell of their difference. Even Freddie, his nephew, the ten year old who likes baby food, he might have some problems . . . but who's to say that he's not deliberately making a statement about what he will or won't eat, not because he's disturbed but because he's defiant, a rebel boy. Yet wouldn't some psychiatrist happily pronounce them all mentally ill because of their tempers, their mischief-making, their refusal to kowtow to authority? Psychiatry, a tool to keep citizens in line, stifles creativity, squashes difference, creates a world of automatons, everyone thinking the same, voting the same. In the past, Annette has wholeheartedly agreed with him about this. He will not be coerced into paying his good, hard-earned money to send his daughter to the office of some conservative, pompous acolyte of Freud's.

In fact, it's for the best that May has some spirit in her, maybe she won't turn out to be just another conventional, dull, sorority girl, which is what he usually sees ahead for her. He looks around the back room, at the exposed light bulbs and recently painted white walls, at the thick wood shelves piled high with boxes and bags of candy, some open, some closed, and he breathes in the familiar scents of sawdust and chocolate, cinnamon, coconut and licorice. A cacophony of scents, each compelling and unique. This is all his. If this were all there was in the world, this room, these scents, he could be content, in his domain where he rules.

He remembers Cookie in his arms, amongst his candies, his scents. With guilt and desire, he remembers their kiss of treachery.

"There's something else wrong with May," Annette says softly into the phone, interrupting his reverie. He blinks. Annette's voice is piercing, a laser gun.

At last, Annette thinks, she is voicing the vague, inchoate thought that haunts her and keeps her up night after night. "She . . . looks unhealthy to me. Her lack of appetite, her eye ..." What *is* it about May's eye that's so different these days? Nothing really. No, something. What has she noticed? She wants to kick herself for not paying more attention, for being so certain that May's refusal to eat her meals is an act of spite, for being so caught up in her own problems.

She wants to tell Leo about the disturbing dream she had the week before, an unusual dream for her, not one of airlessness and suffocation, but one in which May, dressed in some sort of shiny silver outfit, like an astronaut's suit, her eyes shining through like small planets, says, in an uncharacteristically gentle and wistful voice, "Goodbye, everyone. I'm leaving you all behind now."

Leo's bullying voice interrupts her memories of the dream. "There's nothing wrong with May. You're being hysterical." He nearly adds, *like your foolish, hypocritical, meddling mother.* But he stops himself. Proudly, he puffs up, feels strong and in charge.

Annette always accuses him of having no self control. At least this one time he's proven her wrong, even if she'll never know it. "Enough of this foolishness," he says, voice still controlled. He hangs up the phone.

Why did she even try to talk to him? Annette is ashamed of herself, but even more ashamed of Leo for turning his back on his family. The phone, which she cannot seem to let go of, feels as heavy as a brick. It's weighing her down so much her entire body sags. The warning signs of a migraine appear, as if on command: pulsing pain, flashing lights, urgent nausea.

How in the world will she be able to cope with all the trick or treaters who'll be coming by later? Where will she find the strength, while her head is aching and things are in such chaos, to stand at the door and smile while she hands out bag after bag of lollipops, Milky Ways, and Snickers Bars to the Project kids with their demanding, overexcited, needy little faces?

She looks at her watch again—only fifteen minutes since she left the girls alone together in their bedroom. Not a peep, not a whisper, not a rustle, not a sound. She decides not to look in on them, to protect herself—better not to know what they're doing.

Emma, nursing a combination of rage and shame, sits shaking on her bed, knees drawn to her chest, sliding the thin metal zipper of her jacket up and down, up and down. Involuntarily, she grimaces. Her cheek still hurts where May has slapped her. She watches closely as May walks to the closet in her body-hugging dress and removes a slim piece of yellow chalk from the girlish vinyl schoolbag she hangs on a hook inside the door. Tightly gripping the chalk, May totters to the center of the room in her high heels and kneels down.

Up and down goes Emma's jacket zipper, as May, snake-like, begins crawling along the floor, breathing noisily through her nose, her dress riding up her thighs, drawing a line with the chalk, on the floor, right down the center of the room. May's hand trembles as she draws. Her whole arm trembles, in fact. From guilt, Emma thinks, hoping that May feels so guilty she drops the chalk, and then drops dead right there on the spot. Emma imagines May as a comic book vampire, lips blood-red, skin ghost-pale, lying lifeless in a coffin, arms crossed over her chest. *Die*, she thinks, *and set me free.*

Very much alive, in ceaseless, serpentine motion, May crawls along the floor. When the line covers the entire length of the room, she rises from her knees, not in her typical, self-conscious and graceful fashion, but, jerkily, like a marionette gone crazy. Her expression, as she stares at Emma, is one of fierce pride. No guilt at all.

Emma averts her eyes and stares at the chalk line; it isn't even slightly crooked, despite the way May's arm shook like a fragile leaf in a fierce storm. Does this qualify as one of God's "holy miracles" that the Catholic kids speak of?

I will be brave, Emma tells herself, and looks up to meet May's eyes. May, now scowling, is the worst kind of ugly, what Emma and Shelley call *ugoo*, when the ugliness that's inside a person shows on the outside. May has transformed herself into a bona-fide monster, not a bogus Halloween one.

"You see this line, E-Bomb?" May's voice is as cruel and monstrous as her face. "You must *never* cross it. You must never set foot on my side of the room again. Do you hear me?"

Emma refuses to answer. May is not entitled to order her around. A sister, even a monstrous one, is not a parent. Besides, it's a moronic rule, since their shared closet is on May's side of the room, and surely she'll have cross the line every single day to get her clothes.

Enough of this. "I am not your slave," she declares to May, her heart breaking into fragments from the fear, from the knowledge she can never escape, the knowledge that she is unloved. She works hard to steady her voice. "You are no one to me." Holding her head high, she rises abruptly, and the sudden movement causes the scraps of paper that were once her poetry to flutter off the bed and onto the floor. They land on her designated side of the yellow chalk line. She refuses to allow her heartbreak to show, and she walks deliberately and swiftly to her bureau, trying to act as though May doesn't exist. Her brand new trick-or-treat costume, which her father helped her to make last week, is folded, unusually neatly for her, in her middle drawer, the drawer that's always loose and in danger of falling out. She opens the drawer carefully and pulls out the first item—her witch's hat.

She holds it in her hands and caresses it with the joy of meeting an old friend. It's black and pointy, made of thick felt, with red stars and yellow moons pasted on in a wild, asymmetrical, zig-zaggy pattern. She places it atop her head, and then slips off her jacket, ignoring May, whose eyes she feels drilling into her. She loves this outfit. When her father asked her a few weeks ago what she wanted to be for Halloween, she hadn't hesitated. "A witch, witch, witch," she said, deliberately saying the word three times, the number of times that Glinda the Good instructs Dorothy to click her heels in order to go home to Kansas.

Next Emma pulls out her cape, an old black blanket that her father found in the basement of his store, showing her how to safety-pin it so it hung across her shoulders in "bewitching fashion," as he put it.

May's evil eyes continue to bore into her. *You can't hurt me any more*, Emma thinks. *You may be the Wicked Witch of the West, but I'm Glinda the Good, and I'm stronger than you.* If only, like Glinda, she could soar up, up, up into the air and fly away. Instead, she wishes again for May to die, although that's hardly the wish of a good witch. But it is, in the deepest recesses of her heart, the wish she harbors. Flinging her cape dramatically around her shoulders, refusing to meet May's eye, she strides quickly out of the room.

17

Annette, in the bathroom, on her knees, swallowing, retching, sweating . . . vomiting into the toilet, her migraine ritual. Her temples throb. Her throat is dry. Her hands smell. Her daughters will never come to see how she is. They, and Leo, when he's home, avoid her when she's sick like this. Do they detest her for this weakness? Maybe. Worse than that, she detests herself. She flushes the toilet, stands, splashes cold water on her face, and then feels the urgent need once more to vomit.

At the counter, Leo rings up a customer, an elderly Puerto Rican woman who comes in every now and then, always dressed in a long black skirt, shapeless black coat, and a thick black scarf wound around her head. He rings up three bags of caramels, two Jawbreakers, and a copy of a Spanish-language newspaper. "*Gracias,*" she croaks, as Leo comes from behind the counter, to help her to the door. Crookedly, she leans against him, taking small, hesitant steps in her bulky shoes.

"*Gracias,*" she says again, as Leo watches from the doorway to see that she crosses the street safely. He refuses to think any more about Annette's call concerning May. It's already old news, ancient history. Annette, for her own sake, should never again bring up to him May's need for a psychiatrist.

The old woman, safely across the street, waves and gives him a toothless smile. He waves back, and closes the door, suddenly wondering when, if ever, Cookie will return. He hasn't seen her since the day she told him he reminded her of her late husband. Once, when the store was empty, he'd found himself looking up her phone number and dialing it, not knowing what he would say, not knowing what he wanted, but, like a shamefully nervous suitor, he'd hung up before it rang. It occurs to him that he could call her again right now, since he's got no customers. Instead, he busies himself straightening some magazines on the shelf, then sits behind the counter and takes out his notebook. He has decided that the time has come for him to write a novel, loosely based upon his own life, as he has always wanted to do. It will start in the present, with many flashbacks to the hero's childhood. He's already written a few paragraphs of description of the store that the hero owns, changing it from a candy store in the Bronx to a magazine and newspaper shop in Manhattan, but keeping the left-wing politics of the owner, and the modest décor of the store. There will be a character based on Cookie, so transformed that Annette won't recognize her. His desire for Cookie will be channeled into the realm of imagination, and he'll be blameless, following the direction his art leads.

Hoping that no customers show up for a while, he picks up his pen and writes: *A beautiful woman, born in Madrid, enters the store, searching for newspapers from home.*

Emma adjusts her witch's hat and cape and waits for the elevator on the 11th floor to take her downstairs. She holds tightly with one hand to the big shopping bag in which she plans to put her accumulated treats. With her other hand, she grips her mother's broom, the final, perfect touch to her costume. She swiped it from the narrow broom closet in the kitchen on her way out. Her mother won't mind. And so what if she does? Her mother's already furious at her for calling May a fucking bitch. How much more furious could she get?

Besides, as Emma was leaving, she heard her mother throwing up in the bathroom, so, between her mother's headache and the trick or treaters who'll be ringing the doorbell all afternoon, she won't be paying much attention to Emma for a while, at least not until she's feeling better, and that might not be until the following day.

Emma swings the shaggy-bristled, wooden broom back and forth, trying to will it to possess magical powers, but, in her hands, the broom merely feels awkward. If it were truly magic, and not just a cheap thing from the five-and-dime with a wobbly wooden handle and a ragged, coarse brush, she'd be able to figure out some genuinely witchy and magical way to get back at May for what she's done to her poems.

A new mission in her life will be to exact revenge upon May. If this prevents her from ever becoming a good Jew, the kind of Jew beloved by God who doesn't exist, so be it. This lust for revenge has grasped her tight, and she is powerless in its grip. Like faith must be for those who believe, her desire to wound May is greater than she is.

She grabs the handle so tightly, a splinter of wood nicks her. She wonders if this is a message sent from May, who might possess magical powers, herself. Despite what May did, she can always write out her poems again, she can always draw new pictures. The second time around, her words and images will be even more interesting. She could change the line, *The aqua water is like sky*, to *The aqua water is sky*. Instead of drawing just the ocean, she'll draw both ocean and sky, shimmery waves and shimmery clouds, aqua-and-silver tinted, the colors complementing and enhancing each other like loving sisters.

She can't help but wonder, as she waits impatiently for the slow-as-molasses elevator, what it would be like to have a sister who cared about her. A sister who liked her. A sister who maybe even *loved* her. Who sometimes played with her on the grounds of the Projects where everyone could see the two of them together. A sister who laughed at her jokes. Who was proud of her. Who didn't want to hurt and humiliate her all the time. Like Rosemary Mammano's older sister, Victoria. Victoria calls Rosemary "Sissie," an affectionate, sweet nickname, unlike the cruel and condescending "E-Bomb." Sometimes on Saturday afternoons, Victoria takes Rosemary shopping at Macy's, and afterwards they eat lunch at Schrafft's, tuna fish sandwiches and crinkly, salty potato chips followed by ice cream sundaes with sprinkles and cherries and whipped cream. Emma tries to envision herself and May gallivanting about town together, but her imagination fails.

To hell with May! Emma loves the sound of that. It has the ring of poetry. Do Jews believe in Hell? Or is that just another example of Catholicism's wild imagination: fires raging out of control, pitchfork-carrying, scarlet-skinned devils with piercing black eyes and mad,

villainous laughs . . . What *do* Jews believe in? God handing the Ten
Commandments to Moses on the Mount? But what does that tell her
about Jews, other than that they like to follow rules . . . There's
nothing poetic or dramatic about that.

Stepping sideways into the elevator, clutching her broom
closely, Emma joins a bunch of unruly, giggling girls, first or second
graders, in costumes—two nurses wearing blindingly white, old-
fashioned, peaked caps, a ballerina, a gorilla, and a ghost. The pretty
little ballerina wears a fluffy tutu and tights. Her hair is curled into
brown corkscrews like Darla's in *The Little Rascals*. If the ballerina
were her sister, she would call her Sissie, and they'd shop together
every Saturday and eat tuna fish sandwiches just like Victoria and
Rosemary. "Sissie," she'd say, "Come here. Close your eyes." She'd
give Sissie a present, a silver ring with Sissie's birthstone, or a diary
like Emma's. She would show Sissie private passages from her own
diary, in fact, maybe even the one she quickly dashed off last night
while May was in the bathroom, doing what their father calls
"performing ablutions." *I am devastated because I will never again
visit the Virgin Mary*, she had written, and she'd drawn a big
teardrop instead of a period at the end of the sentence.

Emma smiles at the girl, who, in true Darla fashion, tosses her
tightly-wound curls and smiles back, revealing gleaming white,
Chicklet-sized teeth, and then stands on her toes and executes a
graceful curtsy, so delicately and artfully that Emma wants to grab
her and clutch her to her chest and never let go.

To Hell with May, Emma thinks again, the broom at her heart,
careful to let the girls pour out first when the elevator reaches the
lobby. The ballerina waves at Emma as she runs off, her smile quick
and confident. Emma's eyes sting as she waves back.

As planned, Shelley, Rachel, and Rosemary are waiting in the
lobby for Emma, leaning against the long row of heavily dented
metal mailboxes. So awestruck is she by Shelley's costume that
Emma forgets all about her stinging eyes and the little girl in the
elevator. The true incarnation of a fiery gypsy, Shelley wears a long,
ruffled, turquoise skirt and fist-sized hoop earrings that dangle and
jangle provocatively from her ears. Bejeweled bracelets adorn her

wrists, and strands and strands of multi-colored beads are wrapped around her neck. Setting off her dark skin and eyes are scarlet lipstick and a matching scarf.

Emma suddenly feels less confident about her own costume. The old black blanket feels nothing like a cape; her pointy hat is slipping off her head; her mother's broom is just that, a cruddy old broom that's falling apart.

"Hi, Emma," Rosemary says. Emma reluctantly takes her eyes off Shelley to greet Rosemary, whose costume is also perfectly detailed. An angel in a white gauzy dress, she's wearing her hair teased up high, crowned by a plastic halo. Two cardboard wings float from her shoulders. Only a Catholic girl with an unwavering belief in God could transform herself so successfully into such a divine being.

Rachel, standing beside Rosemary, wears a fringed, suede cowgirl's outfit, with pointed boots, a silver pistol holder, and a sharply realistic—at least to Emma—toy gun at her waist. Emma is awestruck by her friend's successful transformation from Jewish schoolgirl to Annie Oakley.

Nervously adjusting her hat and stroking her cap, Emma reassures herself that her costume, although imperfect, is still exceptional and terrific, and that good witches like Glinda possess secret powers and extraordinary strength—like the God who doesn't exist.

Upstairs, on the eleventh floor, Annette lies in bed. She's turned off the lights, and drawn the blinds. The cold compress across her forehead soothes her slightly, but the sound of the doorbell is jarring. Her skin prickles and her head aches. The first trick or treaters have arrived. She groans loudly and clenches her teeth, pulling the blanket over her head, far too weak and nauseated to rise and go to the door, even though it's well-known in the Projects that occasionally, spurned trick or treaters return to splatter eggs on the doors of those who ignore them.

In the lobby, Emma and her friends are debating whose doorbell to ring first. "Manny Colucci," suggests Rosemary, in her gauzy angel costume.

"Good idea," Emma nods. Last year, Manny had given out marzipan as a treat, a nutty, paste-like candy oozing sweetness, a candy her father doesn't carry in his store. *Marzipan*, Emma thinks, should be the subject of a poem.

Behind Manny Colucci's back, Emma's parents call him "Manny, The Garbage Man," because he's a sanitation worker. They profess to feeling sorry for him because he's a "childless bachelor." Yet they themselves are far from happy—that is perhaps the one thing in the universe she has no doubts about—and they have two children, whereas Manny, unmarried and childless, with his wide smile and booming, inclusive laugh, seems completely happy. Perhaps there are secrets about Manny, sad, sorrowful secrets that she's too young to fathom, but her gut tells her that Manny Colucci is a happy man.

"Hi-Ho Silver!" Rachel, the Jewish cowgirl, shouts, reining in an invisible horse before reaching up and ringing Manny's tinny doorbell.

As Emma waits for him to come to the door, she balances her pointy felt hat, swings her mother's broom, and formulates a plan: If the bag of trick-or-treat candy that Manny gives her includes even a single piece of candy corn, one of those truly delicious, orange-and-yellow, sugary-and-waxy, triangle-shaped tidbits, that means there's a God up in Heaven watching over her—and if there is a God, then very soon He'll undoubtedly punish May for what she's done, and then Emma, herself will be relieved of her mission to avenge herself, a mission that is already weighing heavily upon her.

In case He does exist, and in case He's on her side, she pictures Him as a kindly visaged, elderly man—older even than Grandma Thelma was before she died—with a long white beard and twinkling blue eyes. To be on the safe side, she plants a little *yarmulke* atop his large and ancient white head. His skin is rosy, his belly full. He resembles Santa Claus, "another mythic figure, like God," her father had informed her years ago, "although this one is designed purely to give parents an excuse for blatant materialism." On the other side, of course, passionately defending Santa, is Rosemary Mammano. Rosemary says, tossing her hair, "I'll believe in Santa until I'm dead and buried, and it's *your* loss if you don't." Unspoken, Emma knows, is "it's your *Jewish* loss."

At last, Manny opens the door. He looks as though he hasn't shaved in a few days, and he's dressed in baggy grey pants and a white shirt that's buttoned wrong, so that a sliver of his washboard-flat stomach peeks through, but his toast-colored eyes are so warm and his smile so genuine that Emma finds him handsome. Not Tony-Curtis-movie-star handsome like her father, but handsome in a quiet, less obvious way. He looks as if he dances and sings beautifully, despite spending all day among other people's garbage. He is surely a "man of the people," and she doesn't understand why her parents mock him.

"Trick or Treat!" she, Shelley, Rosemary, and Rachel shout together, sounding, Emma thinks, very teenagerish, with their hands on their hips, their knees thrust out, their voices strong and deep— not childish at all.

Manny lets out one of his booming belly laughs. "And a howdee pardner to you, Miss Annie-Get-Your-Gun Oakley," he says to Rachel with a cowboy twang.

To Rosemary he speaks in a hushed, soft voice that sounds like a prayer, "Ah, a heavenly visitor in our midst."

With Shelley, he switches to an elegant Spanish accent, reminding Emma of the male flamenco dancers she's seen on T.V. "*Cuanto le gusta*," he sings, clicking his heels dramatically.

Emma holds her breath as he stares at her for a long minute. Is he disappointed by her makeshift, poor-girl costume? She twirls her cape and swings her broom, trying to appear witchy, powerful, and in-control.

"Double, double, toil and trouble," he finally says, "fire burn, and cauldron bubble."

Emma doesn't understand what these mysterious and ominous-sounding words mean, strung together in this strange way, but she recognizes them as poetry, and she commits them to memory. One day, she promises herself, she'll use them in a poem of her own, dedicated to Manny, who is, perhaps, a poet, himself, which may be why he's happy, despite being surrounded all day by garbage.

Manny turns to a table behind him and picks out four small brown paper bags from a pile of what looks like at least a hundred, each tied with a slim white ribbon. He hands one to each of the girls. "Happy Halloween, ladies," he says, and then gently closes his door. Emma can't stop herself. She immediately unties the ribbon and peeks into her bag. The greatly coveted marzipan, chocolate-coated raisins, honey-colored caramels, and a big round Jawbreaker. But not a single piece of candy corn. And that means: No God. Nobody to punish May, nobody to watch out for Emma, nobody to take on her mission as His own.

No, she decides, unable to resist a quick bite of the thick, chewy marzipan, as oozing and rich as she remembers, she will not give up on God just yet. If I run into Bobby Gaglione in the next five minutes, then I'll know that there absolutely is a God, she tells herself. And if there is a God, He *will* help me to do what I must.

Just thinking about Bobby makes her a little lightheaded—his dark, moody eyes, his black wavy hair. The way he walks, so tough and cool and confident, all swagger and bounce, an Italian *diddy-bop* walk, a walk that's like poetry in motion, a walk that could one day lead him into her arms, although not yet—she knows she's not ready. She will never be as obsessed with Bobby as May is with Marvin Ludwig. May has sacrificed her dignity to her obsession. Nevertheless, she wonders: What would it be like to be kissed by Bobby? Maybe like slowly licking off the icing from a sweet, cream-filled chocolate cupcake.

Emma skips along, up the stairs, with Shelley, Rosemary, and Rachel, loving the energy they create together. Like the Rockettes, those high-kicking, feathered and bejeweled dancers at Radio City Hall, where she's gone a few times with her parents and May. On the fourth floor, they plan to ring Mrs. Williams' doorbell, whose elegant and unusual Halloween candies have been known to rival Manny's.

In unison, the girls stride onto the landing, and there's Charlie

Ludwig, dressed as a pirate with a checkered kerchief around his head and a black eyepatch. Next to him is Bobby Gaglione, masquerading as a Greenwich Village beatnik, a bohemian creature wearing a black beret and a pointy, pasted-on, black beard, carrying a pair of bongo drums that Emma imagines he will play for real one day, in a smoky, dimly-lit Village café, accompanying a beautiful woman poet with long dark hair reading her poetry aloud . . . perhaps Emma herself.

Emma's throat grows suddenly raw and she grasps her broom, realizing that this Bobby-sighting means there really is a God. *Double, double, toil and trouble,* she whispers under her breath, asking God, finally proven to exist, to instill in her a true witch's powers to make her sister suffer in countless ways, as she so clearly deserves to. God will be her accomplice in the total destruction of May.

To Emma's surprise, Bobby, addressing all three girls, but looking directly at Emma, says, "Me and Charlie are heading over to Parkside. You girls wanna come?"

Bobby's interest in her, sudden, unprecedented, and seeming genuine, must be another signal that God exists and cares about her. She's sorely tempted to accept his offer, and her heart briefly flutters with anticipation of their journey together to the Parkside Projects. But Parkside is almost as far away as the Coops, and she doesn't dare risk getting caught walking once again where she's not allowed to go.

"Sorry, Pardner," Rachel says, remaining in character, impressing Emma with her cool demeanor in the face of such interest from the most attractive and desirable boys in their class. "We're not allowed." Rachel places her pistol back into her holster.

The boys nod, and then with a whoop and not a backward glance, run into the staircase. Emma strains to hear them whooping all the way downstairs. Although she's desperately sad to see Bobby go, she's also exhilarated because his presence has proven conclusively that her desire to believe in God has been rewarded. She has been confirmed as a good Jew.

Except, could the lack of candy corn in the bag from Manny the

Garbage Man cancel out the Bobby-sighting? What if Bobby's appearance wasn't really a sign, but simply "a random coincidence," as her father would say?

What she really needs is two out of three signs in order to be absolutely certain of His existence. Okay then: Please, God, don't let Mr. Roshansky open his door the way he always does on Halloween, even though she and her friends never ring his doorbell. Yet whenever they're on his floor, like now because the Williams family lives on the same floor, he always seems to know.

And of course there he is, opening his door right on schedule, with his phony, half-smile, and flat, watery eyes. He waves at them with his bony arms, one of which bears the terrible tattoo that never fails to make Emma shudder. "Girls," he says, in his phlegmy voice, "I have candy. Come. Girls. Here."

Emma, looking down at her feet, remembers the day that he was so kind to her in the elevator, the day he revealed what he knew about May. But she also remembers the times that he touched her, like a clumsy, mauling bear, reaching for her flesh as if he were drowning and her body was the single pole to safety. She doesn't want his half-full bag of stale bubble gum and loose M & Ms. One year, he gave out pennies and toothpicks. She pops a few chocolate-covered raisins into her mouth and holds tightly to her broom as she reluctantly trails behind Shelley, Rachel, and Rosemary. Two out of three, she thinks, her breathing shallow and tight. It's definite now: no God.

At that moment, Leo is selling Pez to a kid in a ghost costume, and thinking of the scene he will write next in his novel-in-progress, which is now twenty-five pages: his hero and the beauty from Madrid unexpectedly meet again in a dusty, old Greenwich Village bookstore, and discover that they share a love of John Steinbeck's novels.

18

May rides the elevator downstairs to Bonita's costume party — a little dizzy again, a little unsteady, but she refuses to let it bother her. She can't wait to tell Marvin about how she stood up for herself and her needs, about how she isn't ever going to allow Emma to ruin her life. She will say: "I did not choose my sister. I disown her." He will respond, "I understand. You must follow your heart." Young as they are, they will craft and fashion a life together that will lead them, inevitably, to a home far from the Bronx, to Hollywood, perhaps, near Kim, or to one of the wealthy New York suburbs, like Scarsdale, where doctors and lawyers and businessmen raise their families, and make no waves.

May has made sure that she's arriving "fashionably late," as she's sure Kim must do whenever she attends Hollywood parties. As she reaches out to knock on Bonita's door, she suddenly grows weak, almost limp, and it's difficult to keep her arm straight out in front of her, difficult to make contact with the door. The air, painfully bright for a moment, undulates and shimmers, and then the brightness pales, and the air spins itself into a blur.

But the moment passes, she sees everything clearly, the unadorned, chipped door, the discolored brass doorknob, and she knocks softly and gently, the gesture of a real lady seeking entrance, not a "wild animal," as her mother has just called her.

Mrs. Taranto opens the door. Smoking a Marlboro, she stands back in the doorway, dramatically, as if she too has been fantasizing about living a Hollywood film star's life. A fleck of ash sits like a perfectly formed snowflake on the tip of her elegant cigarette. Her red hair is combed into a sleek flip, the height of fashion. Her nose is slightly pink, as though she has a cold, which May thinks makes her look even more beautiful than usual, softer and more vulnerable, so different from her own mother, who doesn't smoke, drink, dance, or do anything at all fun or glamorous. Who wears shapeless, cheap *schmatas* and calls them "housedresses." Who mostly complains about everything, and says, "We Rosens are a cursed, miserable lot, destined for lives of relentless Doom and Gloom." Who's too weak to stand up to her own husband. Who crawls into her bed with disgusting migraines.

A man is standing next to Mrs. Taranto, a man with a thick head of sandy hair and a mustache. May doesn't recognize him. In his soft, beige windbreaker, he looks more sophisticated than most of the men May sees around the Projects. Perhaps he and Mrs. Taranto met at a cocktail party somewhere, laughing together over highballs, whatever they are—one day she will know specifically what goes into a highball, and she and Marvin will prepare them for one another on their oversized, wicker-filled patio.

Mrs. Taranto says, "May, this is my friend, Mickey." May sees something fleeting in her eyes, and notes something about her stance. She feels the charged air between them. They have sex. Mrs. Taranto has a lover. Saliva churns fiercely inside May's mouth, and she tries not to slurp or gulp, so they won't know what seeing them is doing to her.

Mrs. Taranto takes a puff of her cigarette, not seeming to notice that the ash falls to the floor, which strikes May as the ultimate in unstudied and effortless glamour.

"May is Bonita's best friend," she says to Mickey, smoothing her already perfectly smooth hair. "She's here today as Kim Novak. Isn't that original?"

May feels herself blushing with pride, almost as if she is Kim.

Mickey laughs and says to May, casually placing his hand on Mrs. Taranto's elbow, "Good choice. Kim's a real looker. And she can act, too."

May stares at his hand, at the easy intimacy between them, something she and Marvin will soon possess. As she steps inside, she immediately notes that the foyer smells of lavender. Perhaps Mrs. Taranto has sprayed a dizzyingly lush, flower-scented perfume up and down the narrow room in order to help Bonita set a dramatic tone for the party, or to please Mickey—or both. May deliberately allows herself to soak in the sexual energy flowing between Mrs. Taranto and Mickey, who are now standing closer together, their hips almost touching, their eyes unashamedly locked. She hopes that the lavender scent will cling to her, and that Marvin will be as drawn to it as she is.

"Go on inside," Mrs. Taranto says, tearing herself away from Mickey, pointing with an expansive gesture to the living room. A late afternoon sun floods the large room, and May smiles because sunlight brings out the blonde in her dirty-blonde hair.

Bonita isn't there. She must still be in her bedroom, changing into her costume, surrounded by her expensive dolls from all around the world, basking in the knowledge that she has the most attractive mother and the most freedom of any girl in their crowd.

So far, Joey Maestre and Francine Goldlust are the only kids in the room, sitting side by side on Mrs. Taranto's sofa, with its delicate design of interlocking pink and purple roses. May guesses that everyone else is planning to arrive fashionably late as well, including Marvin, and she wishes she had shown up even later.

With her phony, padded size C bust, Francine appears self-conscious and nervous as she repeatedly steals glances at Joey, and May suspects she has designs on him. Joey, the only boy in their class who has sideburns and is able to grow a real mustache, is dressed as a farmer: straw hat, baggy dungaree bib overalls, unlit corncob pipe in his mouth. Francine is in a fireman's uniform, probably borrowed from her older brother, who's a real fireman, and it hangs loosely on her. Baggy as it is, the bright red nevertheless accentuates her false bosom, and May wants to touch her own 34-A breasts, to lift them up and add more heft to them, but stops herself before she calls even more attention to that under-endowed area of her body.

May sits across from Joey and Francine in the slightly creaky wooden rocking chair that belonged to Bonita's grandmother before she went into a nursing home, not far from Leo's Candies and the Bronx Courthouse. The rocking movement makes her feel grown up and sexual, the way Mrs. Taranto must feel in Mickey's strong arms, and she likes the way her sequined purse, dangling from her wrist, swings along in rhythm. She feels as if she's dancing in partnership with the chair.

The Beatles' "I Want To Hold Your Hand" is playing on a record player set up on a table in the far corner of the room, next to two large glass bowls filled with those same chocolate-cherry candies in the shape of tulips that Bonita had served at her pajama party, and whose exotic sweetness had so titillated May.

Francine begins to sing along with the Beatles in a tinny falsetto, her British accent as fake as her bosom, and Joey, so manly and forceful, bops his dark head up and down, following along with her, not seeming put off by Francine's inauthenticity and lack of talent.

All the girls in May's class, including Bonita, are wild for the "Fab Four," but when May sees them, she's left cold and unmoved. None of the Beatles are Jewish, for one thing, and for another, their dark Liverpool looks are no match for Marvin's sunny face. All that matters is Marvin. And where is he? What if he doesn't come? And what if the reason that he doesn't come is because he's still trying to avoid her, as he's definitely been doing ever since his parents saw her in her bathing suit on Rosh Hashanah? Her pocketbook thuds into her knee, as she stops mid-swing. Joey, still bopping his head and waving his unlit pipe, joins Francine in singing along with the Beatles. His voice is deep and vibrant, and May hopes that Bonita really does find his particular combination of Puerto Rican charm and toughness as appealing as she claims to. Because May is still worried that Bonita is a liar, and that it's Marvin she really wants, even though she hasn't said so, and even though she constantly says that Joey's accent makes her "weak in the knees."

The song ends, and May turns her head toward the living room entrance, and there's Marvin, and she feels exactly as she had on that June afternoon in the laundry room, as though she has conjured him out of thin air with the ferocity of her will and desire. This must be what Mrs. Taranto is caught up in, this dizzying sensation that wafts from within. She feels weak and breathless.

Marvin, costumed as a doctor, looks perfect in his crisp, tailored, white lab coat, a bona-fide stethoscope around his neck. She remembers the ketchup-scent that emanated from his full lips when he kissed her that afternoon amidst the steamy washing machines and dryers, and she hopes that he's remembering, too, and that he's thinking of kissing her again, right now, right in front of everyone. If he tries, she will return his kiss with a steamier one of her own.

Her head hurts from the intensity of her unwavering gaze upon Marvin. Her eye throbs briefly, then stops.

Joey says, "Marvin, how goes it?" Marvin sits next to Joey on the couch, forcing Francine to squoosh over. If anyone else did that, May would think it rude, but Marvin could never be rude. He's too nice a boy, so brainy and religious and upright. May is just glad that he isn't paying any special attention to Francine and her bosom. Then again, he's also not paying any special attention to her. *Yet*, she tells herself. He's not paying any special attention to me *yet*. He is saving his desire, his need for her, for later.

On an ocean of deep purple silk waves, Bonita floats into the room, carrying a cardboard scepter. Atop her flaming hair sits a delicate crown that looks like pure spun gold. Her brown-black eyes, heavily made up with mascara and eyeliner, glitter—she, too, seems caught in a mist of desire and lust. May watches as Marvin stares fixedly at her.

Milking her stupid moment of glory for all it's worth, Bonita twirls around on her tiptoes. Breathlessly, she comes to a stop. Striving to be sultry, speaking as if she truly is royalty and the rest of the crowd her subjects, she crows, "I just love everyone's costumes!"

"I'm Kim Novak." May's voice is loud and abrupt, even to her own ears. She glances at Marvin, but he's busy tapping, drummer-style, on his stethoscope, and gazing at Bonita, his expression unreadable.

May, still perched on the rocker, although no longer in perfect sync with its movement, wracks her brain trying to come up with something else to say, something to distract Marvin from the pull of Bonita, but just then, Mrs. Taranto and Mickey poke their heads into the living room. Mrs. Taranto's voice is now husky, the overt, unapologetic voice of sex: "Bonita, dear, Mickey and I are off to the movies." Her cigarette drips another ash. "Be good, everyone," she adds, laughing, tipping her head back coquettishly and girlishly, and it briefly crosses May's mind that sometimes Bonita might feel as sickened by her mother as May is by hers.

Mrs. Taranto trusts Bonita and her friends so much that she's going to leave them alone: This is astonishing. May hopes that her parents never find out that she's at a party without "adult supervision." Her father would out-and-out kill her, would skip the beating and just go directly for the kill, but before she succumbed to death, her mother would once more call her "a wild animal," and then be felled by a giant migraine and puke her guts out for May's benefit.

May rocks harder in the chair, which is starting to creak a little too loudly to make her seem sexy. Mrs. Taranto waves goodbye, and then she and Mickey disappear from view. A moment later May hears the front door close. She straightens her eyeglasses, which are not only crooked but fogged over. For the millionth time, she wishes it were Emma, not she, cursed with poor vision and a lazy eye, wishes that Emma was not beautiful.

With Mrs. Taranto gone, the air in the room becomes electric. May rocks and rocks. Marvin rises and stretches his arms above his head, as if preparing for an athletic event. But then he sits down, expression still unreadable.

Francine clumsily removes her fireman's helmet, and she and Joey slowly dance to the Beatles' "'Til There Was You." Joey, holding Francine close, is so light on his feet that he makes even weak-bladdered, fake-breasted Francine look good. Yes, Joey's a good dancer, but not as good as Marvin. Not that May has ever danced with Marvin. But she's seen him dance with other girls. She's watched him dip, sway, cha cha, and twist.

The doorbell rings, and Bonita, not seeming at all upset about Joey and Francine, which sets off alarms in May, sails off to answer it, and when she returns, she's with Susan Gartner, who's wearing a skeleton suit, and Bethie Zimmerman and Bethie's older brother George. Bethie and George are vampires: pointed fangs, bright red lips, shiny, floor-length black capes.

May hopes that George doesn't ask her to dance before Marvin gets a chance. She suspects that George has a crush on her, because at his barmitzvah two years before he asked her to dance three times, more than he asked anyone else. George is a nice enough boy, known for his keen interest in history and current events. He once confided in May his "agnosticism," which made it instantly clear to her that she and he could never be together.

Susan wanders off to the corner and begins dancing by herself, surprisingly confident in her movements, and Bethie smiles and waves at May, which pleases her, because for a while Bethie was angry at her, in a most un-classy way, for dropping her as her best friend. Unlike Susan, who'd been weepy when May had dropped her, Bethie, eyes blazing, had denounced May as "rude and selfish." But time has healed whatever wounds there were, so May feels justified and validated for following her heart.

And then May absolutely cannot believe her eyes: Marvin rises from the sofa, stretches once more like an athlete-in-training, and determinedly, unwaveringly, with long strides, marches right over to Bonita. He removes his stethoscope and places it on the table, then whispers something in her ear. Before May can blink, Bonita and Marvin are slow dancing, like Francine and Joey, except that Marvin is holding Bonita even closer than Joey holds Francine. They're "grinding," rubbing pelvises together, the most overtly sexual thing she's witnessed in person among her friends, something May has never done with a boy—it's much too dirty, too vulgar. What pleasure could such a base act bring? Intercourse between lovers would be candle-scented, slow and dreamy—spiritual, even. Not this animalistic act. How could Marvin want to do such a thing? Obviously, Bonita has instigated it, must be making him do it. May wants to slap Bonita, to bring her down to her knees, to destroy her once and for all. As of this moment, their friendship is officially over.

Marvin, tipping his head forward and down, kisses Bonita. Without a second's hesitation, as though it's the most natural thing in the world, as if their bodies and minds are one, Bonita kisses him back, and it's not just their lips touching, it's a long French kiss, tongues and moans and saliva, more vulgar —incredibly so—than the act of grinding.

May is filled with the most rage she ever remembers feeling in her life. No longer able to sit still, she rocks back and forth, and the chair creaks and creaks, but she doesn't care, because for the first time she wonders if anything she has ever done has mattered one iota to Marvin. Has she been deluding herself completely, making a fool of herself, inspiring Bonita and Marvin to mock her behind closed doors? Is this the first time he and Bonita have kissed? How could it be, considering the blissful, perfect harmony of their gazes and gestures?

Her lazy eye starts to throb, intensely, arrhythmically, like a crazed drum. *I'll kill her*, she thinks. *I'll kill him. I'll kill myself.* Her head hurts worse than it ever has, her lazy eye burns, her stomach turns over and over. She rises, but the floor seems far away and her legs are unsteady. She drops her purse and bends to pick it up, but can't see where it's fallen, things are too blurry, so she leaves it. She tries to run, and she stumbles, her body just won't move that fast. Out of the living room, into the narrow, windowless foyer, where this time, she is revolted by the heavy lavender scent that permeates the apartment, and she gags, doubling over, feeling a river of ropey saliva dripping down her chin.

She manages to turn the lock and open the front door and she's outside, in the hallway, and then, stumbling, bent over, barely able to put one foot in front of the other. She makes it as far as the elevator. The walls close in on her, and she can hardly see. A vise closes in her chest. She bites her lip so hard she tastes bitter blood.

The elevator buttons jump around, her arm won't obey her, her fingers can't make contact. Grandma Thelma's pearls are suddenly too tight, they're choking her, strangling her. Her arms flail uselessly as she tries to pull them off. Her heart is raw and vulnerable, her flesh is melting, evaporating, her boundaries are dissolving, and she hears herself making some sort of sound, a cry so agonizing and heartbreaking it cannot possibly be coming from her own battered lips.

19

Standing in Mr. Roshansky's doorway, Emma, Shelley, and Rachel hang back, just far enough away so that he can't reach them. But Rosemary has gotten too close—maybe her cardboard angel's wings have slowed her down—and he's putting his arm around her waist and moving his hand quickly upward, landing right where Emma is sure that Rosemary's nipples are, beneath her gauzy dress.

Boldly, Emma steps forward and hears herself whisper softly, "No, you won't," although no one else seems to hear. This is the moment to lunge at him with her broom or to yank hard at his beard, but instead, to her own surprise, she places her hand on Rosemary's shoulder where the translucent, fluttering wings are attached, and shouts, "Double, double, toil and trouble!"

Mr. Roshansky, in what appears to be genuine distress, frowns at Emma, his wrinkles following his mouth.

Remembering what she still assumes was his kindness the day he spoke to her of May not being right in the head, Emma feels a pang of guilt but pushes it away, as he lets go of Rosemary. Instead, she basks in the knowledge that she possesses all the power she needs, without anyone's help or approval. Deep inside, she has the soul of a witch, and she has cast a spell over Mr. Roshansky, thanks to Manny the Garbage Man's poem, his true gift to her, beyond marzipan and chocolate.

Now the pale Mr. Roshansky is all business, handing out his wrinkled little bags of candy without a word, hunching his narrow shoulders and shutting the door in their faces, as though he's the one who's been insulted.

"I hate that fucking bastard," Rosemary says, brushing at her shoulders where he has touched her, as if to brush away all residue of his touch. Her angelic cheeks are a bright, fierce pink. "And so does God."

Emma marvels once again at Rosemary's ease with the act of cursing, as well as her ease with her belief that she knows exactly how God feels. But in this case maybe she's right. Why else would God have put Mr. Roshansky in a concentration camp? And why else would he have killed off so many members of Mr. Roshansky's family? Emma reminds herself that, whatever or whomever is responsible, it isn't God. Because there is no God. Her own two-out-of-three test has just proved this conclusively.

"Forget about Mr. Roshansky," Shelley says, waving her hands and causing her multi-colored gypsy bracelets to jangle and click. "Let's go ring Mrs. Williams' bell."

Emma is grateful to Shelley for interrupting her dark thoughts, her endless thoughts about God or No-God, which go nowhere but circles. Together, the girls run down the hall and around the corner, away from Mr. Roshansky's apartment. Rosemary runs the fastest, her translucent halo bobbing up and down.

Mrs. Williams' door is already open. Her skin reminds Emma of rich, delicious chocolate, sweet and quick to melt, and she's handing out candy to a chubby boy and a tiny girl whom Emma doesn't recognize—he's Frankenstein and she's Minnie Mouse. Emma's disappointed because this means that she, Shelley, Rosemary, and Rachel don't get to ring her bell and yell Trick or Treat. But in a second, her disappointment fades when she sees that Mrs. Williams is handing out fluffy, cloud-like marshmallows, and jelly apples that look sharp and pungent, the kind that evoke delicious pain when bitten into.

Emma remembers that Mrs. Williams had seen her wearing her bathing suit on Rosh Hashanah. Does she, despite not being Jewish, think less of her for that? But Mrs. Williams is smiling widely, her mahogany-colored lips parting, handing Emma her jelly apple and marshmallows the same way she does to everyone else.

Frankenstein and Minnie Mouse fly off down the hall, and Emma wants to warn fragile, wispy little Minnie not to ring Mr. Roshansky's doorbell. But she hesitates lest Mrs. Williams hear and her betrayal of Mr. Roshansky be complete. Luckily, Minnie and Frankenstein dash into the staircase, and Emma's loyalty isn't tested.

With a smile, Mrs. Williams closes her door, and Emma nibbles on a tender marshmallow, so creamy and soft in the center, her knees go weak.

"Let's go downstairs to three," Rosemary says, pointing to the staircase, "to the Pierces."

The Pierces are a tight knit Irish family with seven kids, five boys and two girls. The boys are fair redheads, the girls dark and brunette. They intimidate Emma, because there are so many of them. They're like a gang—they have sharp edges, the kind of edge her father often has, that leads to beatings and violence. But one of the Pierce boys is going steady with Rosemary's sister, Victoria, so Emma figures they'll be nice, on their best behavior.

Still, Emma feels wary, since May is supposed to be at Bonita Taranto's party, which is also on the third floor. But she doesn't want to argue with Rosemary, who's just been felt up by Mr. Roshansky, and who therefore deserves to get her way.

Anyway, so what if May's there? They just won't ring Bonita's doorbell, that's for sure. May must be inside, in her absurd dress, mooning over Marvin Ludwig like the crazy creature she is. The three girls race down the one flight in single file, Rosemary taking the lead, her cardboard wings nearly spanning the width of the narrow, unswept staircase. Out of breath, they reach the third floor landing, and Rosemary opens the heavy door. She takes a few steps forward, but then abruptly stops. Emma, Shelley, and Rachel crowd behind her. What, Emma wonders, following Rosemary's gaze, does Rosemary see over by the elevator? And then she, too, sees May on the floor, her body twisted as though she's just had a terrible fall. Her eyeglasses have landed a few feet away from her; her hair has tumbled free from its upswept French twist; her dress is tangled around her waist.

"It's your sister," Rosemary says, her voice a whisper.

Emma is already moving, already by May's side, kneeling beside her. Emma's witch's hat falls off, but she doesn't care.

May's skin is grey. Her eyes are open, but they look large,

almost insect-like, and she doesn't seem to register Emma's presence, even though Emma brings her face right up close. There's blood, and saliva, too, on May's bottom lip. Horrible sounds, rasping and guttural, erupt from May, as though she's being strangled. Emma lifts May's head and holds it in her lap. And then, because she doesn't know what else to do, she screams.

PART TWO

20

In the large, drab hospital waiting room, Leo sits with Annette and Emma. May is undergoing a spinal tap. A week has passed since her collapse.

Leo clears his throat, crosses one leg, then the other, refusing to look at Annette and Emma. He looks straight ahead, seeing nothing, remembering the other May, Annette's younger sister, and how she looked toward the end of her life, her beautiful skin turned yellow and sickly, her eyes filmy and unseeing. He remembers, too, his own father, also dead of cancer, that violent, cantankerous son of a bitch, dying in a way even he didn't deserve, incontinent, his face pinched and grey, his diapers full and foul, howling with pain, his body slack and crumpled, begging to be put out of his misery.

Leo fiercely wishes that he were free and unencumbered, with no depressed wife, no sick child. In a heartbeat, he would run off to Jamaica with Cookie Coke, and they'd make love all day under a hot, fruit-orange sun … eating coconuts and mangos … licking the juice from each other's bodies … He would become apolitical, uncaring about the world outside their tropical paradise. He presses his lips firmly together, trying to hold himself in, as a great thunderous rage fills him — it is too late, much too late.

Sitting between her parents, Emma looks around the waiting room, with its dull, lima bean-colored walls, and notes a smell she doesn't like, sour and sad, like old, decaying food, or Grandma Thelma's breath in the morning, the few times she'd slept over. It's not just this room that has that smell, it's also the lobby and the elevators and the hallway of the hospital. It's everywhere, eating into her skin, her insides. She sniffs her hands, her elbows; they reek, and feel alien to her. Will the stench ever come off, or is she permanently marked as a girl who's been intimate with illness?

She doesn't like anything about this hospital, although she's heard her parents say to each other several times over the past few days that it's "a part of Columbia University," as though this is very important. It's not like them to attach such importance to the status of a place, but they seem to need to reassure themselves of its stature in the world. Her father repeats how lucky they are that the doctors will treat May even though "they don't accept our insurance." It's strange to witness him being genuinely grateful to anyone about anything, and Emma's not sure she likes it ... it's weird, and a little scary, as if he's being impersonated by an imposter who can't get it quite right. His edge has been blunted, mostly gone.

She also doesn't like one iota how cold her parents have been to her since Halloween. Her mother forgets to buy her Bosco and Hostess cupcakes, doesn't strain her milk ten times, doesn't greet her at the door when she comes home from school. Yesterday when she tried to show her father her new poem, *Double, Double, Toil and Trouble*, a poem about the nature of witchcraft, good and bad, he shrugged her off as though she had cooties, or worse, as if his love for her has disappeared along with his sharp edge.

Even worse, earlier today, when he picked her up after school, he barely looked at her. During the long, bumper-to-bumper car ride from the Bronx into Manhattan, as she stared up at the rainy, grey sky through the car window, trying to ignore the slight queasiness beginning in her belly—often the first sign of carsickness—he was completely silent, other than when he explained that they would meet up with her mother at the hospital, where May had just checked in to have a "spinal tap." "The doctors," he said, his voice low and tight, "are putting air into her brain, through a hole in her spine."

How was such a thing possible, Emma wanted to ask, but clearly he didn't want to be bothered with questions. She saw his anger in the way his blue eyes glittered like ice, and in the way he clutched the steering wheel, driving way too fast, cutting off other cars. She understood that May might be very sick, and that her parents were preoccupied. But still, she hadn't done anything to deserve their anger. They couldn't possibly know that she had wished for May to die; they couldn't possibly know of the dark power residing within her, the witchery that had transformed itself from good to bad. Now that she has made May ill, she is simultaneously Glinda The Good and The Wicked Witch of the West; she contains them both.

In the car, en route to the hospital, Emma had moved as far away from her father in the front seat as possible, closing her eyes until bona-fide carsickness began. After that, she tried to focus on the parade of people walking quickly by, dodging cars, jumping over curbside puddles, trying to shield themselves from the rain with their colorful umbrellas.

Now, in the waiting room, sandwiched between her parents, she tries to picture what the doctors are doing to May. What if they blow too hard during the spinal tap, causing May to burst wide open like a balloon? Better not to think about it. Instead, she focuses on the uncomfortable chair in which she's sitting: scoop-shaped, made of hard plastic, colored a sharp toothpaste-green. Her legs dangle, and her rear end is way too small for the chair's scooped bottom; she feels lost and overwhelmed. She unwraps the cherry-flavored Tootsie Roll lollipop that she's been carrying in the pocket of her skirt. She's very careful not to make slurping sounds as she sucks on it, because her father and mother both hate when she does that, telling her it's too "childish," not the way a ten year old should eat. "Unbecoming," her mother says. "Ridiculous," her father says. Not that she's all that inclined to slurp today, anyway, since this lollipop doesn't taste as sweet as she expected it to. It tastes oddly sour, as if the stench of the hospital has permeated the candy.

She swivels in her chair to look up at her father, who's supposedly reading the newspaper comics, but mostly he's running his thumb back and forth along the corner of the page, not chuckling at Li'l Abner's adventures in Dogpatch, the way he usually does. She turns to her mother on her other side, who's sitting as still as a statue, staring straight ahead, her hands tightly clenched in her lap. Totally ignored and superfluous, Emma scrunches down further in the plastic chair.

Just then, another family enters the waiting room and walks to the other side: a mother and two children. The father must be the one who's sick, and, as Emma tries to picture her own father—strong, invincible— shriveled and weak in a hospital bed, she inhales sharply and her throat feels like a knife.

One by one, the blond, blue-eyed family across the waiting room settles into a row of plastic chairs identical to the row in which she and her parents are sitting. They look like the Crowells, the only white Protestant family living in the projects, whom Emma doesn't know all that well, although she finds nine-year-old Mary Beth interesting because during school-wide assemblies, she sits with her ankles neatly crossed and her hands folded in her lap, like a star pupil in an etiquette school.

But this other family neither dresses nor moves like the Crowells or anyone else in the Projects. The mother is stuffed into a fur coat even though it's not all that cold. With her blonde, neatly pinned hairdo and high-heeled shoes, the mother resembles Kim Novak, May's idol, and there's something terrible about this fact, considering that May was dressed as Kim on Halloween when she collapsed. It's like a sign from the God who doesn't exist.

Emma moves her gaze from the mother to the brother and sister, who are whispering together as though they genuinely like each other. The boy, a teenager, is in jacket and tie, and the girl wears a crepe dress and shoes with heels that curve like musical notes. They both look ready for church, ready to pray, perhaps, to converse deeply with the Virgin Mary, who remains off limits to Emma.

Emma finishes the sour lollipop, and then pops a piece of gum in her mouth. Closing her eyes, she concentrates on the gum, expecting sweet juice to fill her mouth. But, it too tastes sour. Opening her eyes, giving up on the gum, she looks at the smudged windows that line the room, and wishes she were far away, in a place where she wouldn't have to worry about being a Godless witch whose evil powers have felled her own sister. If her parents could hear her thoughts, they would surely call her superstitious and feel betrayed by her "irrational, weak thinking." She glances once more at her father; at last he's turned the page of the newspaper.

Leo is at that moment wishing that Emma would stop staring at

him. Nothing he's experienced in his life has prepared him for the
blunt and naked need in his younger daughter's eyes. He's also
completely unprepared for the possibility of losing his older
daughter to a brain tumor—two morbid, terrible words that the
doctors keep using. "Not definite," they say. "But likely." Words he's
waiting not to hear again, but fears he will.

Despite the old saying to the contrary, there are indeed atheists
in foxholes, and he's Exhibit A, with nobody, and nothing, to pray to.
Inside, there is an emptiness. But do the truly religious fare any better
when their children are ill? They pray to God that their children will
recover, and some do, but many don't. Supposedly, God calls those
children to "a better place," "a higher place." But, by doing so, He
has surely, and deliberately, ignored the parents' prayers. Isn't it
worse to feel that God has deliberately chosen not to hear you, than
to acknowledge that no God exists to hear you?

Annette, too, at that moment, is acutely aware that she's all
alone with her fear. She's also aware that she has no energy right
now for Emma, who's swiveling around in her chair trying to catch
her eye, even though it was Emma who first held May in her arms
after she fainted; even though it was Emma's screams that alerted the
Pierces and the others. Maybe one day she'll have the energy to
thank Emma. But not today. Today every bit of her strength must be
conserved; it must go to May. That is how it must be. Annette will
not judge herself as a mother at this moment; any energy expended
on herself is also wasted energy, energy needed for May, to keep her
alive.

And that's why Annette sits so absolutely still. And why,
despite how uncomfortable she is, she won't rise from this
miserable chair and walk across the antiseptic, overly lit waiting
room to the water fountain. Walking demands energy. And she
has none to spare.

Besides, if she gets too close to that other family, they might
attempt to start a conversation with her. How awful if they try to
empathize with her, or try to take their minds off their own
particular tragedy by making asinine small talk. The fear
emanating from their bones might seep into hers, and her own

fear is already more than she can bear.

It's bad enough that she can't stop herself from re-living all that's happened since Halloween, from the moment that Mrs. Pierce, with a plaid apron around her waist and her hair in ridiculously oversized curlers, held in place by a riot of bobby pins, followed by Rosemary Mammano and Shelley in their trick or treat costumes, had knocked on her door. Or was it the other way around—was it the two girls who knocked first? And which of them was the one who said, "Mrs. Rosen, your daughter May is sick." Sick—that's the word she remembers most clearly, although in fact Mrs. Pierce and the two girls said a lot more, but the rest of their words are a blur. Yet she feels desperate to nail it down precisely: Who knocked on her door? Who took her hand and led her to the elevator? Who helped her out of the elevator at the third floor? Why can she remember the bobby pins in Mrs. Pierce's hair, but not what she said, and whose hand she held? There is one thing, though, that's not blurry, one immutable fact: She will never forgive Mrs. Taranto for leaving her daughter alone at that party with no adult supervision. Never. Of course, she will also never forgive herself for allowing May to attend the party when she knew Mrs. Taranto was an unfit mother.

Another fact: The instant she saw May, so helpless, her body twisted on the floor, her head in Emma's arms, her migraine vanished.

The most astonishing fact: As soon as Emma moved aside, and as soon as she herself gathered May up in her arms, May instantly came to. "Mommy?" she cried, slowly blinking her crusty eyes and licking her blood-smudged lips, sitting up with great effort and awkwardly pulling her dress down to cover herself.

A gawking crowd surrounded them. Kids in costumes. Bonita Taranto. Marvin Ludwig. Mrs. Pierce and her unruly children, the five redheaded hooligans and their sneaky sisters. Even pitiful Mr. Roshansky, although he lives on the fourth floor, not the third, so that must be a trick of her memory. "Go away!" May had screamed at the crowd, finding the strength from who knows where. "Go away!" She was so ferocious, they all looked stunned and actually obeyed her, moving back slowly, giving Annette and her daughters some space.

At that moment, Annette hadn't minded seeing May throw one of her wild tantrums in public, not one bit. Because it showed that she was fine, absolutely fine, that whatever had happened to her was a fluke, and therefore Annette had no reason to feel guilty for ignoring her daughter's symptoms. But there hadn't been any symptoms, not really, she reminded herself. After all, May hadn't been losing weight, so Annette had been certain she'd been eating during the day at school. And May's eye ... had always been erratic, lazy. The doctors had told Annette long ago not to worry about May's left eye. Blinking back tears, she held May's hand tightly as they waited, Emma standing behind them, for the elevator to take them upstairs. Annette had refused to turn around, even then, to look at Emma. Emma, now an outsider, would have to take care of herself, at least for a while—for how long, Annette could not say.

That night, like a miracle—not that Annette believes in miracles—May really *was* fine. She took a bath and cleaned herself up. She came out of the bath looking dewy and fresh, sweeter than perhaps she'd ever looked in her life, like an innocent child, much younger than 13. In her pajamas, she had appeared serene, almost untouched by what had happened to her. She'd insisted on ironing Mrs. Taranto's dress. Annette stood over her, her clenched fists balled behind her, biting her lip, terrified that May would be overcome once again by whatever it was that had felled her, that she would drop the iron and scald herself.

May, standing firmly at the ironing board, shook her head and said "No!" when Annette suggested that she do the ironing, not May.

Annette watched May's arm go back and forth with the hot iron in her hand. "May," Annette paused, swallowed. "I have to ask you again. Please ... tell me what happened, what you remember ..."

"I don't remember," May spoke flatly, eyes downcast, intent on her task, relentlessly ironing and smoothing the hateful black fabric. "It's no big deal. Don't bother me about it."

And even Leo, who for once hadn't balked when Annette had called him at work, and who'd rushed home early, didn't insist that May give more details. He looked ... what was the word ... *cowed*. But Annette felt no sympathy for him. Too little, too late.

May hadn't had any appetite that evening. At dinner she refused to eat more than a bite or two, despite the fact that Annette had served mashed potatoes with thick, dark gravy, and extra-rare, bloody steak, May's favorites. But wasn't it only natural that May would be mopey and out of sorts? She was clearly embarrassed by what had happened, by her friends seeing her in such a vulnerable state. And who wouldn't be? Still, sitting across the table from her, Annette was certain that May's eye was out of focus somehow, squinty and uncoordinated. But only for a moment, and then it seemed just fine again. There was nothing, absolutely nothing, to be alarmed by.

And, later that evening, May had grown sulky. But who could blame her for that? "I hate Emma," she'd announced at dinner, watching as Emma took an oversized, second helping of the gravy-drenched mashed potatoes. Leo had thankfully ignored May's outburst, and Annette hadn't the heart to shush her, to tell her to be nice to her sister. For once, Emma hadn't answered her back, had just chewed the potatoes, appearing thoughtful, her mind elsewhere, working her way through three large portions. Her faraway gaze was so intense, Annette wondered if she were composing poetry in her head. Good, that was a good thing. Let her live in her head for a while. Let her absent herself from the Rosens, and let art be her guide.

After dinner, Emma went with Leo to watch TV in the living room. That was the way it should be, since Leo couldn't help with May. Let the family be more divided; again, sacrifices would have to be made. Emma had always been more his daughter than her own; this new configuration would just solidify it.

May remained alone at the table, watching Annette as she began to wash the dishes. The TV was so loud that Annette could hear bullets popping and horses whinnying. Yet, it was keeping Emma and Leo occupied, and that was a good thing. Annette poured soap into the sink, stirred it with her plastic-encased fingers, feeling pleased that May had chosen to remain with her.

Another noise joined the cacophony from the TV, as Annette scrubbed a stubbornly stained gravy bowl. A close-by noise. May, weeping, sobbing. Annette turned from the sink to look at her. "Bonita and Marvin were kissing right in front of me," she sobbed, her mouth a gash of pain.

Annette stopped short in the midst of soaking the stained bowl, stunned by the sight of her thirteen-year-old daughter in such pain over some *pishadink* young boy, as her own mother might have called him. At least though, the mystery was solved: May's collapse had been emotional, not physical at all—brought on by a broken heart. Relief flooded her; her chest grew large and expansive. She gulped air with gratitude and even gusto. So be it: Her daughter wasn't the first female in the history of the world to lose her bearings over a man. Or, was that a rationalization because it was easier to think of May as broken hearted rather than ill? Surely, broken hearts healed more quickly than broken bodies.

Annette wiped her hands on her apron, checked that both faucets were turned off, and then walked quickly to the table where May sat sobbing. She knelt beside her and gathered her in her arms for the second time that day. "There, there," she said, not knowing what else to say, wishing her daughter's body wasn't so stiff and resistant, wishing she were the kind of mother for whom it came naturally to hold her daughter. Their bond was no stronger than before, no more fluid and real.

"I'm tired," May said, after a while, spine rigid as a soldier. "I'm going to my room."

But all night, Annette couldn't sleep. Leo, damn him to Hell, fell asleep instantly, his snores like animals screeching and caterwauling in the night.

The next morning, Annette rose from bed, having slept at most a few hours. In the bathroom mirror, she stared at the deep circles beneath her sunken eyes, sighed, turned off the bathroom light, and went to the kitchen to prepare breakfast. A few minutes later, hair and nightgown both rumpled, May sat down at the table, staring morosely into space, ignoring the glass of orange juice Annette poured for her.

"May," Annette said, not yet having discussed this with Leo, and not caring whether he agreed or not, "you need to see Dr.

Davidson." Roly-poly, bald-as-an-egg, Dr. Davidson, their family doctor, was a gentle, non-didactic soul, beloved by the whole family, other than May.

"I won't go!" May picked up the glass of juice and emptied it on the floor, where it quickly formed an insulting orange pool.

Leo entered at just that moment, dressed in a white tee shirt that showed off his strong arms, and a new pair of crisp dungarees, bought half-price by Annette the week before at Alexander's. Despite herself, Annette noted how good he looked, even as her whole body tensed because he would undoubtedly kill May, sick or not. Only *he* was allowed to spill drinks, throw food, break dishes, when enraged, no one else.

To Annette's surprise, however, he said firmly, "You *will* go to the doctor, and you *will* clean up that mess."

And that was that. He sounded like a man with good boundaries and clear self control. The seriousness of May's situation had brought out the best in him, and Annette found herself hoping that this moment might be a harbinger of a long-term change in him, although she abandoned the hope as quickly as it appeared.

May narrowed her eyes, glared, but got down on the floor, and, on hands and knees, wiped the juice with her napkin, while Leo sat at the table and began eating his breakfast. Annette closed her eyes for a moment in silent gratitude that, for once, a beating had been averted.

Dr. Davidson's office, on White Plains Road, not far from the Five and Dime, was on the ground floor of a small, drab, residential building. He's done his best to make his waiting room cheery, filling it with thriving potted plants and photographs of tropical macaws, cockatiels, parrots, and mynah birds, aloft in the air, dazzling wings outspread. "I admire these birds," he'd once explained to Annette. "They're social, intelligent, beautiful." Annette had guessed that he also envied them — for not having to spend their lives in the northeast Bronx, for having options he would never have.

May, who'd been sulking and silent since she and Annette had left the apartment, didn't greet the doctor when he opened the door to his examining room, and waved her in. Annette had filled him in earlier over the phone, trying to control the trembling in her voice. She yearned to follow May inside, to be present during the exam, but May had said, icily, as they'd walked along White Plains Road, "I will only consent to the exam if you don't interfere."

Annette gloomily studied a photograph on the wall above the sofa of a bright orange macaw spreading its wide wings, and she was flooded with guilt, imagining May, at that moment, being poked and prodded and questioned by the doctor. She picked up a copy of "National Geographic" with a photograph of a fuzzy, pinheaded animal on the cover that apparently was called a "meercat," but quickly put it down. Sinking deeply into the sofa, she felt grateful no one else was in the waiting room with her.

Finally, after an interminable amount of time, the door opened, and May, fully dressed, stalked out, her cheeks flaming. "Mrs. Rosen," Dr. Davidson said pleasantly, bald dome shining, betraying nothing, "please come inside."

Eyes downcast, May took Annette's place on the sofa, as Annette noted how painfully swollen and squinty May's left eye was. Today, there was no denying it.

Inside the doctor's office, Annette sat stiffly on the edge of the firm metal bridge chair across from his desk.

He rubbed his round chin, and sighed, a loud exhalation that made Annette's skin crawl. "There's no easy way to say this. She *may* have a brain tumor. But, even if she does," he leaned forward in his chair, and clearly hastened to add, "it may not be malignant."

Annette looked down at her shoes, trying not to throw up, as Dr. Davidson continued to speak, outlining the steps that Annette and Leo would have to take. He stood, dismissing her, not unkindly, assuring her she could call him any time, handing her a slip of paper with doctors' phone numbers to call, and she forced herself to open the door, and to walk toward May, who sulked and scowled on the sofa, looking, despite her scowls, so vulnerable and young and scared, with her crooked eyeglasses and her failed attempt at a sophisticated hairdo.

Now, a week later, in the waiting room of the hospital, Annette clings to the word Dr. Davidson had used that day. He had said, *may,* her daughter's name, and therefore a lucky word. "Your daughter *may* have a brain tumor." But, suddenly, Annette regrets more than anything, ever having given her child this name. What if the name is a curse, a death sentence? For her sister years ago, and now for her daughter. If so, then it is she, Annette, who is at fault. As always. Guilty of condemning her daughter to an early death. Simply by giving her the wrong name.

All this business about curses, what's wrong with her? It's all just idiotic superstition, the thing she rails against in others, and she, a rational human being who relies on empirical evidence, will not fall prey to superstition—or worse, madness. Perhaps her daughter's illness will drive her over the edge. *The Truth With A Capitol T* is that, despite her predilection for Doom and Gloom, her daughter does not have a brain tumor. Her beloved, precious daughter, unlike her beloved, precious sister, is going to be just fine.

21

Leo, perched on a wobbly stool at the bridge table in his stock room, is taking a break before lunch. It's been a long, slow morning, the only customers a couple of snot-nosed, yo yo-carrying, chip-on-their-shoulder kids with barely any pocket money between them, and a strange guy he'd never seen before, in a three-piece suit who hummed incessantly and took ten minutes to make up his mind, walking back and forth among the aisles like Sherlock Holmes sniffing out evidence, and then buying a measly bag of potato chips. On a slow morning like this, Jorge and Pocho can handle things just fine at the counter.

Leo hunches forward, hoping this posture will help him to concentrate as he tries to re-read Sinclair Lewis' *It Can't Happen Here*. He's hoping that Lewis' words will inspire him to return to writing his own novel, but finally he closes the book, forgetting to mark his place—not that it matters, since he's read the novel numerous times, and knows virtually by heart Lewis' dark, cautionary tale of an America that finds itself governed by a home-grown, fascist dictator.

All Leo can think about is what he had learned yesterday at the hospital, after the spinal tap, that his daughter has some kind of "tumor" on her brain and that more tests need to be done to determine if it's malignant, and what her prognosis is.

He inhales the pungent odor of sawdust which mingles with the far sweeter aromas of chocolate, cinnamon, honey ... His gaze takes in the boxes lining the wooden shelves: *Bit O'Honey; Pez; Bazooka; Red Hots; Baby Ruth; Nonpareils* ... The words seem alien, devoid of significance and meaning.

Shifting his gaze to the phone on the wall directly across from him, he rises, walks across the small room, lifts the receiver from the cradle, and forces himself to dial a number he knows by heart: his sisters' home in California. As he holds the phone to his ear, waiting for Brenda or Evie to pick up, he understands that this is the real reason he took this break, not because business was slow, not because he was in the mood to read or to write, but because he needs to tell Brenda and Evie about May. She's their niece, although they've never met her, and never ask after her. They need to know she's ill; they'll *want* to help—not that he has any idea what they can do, but they'll want to help, and that's what matters. Just as he did as a small child, he needs his sisters to be his allies against a cruel world.

After a half dozen rings, a young boy nasally answers. "Hello?"

His nephew's voice startles Leo. This boy is a complete stranger to him, the same way that May and Emma are strangers to Brenda and Evie. Yet if he were to learn that Freddie were seriously ill, he would do whatever was necessary: close the store; fly to California; meet with doctors; give Brenda and Evie money if they needed it, money that he and Annette don't have. Whatever was called for, that's what he would do—and more—to help his flesh and blood.

"Freddie," Leo says softly, steadying his suddenly erratic breathing, "this is your uncle." How surprising to hear his own voice break; how surprising to feel so moved by the sound of his nephew's piercing, almost feminine, voice.

"Okay," the kid says, sniffling, as if he's suddenly gotten a cold, "I'll get Auntie."

Auntie, Leo thinks, is surely too childish a word for a ten-year-old boy, even for a high-strung boy who eats baby food. Once again, he feels a kind of buoyant pride in his own girls, both independent and strong-willed—even May, who isn't a poet, and who doesn't possess an iota of Emma's feistiness. May possesses another kind of strength; a kind of almost cold-blooded determination. She is single-minded, even in the way she tries to distance herself from the rest of the Rosens, something he's not unaware of. He hangs his head, acknowledging that he hasn't paid enough attention to her, that he long ago chose Emma to be his favorite, his comrade. But that will change. It already has.

After a long moment, Evie comes on. "Hello, Leo," she says. Her bland voice, neither friendly nor unfriendly, disappoints him; he's never been able to rid himself of the habit of expecting to hear some trace of her buoyant, younger self when she first comes on the phone.

"Freddie has a cold," she says, not waiting for his answer, "and Brenda couldn't get the day off, so I stayed home. He's taking a big test next week, and . . . ."

"Evie," Leo interrupts, "my kid . . . May . . . the older one . . . ." Slowly, he finds the words to go on, trying to quell the fury he feels because he has to *tell* her which of his daughters May is.

Abrupt, ill at ease: "I'll let Brenda know when she gets home."

While Leo waits for her to say more, to at least try to offer him some comfort, to say, "I'm sorry," he remembers the way she looked in the last photograph she'd sent to him: average in every way, mousy hair, blurry features, the kind of woman you'd pass on the street without a second glance, unlike Cookie Coke, who turns heads wherever she goes. For that matter, unlike Annette, who possesses a soft, quiet beauty that turns the heads of men who value integrity and know how to think, rather than just to lust.

"Give my ... " Evie hesitates, awkward, "... regards ... to Annette."

That's it. No tears, no *I'm sorrys*, no promises to help, to drop everything, to fly to his side immediately, to hold her niece in her arms.

He cannot stand being on the phone with her for another instant, cannot stand the thought of her. He's not sure he will ever speak to her again. Without waiting for any more from her, he hangs up. Forcefully. The sight of the black phone is an affront. A bitter, medicinal taste erupts inside his mouth. His gut opens, yawning, as if waiting for that comforting, familiar rage, that primal force which, throughout the years, has been like a lover. Instead, he feels wistful, almost melancholic, and he shakes his head slowly and emphatically from side to side, as though disagreeing with what he has just learned about his relationship with his sister. No, he says aloud, harshly. Their lack of love and interest cannot be Truth With A Capitol T. And yet it is.

Startled by a noise, he turns to face the entryway of the room. Cookie Coke, clearly relishing his surprise, and seeming in no way embarrassed about their last encounter, pauses dramatically before entering, flinging her arms out in front of her like a nightclub *chanteuse* seducing her audience. What must Jorge and Pocho think, Leo wonders, of Cookie inviting herself to the stock room.

The close air of the small room is already heavy with her dense perfume, which overpowers the sweet aroma of candy, and she takes a few steps toward him, smiling with her dark-shaded eyes. Watching her, Leo is acutely aware of a blank space inside himself that needs to be filled, a space he had hoped and expected his sister to fill. He notices for the first time a small, cherub-like dimple above Cookie's crimson mouth.

"*My dear,*" she says, moving close to him, stepping over a stray candy wrapper that hasn't been swept up, "tell me what is the matter."

Never before has she called him *my dear*, not even when they'd kissed and held each other. She stands directly in front of him, inches away, body in perfect balance. He tells her about May; the words pour out. When he's finished, she lowers her eyes, and he notes how long and fine her ebony lashes are. She looks up, acknowledging his gaze. "Feel my heart," she says. "It beats on your behalf. Only yours. No one else's. No man from my past." Slowly, she unbuttons her coat and reaches for his hand, placing it over the silky, V-necked dress she wears beneath the coat.

Her rapidly beating heart feels like an extension of his own body, like his own pulse, and he's both awkward and excited as she leans forward and places her lips on his, gently, then with more force.

Gratefully and eagerly his lips receive hers, and she moves his hand slightly, so that now he's touching the smooth, powdered skin in the space between her full breasts, where her plunging neckline falls. He pulls himself out of her grasp and walks to the door of the stockroom, locking it carefully.

Moments later, she whispers his name softly, as if it's a secret word only she knows, and his dungarees are at his ankles, her silky dress above her waist, and they're lying on the floor of the stock room, on top of an old, ratty blanket he's found bunched in a corner.

He's inside her, and her legs are wrapped around him tightly. Her warm breath intermingles with his. They're tangled together, the room churns and spins along with their movements, their rocking back and forth. He covers her mouth with his hand, stifling her sounds, willing himself to remain silent, as they hear Jorge and Pocho laughing loudly up front like two crazed hyenas, perhaps guessing what's going on in the back of the store.

Annette, at the exact moment that Leo's hand rests upon Cookie's flesh, is grocery shopping on the other side of the Bronx, at the A & P on White Plains Road. Focusing intently, she squeezes a large cantaloupe, Leo's favorite fruit, in order to determine its ripeness, when she feels a tug at her own heart, a sudden, painful pressure. She holds her breath and stiffens, dropping the cantaloupe back into the bin. When she touches her chest, her heart feels tender and bruised, as though someone has been squeezing it as hard as she had just squeezed the cantaloupe.

Is she having a heart attack? Will she die here and now in this dusty supermarket with its crammed shelves and narrow aisles? Good, she thinks, because then she will be released from the agonies of her life, from the nightmare of her daughter's illness. No, she will not be sick, she will not die—she will never abandon May, her sick child who needs her so much.

And then the pain passes, the moment is over, and she forgets about it. She twists her wedding ring once, as if for good luck, then picks up the cantaloupe, shakes it, squeezes it once more, decides it's soft enough but not too soft, exactly the way Leo likes it for breakfast, with a spritz of lemon juice in its center, in a large bowl, along with his toast and eggs, everything done to his particular taste.

22

In Shelley's living room, on yet another dull, grey, rainy Sunday afternoon — a week since May's spinal tap — Emma decides that she's absolutely sick and tired of thinking about May, who's still in the hospital having more tests, and who, she gathers from the mood around her, may die. She's especially sick and tired of worrying that she, with her witch's powers, is responsible.

She and Shelley sit side by side on the plump, strawberry-colored sofa in Shelley's living room, watching the movie *Lily* on T.V. Emma concentrates on the movie's high-cheekboned, sweet-smiling heroine, instead of on the images of May that keep flooding her, even though she hasn't yet seen May in the hospital: May, lying on a cramped hospital bed, painfully gaunt, like the concentration camp victims in photos she's seen, gasping for breath while connected to an intimidating array of tubes and machines, like the patients on *Ben Casey*, one of her favorite TV shows.

Lily, the movie's heroine, works in the circus, and is all alone in the world with no mother or father, no sisters or brothers, and Emma understands that this is supposed to make viewers pity Lily, but at this moment, Lily's orphaned and solitary state doesn't seem half bad.

Lily is madly in love with a magician who doesn't love her back, while the handsome puppeteer who does love her is cold and cruel to her in order to hide his true feelings. Emma leans forward on the sofa to better hear Lily sing a beautiful song about the overwhelming sadness of love. Finally, Lily and the handsome puppeteer perform a dramatic dance together beneath a vivid sky, and at last they fall into each other's arms, and Emma wonders if this is how May pictures herself and Marvin Ludwig, eternally entwined. This thought pains her, because Emma knows that this will never happen, and so, before the credits begin to roll, she blurts out, "Idjut, let's go outside."

Shelley yawns so widely that Emma can see the silver glint of her two dental fillings, and she waits nervously, worried that Shelley will say she's being too bossy. Lately, around Shelley, she walks on eggshells. But Shelley smiles and says, with genuine appreciation, "I was just thinking the same thing, Idjut."

Emma wishes she didn't spend so much of her time worrying about pleasing others. She hopes that, when she grows up and becomes a bona-fide poet making her way in the world, she'll be able to be more self sufficient and less dependent upon the needs of others.

Outside, in the rain, Emma's nose starts to drip, but she's forgotten to bring a tissue or a handkerchief with her, despite the fact that her mother constantly warns her never to leave home without one or the other. She and Shelley walk aimlessly and slowly around the grounds of the Projects, from one institutional-looking red brick building to the next. The air smells of wet dirt, and everything looks sad and beaten down: the trees and the grass and the few unsmiling people they pass.

Neither Emma nor Shelley has an umbrella, but Shelley's windbreaker has a hood that ties beneath her chin, so she's not as wet as Emma in her hoodless red jacket. Emma's eyelashes drip along with her nose, and she's totally soaked, but being drenched suits her mood, so she doesn't mind.

As they pass the building directly across from theirs for the second time, Rosemary Mammano and her older sister Victoria walk toward them, each carrying a large brown paper bag of groceries in one hand. Victoria is also holding, with her free hand, a large umbrella over herself and Rosemary, and the two of them are laughing, bowing their heads close together, sharing a joke of some sort. Emma's heart leaps in her throat. Sadness sweeps over her. Maybe they're sharing knock-knock jokes, which Emma adores. Or maybe it's an altogether different sort of joke, something secret and special that only loving sisters can share.

Rosemary waves for Shelley and Emma to come closer. She cracks her chewing gum so loudly that Emma winces. "How's your sister?" she asks Emma.

Suddenly conscious of how the rain is ruining her ponytail, Emma's taken aback by the question. But why should she be, since Rosemary was the very first one to see May on Halloween, lying on the floor by the elevators.

"She's okay," Emma finally says, looking down and kicking at a soaked cigarette butt on the ground. Emma's parents have forbidden her to discuss May's illness with anyone, even Shelley, who luckily, hasn't asked about her yet, for which Emma is grateful. Shelley must sense how taboo the subject is, how much Emma yearns for it to go away.

At least once a day since May's gotten sick, her mother has said to Emma, in a voice as pinched as her face, "Remember, our business is nobody else's business." Harsh and reprimanding, Leo adds, "*Nobody's* business," as if Emma has already violated this new rule.

"Don't worry," Rosemary says, "I'll pray to St. Jude for May. He's the Patron Saint of Hopeless Cases."

Sharply, Victoria says, "Sissie, May's not a hopeless case! That's not nice." She nudges Rosemary in the ribs, and Rosemary cracks her gum and says, "Okay, bye," and blows a much smaller gum bubble, and then she and Victoria walk off.

Secretly, Emma does hope that Rosemary will pray to St. Jude, who for some reason she pictures as big-nosed and wrinkly like President Lyndon Bowel-Movement Johnson, which is what her father calls him.

Shelley joins Emma in kicking at the squashed, wet cigarette butt on the ground. Emma sniffles, not because she's crying, but because the raindrops tickle her nose. Aiming one last time at the cigarette butt, kicking so hard this time it dissolves, she wonders briefly about the draw of smoking, such an unappealing habit. Mrs. Taranto, for instance, has drawn cheeks and smells of old tobacco.

Emma quickens her pace to keep up with Shelley. They reach the building furthest away from theirs, on the other side of the Projects, and at last the rain lightens.

Shelley wipes off a bench with a newspaper she finds in a garbage can, and gingerly they both sit down. Emma bends down and re-ties the loose laces of her wet sneakers, and when she looks up she sees, standing not that far from her and Shelley, but clearly oblivious to them, Bonita and Marvin, holding hands and wearing identical camel-colored duffle coats that are soaked and spotted from the rain, and looking as dreamily in love as Lily and the handsome puppeteer at the end of the movie.

The rain has started up heavier again, more water falling upon the water that's already pooling upon the ground. Bonita and Marvin draw close together and kiss, and Emma's spirits feel as dispirited and soggy as the weather. But then a raging fire starts in her belly, and she imagines that this must be the way her father and May feel whenever they grow so angry they lose all control. It's the way she felt when May destroyed her poetry. "I'm going over there," she whispers loudly to Shelley. "I'm going to tell them they have no right to do that."

"Idjut," Shelley's tone is sharp, "you should M-Y-O-B!"

"Mind your *own* business, Idjut!" Emma retorts, no longer worried about being bossy and offending Shelley. This moment is too big; the stakes are too high.

In a softer voice, Shelley says, almost pleadingly, "Emma, don't . . . ."

Emma rises from the bench. She opens her mouth and tastes the cool rain. It makes her dizzy. Is this what it feels like to drink beer or wine? She's seen drunks portrayed on TV as comical buffoons, but this feels almost exhilarating, not funny or slapstick-y, at all.

Her sneakers and socks are soaked. Her toes are cold. One ankle itches. As she walks toward Bonita and Marvin, she feels a line, an invisible but sturdy cord, stretched taut between herself and May, even though May is in the hospital and hates her guts, and even though she has so recently wished May dead. "Hey," Emma says as loudly as she can, standing before Marvin and Bonita. She wants them to see her as tough and authoritarian, a younger, female version of her father. Her shoulder blades ache.

Startled, Marvin and Bonita jump apart. Marvin's plump cheeks turn red. His broad forehead glistens with rain, and his hair is plastered to his skull. Bonita touches her neck.

"Hey," Emma repeats, not as loudly or sternly. She coughs. Her voice curls way back in her throat, but only for an instant.

"You two shouldn't be kissing!"

"Are you talking to me?" Bonita snaps, adjusting the plastic rain bonnet she's wearing over her fire-red hair, and adjusting the collar of her soggy coat.

Emma looks directly at Marvin, who's looking back at her with a puzzled and earnest expression. Why, she wonders, does her sister love him so much, this broad-backed boy with the snub nose, girlish hair, and flushed complexion. He does nothing for her, evokes no desire in her to be close to him. Yet, for May, he's the most tantalizing person on the planet.

"Marvin Ludwig," Emma says, enunciating carefully, pausing between words, insisting that she be heard over the rain, "you aren't supposed to be with *her*. You're supposed to be with my sister, May Rosen. You know that."

Bonita makes a funny sound, and Emma doesn't know whether she's crying or laughing, or some combination. "Go away, little girl," Bonita says. "Just go away."

Suddenly stunned by the enormity of what she has just done, Emma wheels around, her wet hair clinging to her cheeks and neck, and she runs back to Shelley on the bench, who's waving frantically at her. Her legs feel short and uncooperative, and her heart is thudding in her chest. Now she's sure that everyone—God, if He does exist, and Shelley, her parents, and especially May—are all going to be very, very angry at her for not minding her own business.

23

It's midnight, nine days since her first spinal tap, and May, in her hospital bed, is agitated and can't sleep. For the first time in what seems like ages, she's not feeling weak, dizzy, or nauseated; tonight her vision is clear and focused, hyper-focused, actually, attuned to the details and particularities of everything surrounding her in this unwelcoming and antiseptic hospital room. Her heart leaps around inside her chest like a crazed animal. An itchy, hot bandage is wrapped around her shaved head.

Jiggling her foot beneath the thin white blanket that inadequately covers her, she looks up at the pockmarked ceiling above her bed, wishing she were home. Even being back in her room with Emma would be better than lying here in the hospital, terrified of what will happen to her tomorrow morning, when the doctors are going to operate.

She's trying hard not to think about it, about how they're going to invade her body, but not just her body—her *brain*. Her brain, abstract and untouchable, should never be violated. It contains her feelings, her ideas, her belief in God, her love for Marvin.

What if they hurt her so much, cause her so much pain, that she won't be able to stand it? There must be some degree of pain beyond which she will fold up and die. And what if the doctors find some new way to ruin her looks, something far worse than a lazy eye? What if they ruin her other eye, or scar her face so badly that Marvin would be unable to look at her?

Or what if they destroy her mind, so that she ends up like the kids in the Special Classes at school, "retarded and borderline retarded," as Mrs. O'Reilly used to say. Her parents say, "You'll be fine; lots of children go through this," but their shaky voices give them away—even her *father's* voice wavers and falls, even he knows he is not on solid ground, and this is unbelievable. They look at the floor, the ceiling, anywhere but directly at her. She knows they're lying, and she knows she might die.

No, she won't allow herself to think such dark thoughts. She just won't. But the instant she stops thinking about the operation, she starts thinking about Marvin and Bonita French-kissing so passionately at Bonita's Halloween party, right in front of her, their bodies as close together as Siamese twins, their features rapt and impassioned. How humiliated she was, how wounded she felt, as though they were stabbing her over and over, right through her heart.

And then she can't help but remember her further humiliation: Her face covered with spittle, her eyeglasses knocked clear across the floor, her beautiful dress twisted around her waist, her panties and stockings showing—and everyone, including Marvin, gawking at her, pitying her, frightened of her. She, May Rosen, who has a covenant with God, and whom God should be protecting, lying there helpless and obscene.

She cranks up her hospital bed and sits with her back stiffly against the wall, knees to her chest. Should she pour herself a glass of water from the plastic pitcher on her night table? But why bother? It's not thirst that's troubling her. She just wants things to go back to the way they were before Halloween. But what has happened has happened, and nothing can change that.

Still, just because Marvin and Bonita kissed at the party doesn't mean he prefers Bonita to her. How could he? Bonita is a no-good, deceitful tramp, and a rotten Jew, Sephardic or not. Deep down Marvin knows all this. He knows that it is May with whom he will build a family and a good life, with whom he will grow old and tender and wise. This is not some fantasy, wispy as a cloud drifting through the sky. This is as real as it gets: *Truth With A Capitol T*.

She hugs her knees tightly for a moment, then reaches up and gently runs her finger along her eyelid, feeling the slight bulge there that grows bigger every day. Her hand trembles slightly—a tremor that comes and goes. She listens to the silence outside her room, on the pediatric ward. At night, there are few nurses on duty, and most of the patients are asleep.

What might calm her down, she thinks, would be reading her Bible, the precious book she's been hiding from her family's prying eyes for two years in her bureau drawer, but she didn't bring it to the hospital because her parents would have seen it when they helped her pack her bags. She misses its comforting presence, so she will recite from memory some of her favorite passages. *"If ye will not hearken unto Me . . ."* she says softly, but can't recall the rest, can't concentrate.

She could also try pacing, the way she does at home when she's feeling anxious. But she has to have complete privacy for that, and here in the hospital, at any time, even this late at night, some nosy doctor or nurse is likely to pop in to ask her a question or make a fuss about something.

And then there are her two roommates, Dawn and Suzette, who share this hospital room with her, either of whom could awaken at any moment. Dawn, who's 14, has one blue eye and one green, lives on the Upper West Side, and is what May's parents call an "interracial child," because Dawn's father, who shares May's father's "progressive politics," is black, and her mother is white. Dawn has the same thing as May, something aggressively growing inside her brain, something that has no business, no *right*, to be there.

Dawn's operation is scheduled for two days after May's, so her long dark hair hasn't yet been shaved, and she wears it in two streamlined braids past her collarbone. Her skin is the color of coffee laced with cream, although sometimes in the harsh hospital light it looks ashy and pale, and sometimes her blue eye sags, moping like a sad sack—and then her face is a mirror May can't bear to gaze into.

But even on the days when Dawn looks so pinched and weary May has to look away, May is crazy about her. She has never been so drawn to another female. Bonita is completely bland and uninteresting next to Dawn. From her first night in the hospital, May has been enamored of Dawn, when Dawn, wide awake in her bed, sat up suddenly and said to May in a stage whisper, pausing a couple of times to cough fiercely into a surprisingly fussy and old-fashioned lace handkerchief, "I've got to let you know — in case there's going to be a problem. I'm no Beatles' fan. Paul looks like a girl, and John's a wiseass."

Forgetting for the moment how sick she was, May gasped, "And Ringo looks like Pinocchio." Amazing, she thought, in this oppressive hospital room to have found a kindred spirit. They both love old movies and old-fashioned romance and glamour. They despise beatniks and bohemians. They both believe in God, despite their parents. "My father's an atheist," Dawn laughs, "and my mother's an agnostic, which means she's just dishonest." Dawn can make them both laugh by pretending to be a dazed, vacuous "beatnik chic." "Hey, man," she says, "you rang?" When they're both well enough to go home, when May has stopped feeling dizzy and Dawn has stopped coughing, May will make sure that Dawn replaces the two-faced Bonita as her best friend. She will never, ever dump Dawn, the way she did Susan Gartner and Bethie Zimmerman. Dawn is the real thing. Dawn will marry one of Marvin's friends. Their children will attend the same private schools. They'll live next door to one another in the Hollywood Hills. They'll sweep into cocktail parties together, wearing identical, sparkling evening gowns that fall to their ankles in great shimmering pools.

If Dawn were her only roommate, she might be willing to get up from the bed and pace around the room. But unfortunately there's also Suzette in the bed next to hers; Suzette, with the skeletal face and twig-sized arms and legs. Nobody can figure out what's wrong with Suzette, other than the fact that she's way too skinny, and is obsessed with her weight. She's a bad, broken record: "Am I too fat?" she asks, holding up her pitiful, shrunken arm for inspection. "Am I too fat?"

Suzette has had test after test for her stomach and digestion, but the doctors just shake their heads. Suzette's only visitor is her frowning, thin-mouthed mother, almost as skinny as her daughter, who rarely says a word, and who glares at Dawn and May as if they're responsible for her daughter's condition.

"Psst," Suzette whispers from her bed every morning to May as soon as the doctors finish their rounds, "Am I too fat?" Not responding, May frowns, closing her eyes, shielding herself from the sight of Suzette's taut skin stretched over her bones, praying she never gets as skinny as Suzette, who looks only half alive already.

Suddenly, as though in her sleep she knows that May is thinking unkindly about her, Suzette awakens and sits up, immediately turning on her transistor radio. "*Downtown,*" Petulia Clark is singing, "*where all the lights are bright ... Downtown!*"

Usually May likes that song, but not now as Suzette begins singing along, loudly and out of tune. "Downtown!" she shrieks, snapping her bony fingers. "Downtown!"

Across the room, Dawn, still asleep, cries out in pain.

"Shut up!" May says fiercely to Suzette. "You'll wake her."

Suzette shrugs. "I'm too fat!" she wails, and then continues to sing: "Downtown!"

May turns her head away from Suzette and glances at the bright face of the alarm clock on the nightstand next to her bed: two a.m. She pictures herself pacing around her bedroom at home with Marvin at her side, and she decides that this is what she will do for the rest of the night. She will close her eyes and envision herself doing all sorts of marvelous things with him— pacing and dancing, and lying by his side on a blanket at the beach, and praying beside him at synagogue. She will not allow Bonita, that two-faced bitch, into any of her fantasies.

It's much, much better to think about her future with Marvin than about anything else. She imagines herself with him not as she is, bald with this horrid, hot bandage on her head, but as she was, and will be again, after the operation is over and her beautiful dirty-blonde hair has grown back, when she'll be able to sweep it up once more into a French twist that shows off her swan-like neck.

And these images will calm her down, and she will not allow herself to worry one bit about anything, including crazy, emaciated Suzette, who's still shrieking the words to "Downtown."

Most of all, she will not allow herself to think for one minute about what the doctors are going to do to her on the operating table tomorrow.

24

The night before May's operation, Annette can't sleep. She lies stiffly, hands clenched, nightgown tightly wrapped around her torso. Eyes shut tight, trying to lull herself into a mindless trance, she recites song lyrics, her voice the barest, softest whisper in order not to wake Leo, who, despite everything, is fast asleep beside her, thankfully not snoring for a change. She doesn't care what songs she comes up with, anything will do, one after another without pause, just so long as they block out her thoughts: lullabies she sang to the girls when they were infants; television advertising jingles; Yiddish songs her mother sang to her; protest songs from the picket lines . . . .

Leo, curled up beside her, his strong body in a near-fetal pose, sleeps deeply, and the dream he's having is unusual for him—set in the future, in a bleak world covered with nuclear ash, he's all alone, the only survivor, struggling to find food and water, struggling every moment to stay alive.

Annette hears him cry out. Opening her eyes, she sees him slapping his mouth as though reprimanding himself for being greedy, for wanting too much of something. For a moment, she wonders what it is that he craves so much he feels the need to punish himself. Is it another woman? Cookie Coke, who gives him things she cannot? Or, another family, one without the specter of Doom and Gloom hanging over their heads? Does he crave total freedom from all burdens and responsibilities, as she so often does? She decides not to care. Right now, only May's needs and desires count, no one else's. Not Leo's. Not Emma's. Not her own.

Leo jerkily thrusts his legs out as though he wants to run away from his own dream. Should she wake him? No, with what they're facing tomorrow, he needs his sleep. Besides, if he awakens, he might demand that she offer him comfort, and she doesn't have it in her. *Rockabye baby*, she whispers, *in the treetop* . . . .

Emma, down the hall from her parents, sleeps as deeply as her agitated father, but unlike him, she's not dreaming at all, too tired after a long day spent anticipating May's operation. She has refused to allow herself to believe that anything really bad will happen to May. She has decided not to believe any longer in her own power to destroy. Instead she imagines tomorrow unfolding like the most exciting *Ben Casey* episode ever, with doctors and nurses running around shouting and saving lives, ambulances blaring their sirens, and lots of people paying attention to her, because she's the sick girl's younger sister, and therefore they'll want to take care of her, won't they?

Eyes still shut, Leo wakes up from another dream. In this one, he and Cookie were making love, bodies in sync like high-wire acrobats. His muscles ache, as if from exertion, and he's sweating so much the cotton sheet beneath him is damp. He keeps his eyes closed, and turns over on his stomach, not wanting to face Annette, who, he guesses, has probably not slept one wink, and who doesn't need to know about the dreams he cannot control, the night before his daughter's surgery.

25

Emma sits once again in the hospital waiting room. The room is chilly. She's sandwiched between her parents, her legs dangling like a puppet's, her backside way too small in the uncomfortable plastic chair. They're the only people in the waiting room today. Emma wonders what became of that other family, the Kim Novak mother and her dressed-up children. Perhaps they, unlike the Rosens, have put illness and suffering behind them. Perhaps they have such genuine faith in God, their prayers have been answered.

That rank, sour hospital smell clogs up the air, and she begins to hiccup. Soft, intermittent hiccups, not big loud belches, but still she waits anxiously to see what her father will do, since sometimes something as innocuous and involuntary on her part as a hiccup, a cough, a bout of nose-sniffling, or a fart—which is the worst, because it's also embarrassing—can make him very angry. But he and her mother are, as usual these days, not paying any attention to her. Ever since the three of them arrived at the hospital early this morning, they've been sitting beside her as still as the stiff, awkward mannequins in the windows of Alexander's.

The late morning sun pours in through the narrow windows, making the room feel warmer than it is out on the street. Emma wishes she were wearing a light tee shirt instead of her long sleeved, high-collared, Doctor Ben Casey blouse. The reality today is entirely different from her fantasy the night before: no sirens, no handsome, dark eyed doctors running around, and no one at all paying attention to her. She's bored, and she feels as though she's been here forever, for eons and centuries, two words she's recently added to her vocabulary. Her next hiccup is truly loud, although her parents don't respond.

Maybe if she reads, the time will pass more quickly. She's brought along her father's copy of *Tortilla Flat*, which both he and she love, and which he discusses with her sometimes. She's already read it six times, and what she loves best is how happy Danny, Pilon, and Pablo are, no matter what misfortunes befall them—so unlike the Rosens. Nevertheless, she can't focus on the story, because she can't stop feeling guilty and scared, even at the same time that she's so bored, and she hiccups again, a longer, more desperate sound. Her mother glances at her, but turns away without saying a word.

Emma closes the book and places it on the floor. She writes a poem for May in her head: *For eons and centuries/You have been unkind/Will you ever be kind*? Later, at home, she'll write it down and try to make it better. She sighs, which brings on another hiccup. She tugs at her left earlobe, then her right, left, right, like a game. But that too quickly becomes boring. "I'm hungry," she announces, in a voice rusty and creaky from non-use.

Sighing, not meeting her eye, her mother digs into the large striped plastic satchel she packed this morning, removing a saran-wrapped sandwich. Silently, she hands it to Emma.

Emma eagerly unwraps the sandwich, but this too turns out to be disappointing. In addition to a couple of pieces of lifeless turkey there's some wilted lettuce, but no ripe, juicy tomato, no sharp yellow mustard. Her mother must have forgotten.

Since there's nothing else to do, she forces herself to eat the whole sandwich. "Mommy," she says, her voice still creaky, wiping her mouth after she's finished, wishing she didn't sound so helpless and dependent, although the hospital renders her so, "I want some candy."

Again, her mother sighs and reaches into the plastic satchel, pulling out a box of Good & Plenty.

"I hate Good & Plenty!" Emma shrieks. This is the final straw. After being totally ignored and then fed a dry tasteless sandwich, this is too much. How could her mother not remember how much she hates bitter-tasting Good & Plenty?

"It's all I have." Her mother's eyes are empty, her voice flat. "Eat it or not." Annette is disgusted by Emma's insensitivity. Ten years old or not, why can't she understand the gravity of her sister's suffering, the horror of what they're all facing? How can she be so egotistical, so self-centered, at a time like this?

Emma wants to open the box and fling every single piece of candy onto the floor. Instead, she bravely eats one of the pink ones, pursing her lips, wrinkling her nose, and making a gagging sound. Not that her mother or father cares.

More hiccups erupt from her mouth and tears well up in her eyes. She swings her dangling legs back and forth, back and forth, then tugs at her earlobes, and she's bored, bored, bored. Angry, angry, angry. Scared, scared, scared — scared that her sister is going to die. When Grandma Thelma died, her mother wept and wept until her father slapped her across the face right in front of her and May. He always says proudly, "I've only hit your mother that one time when she was hysterical. I had no choice." And her mother frowns and says, "I was *not* hysterical. You didn't have to do it." What will happen to her mother if May dies? To her father? To her? Will they both die instantly from the shock and loss, leaving her, the perpetrator, all alone in the world like lovely, waifish Lily from the movie?

Her father stirs in his seat, like Rip Van Winkle finally waking up. Her hopes rise: Maybe he's going to pay attention to her at last, discussing with her what he calls the "social message" of *Tortilla Flat*, or maybe he'll offer to go off to find a vending machine and buy her some candy she likes, to make amends for the atrocious Good & Plenty?

Ignoring her, he looks at his watch, and mutters under his breath, as if he doesn't care whether she and her mother hear him or not, "I'm going to find someone in this hospital who can tell us what the hell is going on."

Emma hears the edge of fury in his voice. His forehead is tight with tension, and he's out of his chair in a flash, his large body moving much more quickly than usual.

Now there are a couple of other people in the waiting room — in the far corner, a frail, bent old man clinging to a cane, and a few rows away, a man and a woman her parents' age, holding hands, and they all look up, seemingly startled by her father's abrupt movement.

But Leo is unaware that he's caused any commotion. All he can think about as he strides down the empty hospital corridor is that he'll go berserk if he doesn't get some news of May from someone, a doctor or a nurse, even a janitor. His daughter's skull is in the process of being opened up, and if this isn't done successfully, she will die from the pressure of the tumor pressing against her brain. Turning a corner, he comes upon a closed door with a huge sign, *Dangerous: Do Not Enter.*

He wheels around, suddenly feeling fury at the doctor who first told him, nine days ago, about the need for the operation. Dr. Brophy, who stutters slightly and has a bulbous, heavily veined nose, had said, "The tumor might turn out to be benign. And then again," he added, taking out a handkerchief and loudly blowing his thick nose, "maybe it's not even a tumor. Maybe it's just a cyst."

On the other hand, he warned Leo, May could die of loss of blood on the operating table. Or the surgeons could inadvertently destroy what is healthy in her brain. And then, Leo doesn't need to be told, she'd be better off dead.

Finally, a doctor Leo hasn't seen before is walking down the corridor toward him, taking brisk, long steps. Leo holds his hand up as though stopping traffic. "My daughter," he explains, "is being operated on." The doctor, not breaking his stride, points in the direction of the elevator down the hall, as though that's where Leo should go. Not knowing what else to do, emotionally wrung dry, almost spent with anger, Leo begins to walk in that direction, slowing his pace. Why bother to rush? No one is going to be helpful.

He stands in front of the elevator but doesn't ring the button, remembering how he had ignored Annette when she'd first told him over the phone that she thought May was ill, and he refused to listen. Annette had allowed herself to see what he had been blind to. He thinks of Emma hiccupping back there in the waiting room, making those helpless-sounding sputtering sounds, and he feels the same rush of love for her he feels for Annette, followed immediately by an attack of guilt for all the times he has favored Emma over May. If he could wipe the slate clean, he would start all over and become a *tabula rasa* of a father, with no shameful history.

There was the morning, for instance, not so long ago when he told the girls, as they silently ate their breakfasts across from each other at the table, that being a poet was one of the greatest things a person could be, far more important than being a scientist or mathematician. "I'd rather have been Edgar Allan Poe," he'd said, "than Albert Einstein." Emma's little face had flushed with pride, while May's shoulders drooped and her lazy eye started to wander, as though panicked.

Why had he said that, knowing how much it would hurt May? Because he feels close to Emma in a way he's never been able to feel toward May, and because he blames May for this. It's her own fault, he has always felt—irrationally, of course, even he knows this—that she's never been the imaginative, creative daughter he had imagined for himself, the daughter Emma has turned out to be. Such disappointment the very first time he beheld her, newly born, wrinkled, red-faced and squalling.

He will never again favor Emma over May, will never again lose his temper with either of his daughters, will never again lay a hand on them, will never again act on his desire for Cookie Coke, whom he has not seen since the day they made love on the floor of his stock room, or any other woman not the mother of his daughters. He will be a changed man, a far better father, a far better husband. He will do this, he will bargain for his daughter's life if that's what it takes to save her, even though he has no idea with whom he's striking this bargain.

A nurse he vaguely recognizes seems to appear from nowhere. She stands next to him. "I'm waiting for news of my daughter," he says. "It's been hours." His voice is shaky. He doesn't sound like himself.

The nurse has soft grey eyes. She touches his shoulder. "Go back to the waiting room, to your family. We'll come to you as soon as there's news." The elevator comes and she steps inside.

Leo continues to stand in front of the elevator; he hangs his head. He wants to shout, to fight, to murder someone. But it's useless. He begins walking slowly, retracing his steps, and suddenly he's thinking once more about Cookie, as he hears the sound of the elevator stopping at a lower floor, and at last he pushes the button.

When the elevator arrives, he steps inside, but he can't help himself, he's picturing Cookie naked, the mass of thick, tangled, jet black hair between her legs, her gently rounded stomach, her full, slightly sloping, caramel-toned breasts. He shakes his head to clear the image. Of all times to have such thoughts—while his daughter is lying helpless on the operating table. What the hell is wrong with him?

In the waiting room, Emma tugs at her earlobes, and wonders what's keeping her father. At least a hundred-million more eons and centuries have passed since he left. Maybe he's abandoned her and her mother. Or maybe he's gotten into a fistfight with someone and been killed, and she'll have to live alone with her unhappy mother and her sick, deranged sister for the rest of her life. Or, if May dies, alone with her mother, whose migraines will undoubtedly grow worse and worse.

Annette, staring into her daughter's hiccupping, pale face, now wishes so much that she hadn't brought her to the hospital, although this morning she had believed it was the right thing to do. She'd wanted the whole family to be together. She'd genuinely believed it best for Emma. But now she sees that Emma really *is* far too young for this, far too young to comprehend the nightmare, the living hell, they've all been plunged into. But there's nothing to be done about it now. Acknowledging this to herself, she still cannot bring herself to touch Emma, she cannot offer her any comfort.

She looks at her watch: The doctors have been operating on May for six hours. She looks up to see Leo at last coming through the door. Half rising from her seat, she feels her body grow stiff as a board, and her heart crashes against her chest. But he shakes his head as he rejoins them—no news. She looks at Emma, who in the last two minutes has managed to do something absolutely amazing: She's fallen asleep, her head tipped back, her mouth open. Annette is flooded with a great urge to gather her sleeping, healthy daughter in her arms. But she resists the urge. Call it superstition, madness, whatever, but she simply cannot shake the belief that the more attention she gives to Emma, the worse things will get for May.

A few moments later, Dr. Brophy enters the room. Leo hears

Annette intake air sharply, and he's aware that he's doing the same. Dr. Brophy is heading directly toward them. Surprising himself, Leo takes Annette's hand in his and holds it tightly.

"The good news is that we've removed half of it," the doctor says with his slight stutter, and no preliminary small talk, which Leo appreciates. "This is how big it was." He makes his fist into a circle.

"As big as an orange," Emma says, excitedly, startling Leo, who hadn't realized she'd woken up. Does she even know what they're talking about? How can she understand? Why in the world did they bring her here? It had been Annette's idea. One of her stupid ideas, he thinks, grimly, no longer remembering his recent rush of love and gratitude toward her.

The doctor's exhausted face breaks into a smile. Leo feels irked by the doctor and Annette, and at the same time proud of Emma for trying to be a part of what's going on. He feels newly in love with her innocence. Mostly though he just feels weary and scared and shell-shocked. He tightens his grip on Annette's hand, no longer caring that she'd had a stupid idea, because she's all he's got.

"The tumor," the doctor continues, tearing his gaze from Emma and no longer smiling, "is malignant, and it's a fast growing type. And that's not good news."

Leo can't think, can't absorb the doctor's words, yet already the doctor is instructing them to follow him to the ICU. "If," he says warningly, "she should wake up—which she won't, but if she should—don't let on that you know how she looks. The operation . . ." he paused, ". . . leaves . . . temporary marks."

"I can't see her yet," Leo hears himself mumble, abruptly standing still. "I'm not ready."

Annette feels so much fury at Leo's cowardice—so typical for him!—she believes she will explode. But as always, she doesn't know how to express her anger, not even now, when he has so completely and finally betrayed her and their daughter. Would he be able to do it if Emma were the one who was sick? Would he find the courage then?

"Fine," she says, flatly, "you two stay here and wait for me." She nods in Emma's direction, and for an instant she registers the terror that's crossing Emma's features, but there's no time for that now.

In the center of the ICU, May is lying on a bed, surrounded by other bodies on other beds—Annette thinks of them as *bodies* because it's too painful to register them as individuals—in similar states. Annette tries not to look at these others. A needle protrudes from a vein in May's arm. At her bedside, there's oxygen and some complicated, menacing-looking paraphernalia that Annette doesn't recognize. Wordlessly, she points at it.

"For blood transfusion," Dr. Brophy explains. "May has lost a couple of pints of blood."

"May will remain unconscious," he continues, until tomorrow morning." But there is more good news: They're pretty sure that the surgery hasn't made her blind or deaf, or caused brain damage.

Annette half-listens to what he says as she stares at her daughter, who still wears that big turban of a bandage. May's eyes are stuck closed, and her face is black and blue as though someone has been beating her relentlessly for the past six hours. Annette's heart beats in her ears. She feels betrayed, and furious, and her sorrow is immense and unyielding. This is not what she expected when she got married, not what she expected when she bore children. The happy life she had envisioned for herself has completely dissolved. Even the fantasy of it can never be resurrected. Wasn't having a family supposed to give her joy, to expand her world, not to empty and deplete her, not to cause her agonies beyond any she had ever experienced? Not to make her feel so all alone.

She hears herself whispering words that sound almost like prayer. *Take care of my daughter,* she says. Who is she addressing? The doctors? Herself? Nobody at all? *Take care of her,* she whispers again, as she gently strokes her daughter's terrible, battered face.

26

Leo's hand trembles as he drops a coin into the phone. He closes the phone booth door securely and pulls up the collar of his fleece-lined jacket. He's afraid to call Cookie from the phone at Leo's Candies, and he's ashamed to be skulking around like this, like a common criminal—with his daughter operated on just yesterday. "I'll be gone a couple of hours," he'd told Pocho at the store, putting on his gloves and jacket.

Pocho nodded soberly, in keeping with Leo's demeanor. "Anything I can do for you, Leo, anything you need ..."

Clearly, Pocho had assumed that Leo's mid-day errand had to do with May's illness. Well, wasn't that precisely what Leo had *wanted* Pocho to think? Okay, yes, Leo admits to himself as he picks up the receiver, but he's not proud of this fact. He'd forced himself to nod at Pocho, to let him know that he appreciated his offer, and also to convey wordlessly his even greater appreciation for the fact that neither Pocho nor Jorge have said a word to him about the day that he and Cookie were alone together in the stock room.

Leo reads Cookie's number from the scrap of paper he's scrawled it on, and dials it quickly. He pulls his jacket collar up higher, half-hiding his face. Not that what he's doing is anyone's business, but you never know. *Yentas* like Mrs. Gottleib, for instance, who might hobble by with her cane, cannot be trusted.

The phone rings a second time. It's growing warm in the closed, airless phone booth, and he begins to panic, fear spreading outward from his chest. He forces himself not to hang up. How little he really knows Cookie, despite the way his body had, that day in the stock room, known her body so intuitively and intimately. He knows that she works nights, but he doesn't have any idea what she does during the day when she's not visiting Khenan's family or his store. Will she even be home?

On the fourth ring she picks up. "Hello?" she says, her question a direct invitation, and desire arrives like a shocking thunderbolt inside him. He nearly moans, picturing her lying in bed, wearing only a flimsy, sheer nightgown that shows off her nut-brown skin.

"Cookie," he says. His tongue is slow and clumsy. He's spoken so softly that he's not sure she heard. Loudly, he clears his throat before she hangs up. "Cookie," he says more firmly, aware for the first time of the intrinsic sweetness of her name itself. What to say next? He doesn't want to say, *We must talk!* like a bad actor in a bad movie, although he acknowledges that hiding in a public phone booth does reek of such a movie.

"Can we meet?" His voice is so tentative and unmanly that he cannot believe it's his own. He names a diner on Pelham Parkway, a neighborhood known for its good schools, far better, he and Annette have been told, than the schools that May and Emma attend. Pelham Parkway, also known for a large Jewish population—*so-called Good Jews*, Leo thinks—is not one of his favorite neighborhoods. But, it's close enough to the Projects for Cookie to get there easily, and close enough to the store for him to do the same, and yet, it's far enough away from both so that they won't likely be spotted together by anyone either of them knows.

"Of course," she says, her enunciation perfect and formal. "I will meet you wherever you wish."

He arrived early, and sits alone in a booth for fifteen minutes before she slips into the red vinyl seat across from him. The diner is large, and, at lunch hour, bustling with neighborhood housewives, local businessmen, and a few small groups of *yamulke*-sporting Jews, who must be very careful, Leo thinks, to order Kosher from the menu—unless they're cheating, which he wouldn't put past them. The diner is noisy and colorful, with yellow balloons hanging from the ceiling, and amateurish paintings of the Acropolis and Parthenon on the walls.

Leo sips his extra-strong coffee, and greets Cookie uneasily, but before he can say more, a waitress appears to take their food order, and, suddenly ravenous, Leo orders roast beef on rye, with French fries.

"Tea," Cookie says softly to the waitress, whose bouffant hairdo seems almost high and pointy enough to puncture the hanging balloons. "That's all."

Trying not to be too obvious about taking in every detail of her appearance, Leo notes that Cookie is dressed uncharacteristically simply and casually—a skirt and a cardigan sweater that reminds him of the conventional schoolgirl sweaters May and her friends wear, with clean lines and small pearly buttons down the front. Her hair is loose, and she's combed it so that it flips up at the bottom, and the earrings she wears are modest gold dots that match the whisper-thin, golden bracelet on her wrist. There's nothing overtly gypsyish about her today, but then she unbuttons her cardigan and reveals a low-cut, deep red, silky blouse, letting him know that the gypsy within her is alive and hungry.

"Leo," she says, after the waitress places their orders in front of them, leaning forward with both elbows on the chrome borders of their table, showing so much cleavage he's dizzy for a moment and has to look away, "how is May?"

"Recovering." His throat is throbbing, and he takes a large bite of his heaping roast beef sandwich.

Cookie sits quietly for a second, leaning forward, watching him chew. Then she leans back and removes the soggy teabag from her cup, setting it down on the rim of her saucer.

He doesn't want to go into any more detail about May, doesn't want to share her grim prognosis or the fact that he hadn't had the courage to go into the recovery room to see his own daughter. "Annette is with her now," he forces himself to add, saying, for the first time, his wife's name in Cookie's presence. He sees her flinch, and although he's instantly guilty for hurting her, he's glad that he was brave enough finally to speak, even if indirectly, of his marriage.

"I pray for May," Cookie says quickly, recovering her poise, pouring two large spoonfuls of sugar into her anemic-looking tea, then gently stirring the liquid with her spoon.

Spare her your useless prayers, he thinks, and dares himself to say it, so that Cookie will understand that, for him, the concept of prayer at such a time is no more than an ugly joke, and she'll end things between them, and then he won't have to.

Instead, he takes a deep breath and says, "Cookie, I can't be with you — can't see you — any more." His voice is sharper and edgier than he intended. He has crossed the line, has become what he's dreaded becoming, a real-life character from a trashy movie.

Her round face flushes. Her eyes open wide, and the whites become severely pronounced. "You are cruel! You are wrong!" she cries out, loudly enough for the *yamulke*-wearing, thin-lipped man sitting alone two tables over to look up from his newspaper and frown in their direction. "I am a good woman, and you have used me!

He's amazed that she moves so quickly into the cold white heat of rage, a state he knows all too well in himself, but which he has never witnessed in Annette. He turns up his hands, as if in entreaty, unsure if he's asking for forgiveness, or simply acknowledging the truth of her words. It's not a distinction that matters to her, as she rises from the table, grabs her purse and jacket, and stalks out of the restaurant, her tea untouched, the teabag limp on the saucer's edge. He looks out the window, hoping for a final glimpse of her but sees no one other than a bent-over couple, holding hands and shuffling slowly together down the street, their expressions so tired and hopeless that he pegs them as concentration camp survivors, and quickly turns away.

"Anything else?" the waitress asks, sounding bored, and Leo becomes aware that she's standing over the table, clearing his plate. Five minutes later, she returns with the largest hot fudge sundae he's ever seen, a brick-size brownie topped with two ice cream scoops, covered with hot fudge and a glowing red cherry. As he rapidly devours the sundae, returning the hostile stare of the jerk with the *yamulke*, he promises himself that when he gets back to the store, he will call home to see if Annette has gotten back from the hospital.

27

It's a Sunday afternoon, almost two weeks since May's operation, three days after Thanksgiving. Emma is still disappointed about the fact that there was no turkey and stuffing and cranberry sauce this year. Usually her mother shops for days before Thanksgiving. "The one holiday," her mother says every year, "we celebrate because we have things to be thankful for, even if we don't attribute them to God." She never says what it is that she believes the supposedly cursed Rosens, destined for lives of unmitigated Doom and Gloom, have to be thankful for, and Emma never asks, because she suspects that her mother would probably just shrug and say something like, "Now that you ask, absolutely nothing."

Nevertheless, her mother usually spends the entire day itself cooking, and then in the evening her father proudly carves the bird with swift, sharp strokes. All of them, even May, devour everything on their plates. But this year when Emma said, "I want a big turkey," her mother frowned and ran her hands through the white streak in her hair. "I don't have the energy," she said, "so don't ask me again."

The weather is warm, almost spring-like, the kind of weather that usually makes Emma's heart soar. But today, she's about to visit May for the first time in the hospital, so she barely notices it. She is here, standing outside May's room, only because her parents insisted. "It's time for you to visit May," her mother had said this morning, while serving breakfast to Emma and her father. "Sisters should be close," she said, setting a plastic pitcher of orange juice squarely in the center of the table, "the way my sister and I were."

"No," Emma said, pouring herself a glass of the thick, pulpy juice. "I won't go. May and I can't stand each other. We're not you and *your* May." She noted the pain that crossed her mother's face when she brought up this long-dead Aunt, but she couldn't stop herself. "I don't love her," she adds. "I just don't."

Her mother stood over the table, coughed into her hand, looked into the distance, and whispered, "May loves you. She just doesn't know how to show it."

Liar, thought Emma, amazed at her mother's hypocrisy. Or, was it pure ignorance? "I'm not going," she insisted, chomping as loudly as she could on a slice of rye toast.

Her father looked up from his plate of runny scrambled eggs, exactly the way he likes them. Her mother still caters to his "culinary needs," as she calls them, although no longer to Emma's. "Yes," he said grimly to Emma, his blue eyes flashing, "you are going to see your sister." And that was that.

But then to make matters worse, as soon as she and her parents got to May's hospital floor, her mother said, "We're going downstairs to the cafeteria for coffee. You go on in." She pointed with her chin toward May's room. How deceitful they were, engineering this whole thing to leave her alone with May. "In politics," her father often says, "the end justifies the means." But to what "end" is this scenario?

Now, in the doorway of May's room, she nervously unzips her jacket, and the thick metal zipper catches and almost breaks halfway down, but she finally manages to unzip it all the way. She forces herself to walk slowly into the bleak room, where she's startled to find May, looking like herself but not, pale, with a thick, pirate-like bandage wrapped around her head. At least her eye isn't sticking out and drooping any longer, the way it had been. In fact, she looks better than the last time Emma had seen her, the morning she'd left for the hospital. Now she's sitting up tall in bed, holding an envelope on her lap, looking at Emma expectantly, as though she's been waiting for her.

A fierce, burning itch suddenly spreads across Emma's face, down her neck, across her stomach … she wants to scratch herself in a million places. But if she does, then May, who won't stop staring at her, will undoubtedly say she has something incurable, like rabies, and, despite herself, Emma will grow frightened, convinced that death by rabies will be her punishment for wishing May dead on Halloween, and for leading her, ultimately, to this bleak, cheerless hospital room. Controlling her desire to scratch herself, Emma eases her body carefully into the single visitor's chair at the foot of May's bed, and folds her burning hands neatly in her lap.

Both of May's roommates have their privacy curtains drawn around their beds, making Emma feel more vulnerable and nervous, especially since May now has an eager expression on her face, as though she's actually glad to see her. Trying to ignore the sick-smell that permeates the room, Emma stares at a lone, silver-colored balloon attached to May's bedpost, and then at the envelope on May's lap, which May, with a trembling hand, picks up and thrusts eagerly at her.

"For Marvin," the envelope says, in an unfamiliar, shaky handwriting, completely unlike May's former meticulous script.

"I want you to give this letter to Marvin Ludwig," May says, sounding far more bossy and imperious than Emma is sure she herself ever sounds, despite Shelley's complaints,

"Why should I?" Emma's knee itches ferociously through her denim blue jeans. As surreptitiously as possible, she unfolds her hands and scratches gently, but that only aggravates it. She's startled by May's request. Does this mean that her mother is right, and that May *does* love her? Or that she at least trusts her? Why else would she want to involve Emma in her love life?

"I'll tell you why," officious May says, in her strict schoolteacher's voice, reminding Emma of Mrs. O'Reilly, adjusting the bandage on her head. "Because you owe me big time for what you've done to me."

Emma flinches and scratches at her other knee, which is now itching worse than the first. "Oh yeah? What have I done?" She tries to sound brave. Is May on to her? Does May know that Emma, with witch-like accuracy, wished her dead?

May looks coldly at her. Her lazy eye slowly begins to drift inward. "You have done nothing but ruin my life since the day you were born."

Emma crosses her legs and scratches at the top of her ankle, above her sock. She still can't be sure: Does May know or not?

May goes on. "So here's what you have to do. You have to

promise that you'll give my letter to Marvin. Promise!"

Emma tears her gaze from May's, which has been unwavering, and looks at the door. She's hoping to see her parents returning from their coffee break, but instead she sees a toffee-colored nurse with liquid eyes, who resembles Cookie Coke, her father's beautiful friend. The nurse looks in and smiles widely at Emma as she passes, and for a moment Emma thinks that instead of becoming a poet when she grows up, she'll become a nurse and heal the sick. Not realistic, though, because she couldn't stand having to be around this nauseatingly sour-sick hospital smell all the time.

"Promise," May demands. "Promise that you'll give it to him tomorrow."

"I promise," Emma says, scratching at her elbow. *Oy vey,* she thinks, *what have I gotten myself into?*

"Good," May says, smiling. "And remember that God will strike you dead if you break your promise."

May believes in God? Since when? Is this something new, since she got sick, or has she always believed in Him, without any of Emma's own wishy-washy-ness? Did she and Grandma Thelma whisper together about how they were the good Jews in the family? Had Grandma Thelma loved May more than she'd loved Emma? And, if true, what does this reveal about May, who is so near death — that she had displeased God somehow?

May watches Emma, who's been twitching and scratching so peculiarly ever since she arrived, and wonders whether she can trust her. Yesterday, when her parents told her that Emma would be coming today, she had protested. "Keep her away from me," she said. "I'll destroy her if she sets foot in this room." "She's coming," her father insisted. May turned her face away, her cheeks stinging, but, at that moment, from seemingly nowhere, came the idea of giving Emma the letter, of putting Emma to use. She turned back to her father. "Fine," she said. "So be it." She turned away again before she could see his expression.

And now that Emma's here, she wonders if maybe she's misjudged her all these years. Maybe Emma isn't totally evil and awful. If Emma proves herself to be an honorable and righteous person by giving Marvin the letter, then once May is home from the hospital, she might take Emma with her to the movies once in a while, or discuss TV shows or books before they fall asleep. But they will never be close, and she will never love her.

In the meantime, as she fixes her gaze upon her twitching, scratching sister, she thinks about the things she will be able to do, upon her release from the hospital: go to the movies; shop at Alexander's for new winter clothes, maybe with Dawn by her side; return to school and quickly catch up on her work, impressing everyone; and, most important, date Marvin, who must have, by now, figured out what an unworthy and hypocritical skank Bonita is, and dumped her without a backward glance. Bonita must be sitting at home, crying her eyes out, looking for solace from her silent, ungiving dolls.

May knows that she's growing stronger every day, and that it's just a matter of time until the doctors say she's well enough to go home, to begin her life anew. From here on, her life will be composed of perfect, magical moments.

Not that there haven't been times since the operation when she's been absolutely terrified. She was terrified, for instance, when her eyes were shut tight, and wouldn't open at all, for two full days after the operation. Despite her parents' assurances that this was just temporary, she was convinced then that she was blind, that she would never again see the sky, the sun, her own reflection in the mirror, Marvin's fine-spun golden hair.

Then she was frightened that the doctors had destroyed part of her brain, because she had tried, a few days after her eyes finally opened, to do some math problems in her head, simple arithmetic, addition, subtraction, the easiest multiplication and division problems imaginable. But her thoughts were vague and undirected, and she couldn't remember the most basic rules of addition and subtraction.

And then a day or so after that, she tried to walk unaided to the bathroom, but fainted in the corridor, although she has no memory of doing so, and when she came to, a frowning nurse with bottle-cap eyeglasses held her in her arms and said, "Young lady, you must understand your limitations!"

Still, only eight days after the operation, May had a large enough appetite to eat half of a steak sandwich rare, the way she likes it, sitting up while her father sat at her bedside and told her one of his silly rabbi-priest jokes. And that same day, when she braved looking at her math workbook, she aced every single problem she tackled, including the most complex and challenging. As for walking the hospital corridors by herself, well, most days now she can do it pretty well, despite what that ugly and unpleasant nurse said to her, and despite an occasional bout of dizziness.

May glances away from Emma and sees her mother and father walking through the door, holding their unopened coffee cups, smiling identical, grandly insincere, frozen smiles. Rarely, do they ever appear so in tune with each other, and May finds the sight of them strange and disturbing, knowing that it's her illness that's bringing them together, and she doesn't like what this suggests about the true nature of her illness. No matter—she has something urgent to attend to. Quickly, she whispers to Emma: "My letter is for Marvin's eyes only. *Do not open it!*" If Emma dares to disobey, she won't hesitate to kill her on the spot, in cold blood, and to make her suffer while she does so. Her sacred letter is meant only to be read, with reverence, by her beloved.

Emma scratches her twitching nose. "I promise."

Again, May thinks: *Maybe Emma's not so bad.* It's not a thought she can hold onto, though, because it would mean that the entire house of cards that is her life would crumple, and she cannot allow that to happen, especially now, while her life itself is so tenuous.

28

In the middle of December, two weeks later, Leo is dreaming one of his typical dreams, a scene drawn from his childhood, his *zaftig*, fleshy mother slapping him repeatedly across the face because ... Because of what? What had he done? In bed, Leo groans loudly, and Annette, asleep beside him, wakes for an instant but then falls right back to sleep. At last, she's been able to sleep again most nights because her exhaustion trumps her anxiety.

In Leo's dream, his florid-faced mother shouts, "You are a terrible son!" Leo kicks angrily, and the blanket he and Annette share is thrust toward the end of the bed, but neither awakens.

Down the hall from her parents' bedroom, Emma lies in bed, wearing an old tee shirt and a pair of pajama bottoms, unable to sleep. Even with her bedroom door closed, she hears her father's loud, ragged snores coming from his room down the hall.

Leo's snores increase in volume, and Emma places her hands tightly over her ears. Ever since May handed her the letter for Marvin, Emma has hardly slept because she can't stop thinking about it. Despite her promise, she hasn't given it to him, although she carries it with her everywhere, folded neatly inside her jacket pocket. Luckily, she hasn't been forced by her parents to visit May again in the hospital, so she hasn't had to lie to her yet and say she's given him the letter.

She hasn't lacked opportunity. Just last week, on one of the very few cold days of this unusually warm winter, as she and Shelley were walking home from school, their noses turning red from the unexpected wind, they both spotted Marvin at the same time, across the street, walking with his tall, skinny father.

"There's Marvin Ludwig," Shelley said accusatorily, pointing with her thickly gloved hand.

Emma figured that Shelley's tone of voice meant that she was still annoyed because Emma hadn't "minded her own business," on the day they'd come upon Marvin and Bonita kissing. Emma averted her gaze from the sight of Marvin and his father; her heart beat rapidly as she stared at a swaying, bare tree, hoping to distract herself. But then, unable to resist, she stole another glance, and noted that Marvin wore the same camel-colored coat he'd been wearing when he held Bonita in his arms. *Do it*, she told herself. *Just cross the street and give him the letter.*

A brisk wind hit her in the face. As usual she'd forgotten to take her handkerchief with her, and she needed to blow her nose. She shrugged again as she and Shelley walked on, and she felt guilty for not honoring her promise to May. But she would not turn back for one more look at this boy who is part of her sister's madness.

And now late at night, lying awake in her bed, restlessly tossing and turning, her hands over her ears to block out her father's snores, she acknowledges to herself that one of the reasons she hasn't yet given the letter to Marvin is because she wants to read it herself. How she has gone this long without tearing open the envelope, she doesn't know. These past few weeks, she has lusted to know what May had written, but she's resisted, an act which must constitute what Catholic Rosemary calls "a holy miracle."

She rises from her bed, turns on the light, and looks across the room at May's perfectly made bed, untouched for so many weeks. Gingerly, she tiptoes over and lies atop the soft, delicate bedspread, her heart racing, her eyes clenching shut, then popping open as if in terror. What if, when May comes home from the hospital, she senses that Emma has dared to lie in her bed? Emma jumps up in a panic, trying to smooth the bedspread, hoping to erase any trace of her own flesh. She's already responsible for May's illness. How much more guilt and grief could she stand?

She turns the light off, and gets back into her own bed, burrowing beneath the covers, shutting her eyes tightly and then opening them immediately. She sighs, sits up, turns on the light, shuffles like an old woman, like Mrs. Zelig, the few steps to her bureau, pulls out the envelope from her top drawer. Her hand trembles almost as much as May's as she tries to open it without tearing it. Amazing: she does a decent job. Unfolding the letter, she reads:

Dear Marvin:

You are my destiny, and I am yours.

We both know this. You must come to me at once.

I have been sick, but I promise that I will be well soon.

Forever yours,

   May.

Emma sits heavily on her bed, hunching over, elbows on her knees, feeling ancient and bowed. How can May be so certain of her destiny? Is it because of her faith in God? But she's wrong, anyway, because Marvin will never love her the way she loves him. Maybe he loves Bonita that way, but not May. No boy, no man, is worth such anguish. She promises herself that she will grow up to be as different from May as she will be from her mother.

Emma re-reads the letter, this time speaking May's words aloud, as if she's an actress in a play, although the words remain at a great distance from her: *You are my destiny ... Forever yours ...* If May is able to love Marvin so passionately and completely, why is she so unable to love Emma, her own flesh and blood? What about herself is so repulsive? Still, May has entrusted the letter to her, and she would never have done that if she didn't, deep down, care for Emma at least a little bit, would she? And if this is true, then Emma is a terrible person, as terrible as May so often says she is, a bona-fide, destructive E-Bomb, betraying her sick sister's fragile, burgeoning trust.

Carefully, she refolds the letter, placing it back inside the envelope. Only now does she see that it's impossible to simply reseal it—all the glue is gone. Tomorrow she'll have to sneak into her father's desk drawer and take out a business envelope, and try to copy May's shaky handwriting on the envelope as accurately as possible. Her skin begins itching all over, face, hands, chest, knees. If she ignores it, perhaps the itch will stop on its own, since scratching never really seems to help. These fits have plagued her since she day she visited May in the hospital, as if a swarm of invisible mosquitoes that had attacked her there have never left her side.

She returns the letter to the drawer, turns off the light, and slinks guiltily into bed, pulling her blanket to her chin and shutting her eyes, but still she can't relax enough to fall asleep—because she knows very well that she has already irreparably betrayed May's trust by wishing her dead. Her flesh is consumed, burning, itching, worse than when she had chickenpox in first grade. Listening to her father's foghorn snores, she gives in and scratches until her skin grows red and chafed.

29

On the third day of the new year, two weeks since May's release from the hospital, Leo is driving her back there for her daily x-ray treatment. At a red light, he glances at Annette sitting beside him in the front seat, her head turned away, her hands rigid in her lap. In response, his own hands grow tight and rigid on the wheel, and he wonders, not for the first time, if Cookie, to get back at him, has called Annette and told her about what happened between herself and Leo, and if that's why the distance between himself and Annette seems greater than ever. He didn't want to hurt Cookie; he doesn't want to hurt Annette.

Someone's car horn honks, and Leo flinches. *Do not think about Cookie*, he reminds himself silently and reflexively, as he has reminded himself at least once a day, every day, since he last saw her at the diner, and he steps down hard on the accelerator.

In the rearview mirror, he catches a glimpse of May. With a scarf tied tightly around her head to hide her baldness, and her lopsided eyeglasses, she looks lonely and vulnerable and childish, younger than her thirteen years. A lump forms in his throat, and he swallows hard to dissolve it. Seeing her like this, he's newly convinced that he and Annette have made the right decision not to tell her the truth of her situation: brain cancer, with little chance for recovery.

For the first time, he wishes that he and Annette had been able to provide May with a large extended family, with lots of loving uncles and aunts and cousins to play with, to feel close to, like those ideal families portrayed on TV sitcoms. Annette has no living siblings, and just one cousin, a boring, synagogue-attending Republican out in the suburbs, whom she barely keeps up with. He has only Brenda and Evie, three thousand miles away in California, and, toward them, his heart is hard. They deserve no forgiveness.

Neither of them has had the decency to call him. All he has received from them is a messily typed letter from Brenda on stationery bearing the letterhead of the drug company that manufactures her arthritis medicine. "Evie told me about your daughter," she wrote. That was the extent of what she had to say about May; the rest of the letter was her usual litany of complaints: her joints were inflamed; a neighbor's German Shepherd had frightened Freddie; her anti-Semitic boss had refused to give her a raise; her car was on the fritz.

Leo drums his fingers on the steering wheel, silently cursing his sisters who once, a long time ago, were his best friends and would have done anything for him. Why have they become so cold? Because he reminds them too much of a miserable past they've conspired together to forget? Because he has chosen a path unlike theirs, and is therefore a living, breathing affront to them? Because his children are reminders that Freddie isn't so perfect after all? He doesn't know why they behave toward him as they do—they themselves may not know why. Just as he's not always sure of why he does what he does—makes love to another woman; beats his own children.

May, in the back seat, wishes her father would calm down. She can tell by the stiffness of his neck and by the way his fingers gallop along the wheel like wild horses, that he's growing impatient, and this makes her fearful, since so often his impatience leads to a temper tantrum. She wishes that her recently shaved scalp would stop itching. She refuses to scratch, though, unlike the inelegant Emma, who seems to have caught a case of fleas.

Finally, both of May's wishes come true: the light changes, so that her impatient father can zoom off, at least until the next red light; and her itch gradually abates. She stares at a jewelry store on the corner, in whose window a bright red-and-green lettered sign reads, *Big-Blowout After-Christmas Sale*, reminding her that Christmas has been over for a week, and that Hanukkah too has come and gone. And, that her parents had refused to celebrate the Jewish holiday, not even willing to make an exception this once because of her illness. "We don't observe," her mother had said. "But," she added, "think of your new bathrobe and slippers as a

Hanukkah present, if it makes you happy."

So okay, it was true that her parents had given her a fluffy pink robe with glamorous, glittery, matching pom-pommed slippers to wear in the hospital, and she knows how difficult it must have been for her mother to purchase such clothes that violated her core beliefs. Still, she wants more, much more than the robe and slippers. She wants her very own black Kim Novak dress, so she'll never have to borrow one again. She wants her own strand of pearls, pearls chosen to fit her neck perfectly, so she'll never again have to wear Grandma Thelma's fakes and feel choked and strangled. She wants spinning *dreidels*, lights, music and a joyous, big celebration, the way she imagines that Marvin's family celebrates Hanukkah. One day, of course, Marvin's family and their celebration will be hers, but she's tired of waiting.

Despite this disappointment about Hanukkah, May is hopeful that the new year will turn out to be a terrific one for her, filled with love, good health, happiness. Even though at this moment, things are far from terrific: Her head is starting to itch again, and she has to have these awful x-ray treatments for another few weeks. Luckily, she's had no "side effects," a fact that very much pleases her parents and Dr. Brophy. She hasn't asked what these side effects might be, in case the answer is too terrifying. Usually she and her mother take a taxi to the hospital, but today her father has volunteered to take off a few hours from work to drive them. But he's driving really crazily, so typical for him, speeding and weaving in and out of lanes, causing Emma's stupid Puke Bucket, on the floor in the back with her, to keep knocking into her legs. What would it take to calm him down the way other fathers are calm, like Marvin's father and Dawn's? She has no idea; he's always wired to explode.

Neither her mother nor her father, sitting together in the front seat, have said a word since the ride began, so she stares out the window and looks at the same old boring things she's been looking at every day: garbage left out on the streets; pedestrians bundled in unflattering winter clothes; storefronts with bedraggled holiday lights and wreaths left over from Christmas.

Her father brakes abruptly at another red light, and she

manages to grab onto the plastic bucket before it bangs against her shin. If she asked him to slow down, he would surely interpret that as criticism of his driving, and then the rage could start. And, since she's been sick, he's been more attentive to her than usual, and she doesn't want to rock this fragile new boat of his love.

But her mother says timidly, finally breaking the silence, "Leo, maybe you could slow down a little?"

"If you don't like my driving," her father shouts, "why don't *you* drive?" He takes his hands off the wheel for a dangerous instant, and her mother, who's never learned how to drive, is clearly panicked. "Okay, enough, I'm sorry," she says, almost choking with fear.

May is relieved when her father grabs the wheel again. In an overly controlled, calm voice, he says, "May, sweetheart, everything is fine now. Just relax. Ignore your hysterical mother."

Why, Leo thinks, does Annette always have to butt in and criticize him, so much like her own mother, Thelma Baum, the *yenta*? Two such negative women, naysayers, chronic harbingers of Doom and Gloom. Cookie, on the other hand, is the kind of traditional woman who honors her man . . . *Do not think about Cookie . . . .*

Isn't he supposed to be working on being more forgiving, on not exploding the minute someone says something not to his liking? Hadn't he, in the hospital on the day of May's operation, promised himself that he wouldn't be so quick to explode? Yes, but this is different. Annette can handle his anger, can handle whatever he does or says. She isn't a child. She can take care of herself. *Drive*, he tells himself. *Just drive.*

In the rear view mirror, he sees May again, looking vaguely dramatic with that scarf wrapped around her head, like a gypsy—his unadventurous daughter who has never been gypsyish in any way, unlike Cookie, with her exotic beauty ... *Do not think about Cookie.*

He returns his gaze to May. The bruises on her face have healed, and she looks almost pretty again. Scratch that. Not *almost*. She's his daughter, and she looks—*is*—pretty. It's not immediately evident how sick she's been, not immediately evident that she has a malignant brain tumor. *Has*, he repeats to himself in a sudden panic, not *had*, as he yearns to be able to say. She still *has* the brain tumor. Only half of it was removed. The other half, according to the doctors, will quickly resume growing. "Aggressive," they call it. "Fast growing."

He intends to be there for his daughter, to take care of her, to make up for the times he's felt cold and closed off to her, such as the night not long ago that he sat on the sofa with Emma on his lap reading Shakespeare to her in the living room. May came in and stood in front of them, her eyes wide and filled with hope. "You're a numbers girl," he waved her off. "This isn't for you." The shadow that fell over her face both thrilled and horrified him. She retreated to her room, and didn't come out again.

From the back seat of the car, May looks at the back of her father's thick neck, at the way a vein is bulging, which could mean either he's still angry or is concentrating on his driving, she isn't sure which. And then her mother turns around to look at her, clearly upset, her mouth a tight line, her eyes cloudy. May expects her to turn back to the front of the car once she sees that May is fine, but instead she keeps staring, which May doesn't appreciate at all, and she snaps, "Why don't you take a picture?"

Annette's need, however, at this moment to memorize everything about her daughter is greater than her need to please her daughter. She wants to remember, for as long as she lives, the colorful scarf around May's head and how May's skin appears luminous, lit-from-within, rendering her almost saintly, but that's an image Annette immediately shakes off, because even she, an atheist Jew, knows what happened so often to those who became saints: the terrible deaths of martyrs.

Another reason she should stop staring at May like this is because it must unnerve and scare May, but she finds it increasingly difficult to behave normally when her own heart is so unbearably heavy with the burden of what she and Leo haven't said. How in the world can they tell a 13-year-old child that, according to her doctors, her chances to survive more than one more year are extremely slim? How can they tell her that she won't live to graduate junior high school, won't get married, won't start a family?

Last week when she and Leo were alone with Dr. Brophy, he

had said, after blowing his heavily-veined nose so hard Annette felt herself wince, "We all need to bolster May's will to survive. That way, maybe she'll be one of our miracle cases."

And that is the hope Annette clings to as Leo cuts across three lanes of traffic, ignoring the shrill honking of car horns all around him. She wills herself to believe that May is going to be a miracle. Not a miracle sent from a glorious Heaven above, but a miracle nonetheless. A miracle created by herself, and by Leo, too, who, despite his temper and cowardice, possesses a great and enduring love for his daughter. But most of all, a miracle created by May, whose will to survive is ferocious.

Her mother continues to study her as if she's a lab specimen, and May cannot figure out what her mother's problem is, since everyone knows that she's getting better. Just last week Dr. Brophy made a big point of telling her, without stuttering even once, that she's making a "wonderful and quick recovery."

True, she's not yet allowed to go back to school or to venture outside on her own, and some days she feels weak and faint, and then it's difficult to walk. But surely it's the piercing and dangerous x-rays, themselves, that cause this, even though supposedly she has no "side effects."

True, her eye is back to normal, but the tremor in her hand hasn't gone away; sometimes it seems to be getting worse, and then she wants to scream because her body is like a chaotic, alien thing over which she has no control.

True, too, there's the terrible flap on her head, a soft spot that requires her to be very, very careful. "Do not," Dr. Brophy warned, "allow yourself to fall or injure it in any way. The doctors had left open an area in her head about the size of her hand, covered only by a flap of skin. That way, if the tumor grows back, it won't grow inward, which is "far worse than outward," she'd heard a doctor explaining to a nurse when they thought she was asleep. But why *should* it grow back? She's baffled; everyone keeps telling her that it's all gone and, anyway, that it wasn't even cancer.

Frequently, it occurs to her that she is being lied to, that neither

her parents nor the doctors are telling her *The Truth With A Capitol T,* and maybe she does have the Big C, like Mrs. Aptheker, the Assistant Principal who got sick and died when May was in fourth grade. And like her mother's sister, who died before she was born, and for whom she was named. But her parents have repeatedly told her that her tumor was "benign, not malignant," and that this is a very good thing. The only reason she needs all these x-rays, they say, is because the doctors want accurate pictures of her brain in order to monitor her recovery.

At the next red light, she sees a black man and a white woman sitting in the car stopped alongside theirs, and her heart cries out for Dawn, her interracial best friend, who was sent home from the hospital just a few days before she was—on the same day the creepy, bonier-than-ever, Suzette also went home. May has called Dawn twice since then, but both times Mrs. Winston, sounding exhausted and dazed, said, making May's heart clench, "Oh, honey, Dawn will be so happy that you called, but she isn't well enough to come to the phone." May asked her own mother what was wrong with Dawn. "Don't lie to me," she'd warned, but all her mother would say was, "Dawn's operation wasn't as successful as yours. Still, don't worry, she'll be fine."

Her father cuts wildly in front of a thick-mustached taxi driver who gives him the finger. Luckily, her father, who's already absorbed in trying to veer back into the lane he just came from, doesn't notice. In the past, he has pulled over and started fistfights with drivers who disrespected him—or whom he *believed* had disrespected him.

May stares out the window and sees a boy her own age standing on the corner, wearing a wool cap pulled tightly over his ears, and she suddenly yearns to know what kind of winter hat Marvin is wearing this year. In sixth grade, he wore furry grey earmuffs; in fifth grade, a herringbone cap with flaps. If only he would come see her, the way he's supposed to. It crosses her mind that Emma hasn't given him the letter, although when May questions her, Emma scratches her nose, chin, and neck and says, "I swear." But why should she trust Emma, the girl who would do anything to hold onto her place as the favorite in the family?

Of course, May knows that it's within her power to pick up the phone and call Marvin any time. But she won't—he must rid himself of all feelings for Bonita, and he must be the one to come to her. He must be cleansed of all his dirty thoughts; he must come to her fresh and new.

Still, if he visits her, he'll see the horrible flap on her scalp, her short, choppy hair, and her trembling, old-lady's hand. Nevertheless, God will make sure that he finds her beautiful, and that he understands her state is temporary. God will show Marvin that, having suffered like Job and met His challenges, she will be an even better wife and mother.

Instead of Marvin, however, it was Bethie Zimmerman who'd called last week and asked if she could come to visit, but May said, "Not yet, Bethie. Soon." It was crucial that Marvin see her before any of their peers, so that he didn't hear about her looks second-hand from anyone else. But, she was glad that Bethie cared. When she was better, she would introduce Bethie to Dawn, since Bethie had proved herself to be loyal and worthy. As for treacherous, two-faced Bonita, May would never speak to her again.

She has received two get-well cards since she's been home. One from Mr. Dirty Old Man Roshansky, of all people. "To a fine young lady," he'd written in a script as precise and elegant as her own used to be, "feel better soon. Yours truly, Samuel Roshansky." Her ears rang loudly as she read his words, and she wondered if he had guessed that she now looked like a survivor of the camps: bald head; haunted, disbelieving eyes.

"Isn't that nice of him?" her mother asked, smiling as May read the card. May was too confused to respond; was he sincere, or did he just think that this would make her more inclined to let him grope her breasts in the future?

The second card had come yesterday, from her homeroom class. *We Miss You!* it said in raised gold letters on the outside, and on the inside, spread across a fuzzy watercolor image of a butterfly, her teachers and all her classmates had signed their names. It was juvenile, an inappropriate card for their ages. Marvin's signature on the butterfly's pale pink wing, dangerously close to Bonita's, had been an insult, and she'd angrily thrown the card away. Had he and Bonita sat close together, side-by-side, thighs grazing, hands finding each other? Did they mock her behind her back, make fun of her lazy, wayward eye? Just thinking about it now, her stomach hurts, and she sighs loudly as her father turns a corner, causing Emma's Puke Bucket to smash hard into her ankle.

She has, however, actually had one visitor, her father's friend Cookie Coke, who simply appeared a few days ago, ringing the doorbell, apparently startling her mother so much that she'd led Cookie into May's bedroom, although May had explicitly told her, "Other than Marvin, I want no visitors."

May was sitting up in bed, wearing her least favorite nightgown, a mustard-colored, jersey number purchased by her mother. Halfheartedly, she was playing a game of solitaire, when Cookie burst into her room, grinning widely and wearing a bright yellow dress that revealed what May's mother would call, "much too much" of her breasts. She strode toward the bed and sat down beside May, fluffing out her yellow dress so energetically her silver bracelets rattled. Turning her face to look directly into May's eyes, she said, "Honey, trust in God, and there will be bright times ahead. Just look at me, a lonely widow getting married again!"

Astonished, May sat rigidly against the headboard, not wanting to crowd Cookie, breathing in Cookie's intoxicating, fruit-scented perfume.

"I, a woman with few prospects," Cookie went on, taking May's hand in her own, "met a man from my country, who asked me to marry him, but I said no, because there was another man . . . ." Cookie's large brown eyes grew watery, and May quickly shut her own eyes, not wanting to see Cookie as anything but exquisitely happy.

"But it was a mistake for me to say no to this man," Cookie went on, and May opened her eyes to see Cookie's full lips curving into a wide smile. "So I called him and said, 'God calls me to you.'"

May ran her fingers through her short, butchered hair, hoping that Cookie, sitting so close, wasn't turned off by how she looked.

"And you, my dear girl," Cookie went on, staring into May's eyes with increasing intensity, now softly stroking her hand, "your dreams of love and romance—all your dreams!—will one day come true!"

May closed her eyes again, content to feel Cookie's soothing hand upon her flesh, and wishing that Cookie—religious, sexy, and un-migrained—were her mother. A loud noise startled her, and she opened her eyes to the sight of her real mother in the doorway, wearing her ugliest housedress, a ballooning, stained monstrosity. Her hair was a mess, her face pale and tired. "Cookie, thank you for coming." Her mother's voice held no warmth.

Cookie's cheeks turned red, but she rose graciously. "Of course, Annette," she said, surprising May by knowing her mother's first name.

As her mother coldly watched Cookie sidle past her, out of the room, May saw that her mother was as jealous of Cookie as she, herself, was of Bonita. Mother and daughter were not so different, after all, when it came to affairs of the heart. And yet, her mother was more of a stranger to her than the exotic Cookie, whose mysterious, unexplained visit today was a "Get Well Gift" from God.

30

The late afternoon winter sky is streaked bright orange and pink. Almost a month has passed since May's release from the hospital. Emma and Shelley's thighs stick to their shared seat inside the school bus that's bringing them home from a class trip to the Hayden Planetarium at the Museum of Natural History. Viewing the stars, glittering like sugar cubes, in the Planetarium's vast velvety sky dome, had made Emma shiver with delight.

"Children," Miss Harper, eyes dancing, had announced that morning, as the class piled into the school bus taking them to the museum, "For homework, I want you each to select a constellation from the Planetarium's sky, and to write a poem about it."

Now, homeward bound, the bus wheezes to a stop at a red light near the Bronx Zoo, and Emma feels sorry for the young, acne-ridden driver who has to maneuver such an ancient vehicle through the bumpy, pothole-filled streets of the Bronx. Just then, Shelley taps her hard on the knee. "My poem is going to be about Orion's belt," she announces sternly, "so you'd better choose a different constellation."

Emma is impressed at Shelley's attempt to be the bossy one, although she bristles a bit at being told what to do. Nevertheless, *The Truth With A Capital T* is that she doesn't care which constellation Shelley chooses to write about, since she's already decided to write about the Big and Little Dippers. She's silently composed a first draft: *You are like sisters/Traveling together through the thick blanket/Of the nighttime sky.*

The plodding school bus starts up again, lumbering slowly through traffic, beneath the elevated subway tracks along White Plains Road. Bobby Gaglione and Charlie Ludwig, sitting directly behind Emma and Shelley, loudly start to sing "One Hundred Bottles of Beer On The Wall," and then Shelley joins in, and all the other kids do too, except for Emma, because her nose suddenly itches, and she needs to scratch.

She smells gasoline and starts to feel slightly carsick, and, still scratching, breathes through her mouth. She remembers when this damned itching began, back at the hospital when May handed her the letter to give to Marvin, which she still hasn't given to him, although she's not sure why. Is it because she fears that all he'll do is sneer? And that he'll show it to Bonita and they'll laugh and mock May, with her trembling hand and that awful soft spot on her head? If either of those things happen, May would just lay down and die, and then her blood would definitely be on Emma's hands.

Or, maybe she's not concerned about May at all, maybe it's the bad witch inside her that is still not satisfied, that craves even more revenge, and keeping this letter from Marvin is one more drop of vengeance upon May, beyond death, into eternity.

Or maybe it's some of both, good witch mixed up with bad. Will she ever truly know her own heart? If she became a good Jew, would she at last know herself in all ways?

At last, the bus comes to a lurching stop on Magenta Street, and everyone stops singing. The gasoline odor fades, and Emma resumes breathing. Miss Harper, wearing a pretty paisley scarf tied under her chin, in the style of one of Grandma Thelma's *babushkas*, stands up, thanks the driver, and says brightly, "Remember, class, write your poems tonight. And I'll see you all tomorrow!" Miss Harper is so ceaselessly enthusiastic and perky, that for the first time Emma wonders if Miss Harper is insincere, only pretending to be such a fun sort in order to win the children over. She hopes not. She prefers to think that Miss Harper's love for poetry, teaching, and children is genuine.

When it's their turn, Emma and Shelley step outside into an almost stormy, brisk wind. Emma finds herself staring directly into the almond-colored eyes of Marvin Ludwig, who's wearing his duffle coat, and a Yankees baseball cap that doesn't cover his bright pink, cold ears.

Emma gasps. Has God sent him to meet her? Is this an opportunity? Or a punishment? Or, as her father would have it, "random coincidence?" No matter, she knows that she has no time to waste. The time has come, and she must act, whatever the consequences. Urgently, she whispers to Shelley, "Go ahead without me. I'll catch up."

Shelley looks bewildered until she glances at Marvin, and then back at Emma. She opens her mouth as if to speak, but then, with a loud exhalation, closes it and obediently starts trudging up the hill.

Fumbling slightly, Emma reaches into the pocket of her pea jacket and pulls out May's letter, which she's been carrying everywhere with her, even though it has crossed her mind a number of times that May one day might discover it on her, might sniff it on her like a dog hunting for food. And then May would know that Emma had repeatedly lied to her, and whatever fragile, beginning trust had been building between them would be shattered. But what choice did Emma have? She'd had to take that risk, just in case she ever spotted Marvin again and was able to find the courage to act. And now is the time, before Charlie steps off the bus and spots his brother.

"Marvin Ludwig," Emma says, her voice cracking, "this is for you." She thrusts the letter at him. Her chin is itching like mad, as if a thousand bugs have alighted on it. Politely, Marvin says "Thank you." He seems remarkably unfazed, so matter of fact that Emma wonders if he's been expecting this all along. Is it possible that he and May really do have some kind of quiet and private understanding?

A few isolated snowflakes are starting to fall, and one lands on his long eyelashes. He blinks, his eyes shine, and for the first time Emma, seeing how handsome and glistening he is, recognizes what May sees in him, this golden boy, sweet and polite to all, even to younger sisters who have previously made fools of themselves in his presence.

He pockets the letter, before walking past her. "Hey, Charlie," he says, not missing a beat, "Mom wants us to go to the store."

Emma's heart feels sunlit as she runs off to catch up with Shelley, who has already made it halfway up the hill without her, despite the wind.

31

Awakening side-by-side in bed, Leo and Annette yawn and stretch in unison. It's Saturday, a few days since Emma, unbeknownst to them, gave Marvin Ludwig May's precious letter. Moving as one, they lean against the wide, wooden headboard of their queen-sized bed, and turn, again in a silent unity that feels to Annette pre-ordained, although that's not possible, and she knows it. Together, they look out their bedroom window, at a stunning, blue-black, pre-sunrise sky.

To Annette's surprise, Leo reaches for her hand and begins to massage it, the way he often used to when they were first married, when he readily held her hand at the movies, during long walks in Prospect Park, at political meetings and rallies. Rhythmically and urgently, his fingers rub her palm. "May is strong," he says, "and she'll pull through."

So rarely does he speak like this to her, revealing his thoughts about himself or their children, that she doesn't know how to respond. A lock of dark, wavy hair falls over his eyes, and he looks like a Jewish street kid all grown up into a sexy, moody leading man.

Even as she allows herself to fully experience the unexpected tenderness of this moment, she wonders whether Leo is saying this about May because he believes it to be true, or because he wants to encourage her, to give her hope, to lift her spirits with a lie. Either way, she's deeply moved, and grateful. With her free hand, she strokes his strong, muscled arm, her way of saying thank you. She will choose to believe in what he is saying, that it is his new gospel, his new *Truth With A Capital T*. And so it shall also be hers. Their daughter will pull through.

Leo, who's enjoying his unguarded moment of intimacy with Annette as much as she is, believes, absolutely, at least for this moment, in what he has just said about May. As he continues to massage Annette's hand, still soft and youthful despite years of washing dishes and scrubbing floors for her family, he hopes that, for his daughter's sake, this godless world will prove itself to be a just and fair place, and that he, and his family, and Cookie, will all find their way to happiness.

Just the day before, Cookie's brother, Khenan, had come into the store with his wife, a plump, quiet woman, and their three sons, aged three to nine. The boys strutted like peacocks in identical navy-blue coats and derby hats. All three were handsome, but the middle son had toffee-colored eyes and an irrepressible grin that reminded Leo of Cookie. Looking at the boy standing tall and proud, his hat at a jaunty angle, Leo felt sore all over—even his mind, he thought, was sore and aching and bruised.

"We're on our way to visit Jennie's cousin," Khenan explained to Leo, pointing with his chin at his quiet wife, and taking a puff of his fat cigar, "and we need some goodies for the trip."

From behind the counter, Leo watched Khenan warily, waiting for a sign that he knew, but he seemed friendly and natural … Unless it was an act, to trick Leo into … what?

Khenan leaned over the counter and clapped Leo heartily on the back. "Have you heard the news about my sister?"

Immediately, Leo leaned back, out of Khenan's reach, hiding the tumult of emotions within him. Khenan did know, which meant Cookie wanted revenge—which Leo didn't fully blame her for—and soon Annette would know, too, and then, on top of living with the knowledge that her daughter is dying, she would have to live with the knowledge that her husband has been with another woman. Leo feels impotent, powerless, and he hates himself for feeling this way.

"Cookie," Khenan went on, walking over to his wife and wrapping his arm across her shoulder, "is affianced."

Affianced. The old-fashioned word brought Leo up short. Had he misheard? Dizzy with nerves, he waited.

"To one of my husband's boyhood friends." Khenan's wife spoke for the first time. Her dark eyes lit up, transforming her passive face into an animated and beautiful one.

Khenan waved his cigar around expansively, and his three boys giggled at the sight. "They're fascinated by my smoking," he said to Leo, rolling his eyes in mock exasperation. The boys giggled harder, but then grew wide-eyed and serious as Khenan paid for three bags of jellybeans and three bags of potato chips.

Khenan's wife lingered after the others had gone. "Cookie told me ..."

Leo steeled himself: So, it was the sister-in-law in whom Cookie had confided her affair with Leo; it was the sister-in-law who would betray him to Annette.

" ... about your daughter. I am so sorry." Slowly, she shook her head from side to side, and then followed her family outside.

Now, in bed next to Annette, he gazes once more at the stunning morning sky, then lifts her hand to his mouth and allows his lips to graze it, an old-fashioned, courtly gesture that seems to surprise them both equally. *Do not think about Cookie.*

Emma, in her bedroom, awakens just a few moments after her parents, and she too sits up and stares out her window at the same black winter sky. Like them, she is stirred by its beauty. Surely a sky like this means that today will be an important day, a day of reckoning of some sort, although she doesn't fully understand the meaning of the phrase. She stares at May across the room from her, fast asleep in her bed, her short, growing-in hair sticking out in funny little tufts, breathing heavily and coarsely in a way she never did before she got sick.

Suddenly Emma knows exactly what she must do. She must return to the Immaculate Conception churchyard; she must pay another visit to the statue of the Virgin Mary, because Mary is the only one who will tell her once and for all whether she has caused her own sister to fall ill. Real or imaginary, true Mother of God or inert statue, it doesn't matter — Mary sees inside Emma's head. There is no one else to turn to.

Despite the fact that she knows it's dangerous for her to venture back to the Church, she must brave returning. And this time, if she's turned into a Catholic, and if she isn't able to wash the Catholicism from her skin with Jewish water, so be it. It is meant to be, and she will have to reconcile herself to a life as an outcast from the Jews, an outcast from her family, and perhaps even from her self.

Quietly, she rises, grabs her blue jeans and a turtleneck sweater from the floor where she'd thrown them the night before, and tiptoes to the bathroom. She brushes her teeth with greater care than usual, then washes her hands and face, again with uncharacteristic diligence. She will be fresh and sparkling as she faces Mary, a young girl open to an infinite array of endless possibilities.

As always since the onset of May's illness, she studies herself in the mirror, touching her scalp and forehead, worried that something invisible and tiny, unwanted and unbidden, may be growing there. How can she be sure that she doesn't have what May has, that "tumor," her parents call it, mumbling and barely able to speak the word. Does what May have grow in families, in sisters, especially, even those not bound by love?

At least there's nothing visible, no bulge, no drooping eye. She's probably safe for another day. She dresses quickly, then walks to the kitchen, putting on her most innocent face so as not to arouse the suspicions of her parents. Not that they care what she does these days. Their whole world is consumed by May. She sits across from her father, who's reading the newspaper, or, more likely, pretending to read it, using it as a shield against his family, as he so often seems to do these days, and gulping down the last spoonful of thick, milk-oozing, nutmeg-and-cinnamon-laced oatmeal in his bowl.

"After breakfast, I'm going to Shelley's," Emma lies, spreading margarine on the toast her mother silently places before her.

Her father doesn't say anything, doesn't look up from the paper, because he's busy trying not to think about May, trying to absorb himself in the news, to pay attention this morning: the latest racial incident in Alabama; LBJ approving air raids over North Vietnam; a liquor store two blocks from his own store robbed by three armed men in masks, and he wonders whether it's time to apply for a gun license, whether his store will be next.

There's no question in Emma's mind that he has lost all interest in her, in her day-to-day activities, in her poetry, in her art, in the way she looks ... He no longer calls her his "Semitic beauty," no longer compares her face to Helen of Troy's, "that launched a thousand ships." Something she never dreamed could happen, has happened: She is no longer his favorite child. This is both terrible and wonderful. She is sadder, and freer, than she has ever been.

Her mother, sitting at the table sipping a cup of unappetizing looking black coffee, also pays no attention to Emma's announcement, and simply continues to gaze into the distance. Emma feels like a ghost of a child, existing outside of everyone's vision and concern. If she became a Catholic this time, no one would care.

Annette, perfectly aware that Emma wants attention, blows on her coffee, wondering whether one day in the future Emma will make her pay for these days of disengagement, but it's a risk she must take.

Emma rushes through her breakfast, chomping down on her toast, eating so fast she practically chokes. Would either of her parents notice if she turned blue in the face and couldn't breathe and died right before their eyes? She tosses her napkin onto the table, trying to stifle her anger. Best to remain beneath whatever remnants of Emma-radar either of them might still possess. She walks quickly to her room, throws on her jacket, and then is flying out the door, now eager to get away from them.

Far too impatient to wait for the elevator, she races down the eleven flights of stairs, holding the banister, leaping over two-three-even four steps at a time, flying across landings as if she's truly grown wings.

Outside, the morning sky is still that eerie blue-black color. True winter weather has finally arrived, and the air is so cold that, despite thick woolen mittens, her fingers are already feeling icy. Not many people are out, just Manny the Garbage Man, who's getting into his car and doesn't see her, and an elderly woman in a coat that falls all the way to her ankles, who reminds Emma of Hannah Zelig. Could she be Hannah's sister, coming to pay an early-morning visit? Emma has heard from Rachel's mother that Hannah Zelig has a terrible, lingering cold. "Poor Hannah," Rachel's mother tsk tsked, "such a life she's led. Why her, why not us? Who knows?" Emma knows perfectly well that Hannah's family was killed in the camps, and that she's all alone in the world. Well, maybe this woman is an old friend of Hannah's, even if she's not a sister, and maybe her visit will help to cure Hannah of her cold.

The elderly woman pays no notice to Emma, and Emma focuses once more on her own plan. She crosses the street, careful to look both ways for cars. She cannot risk being hurt on this momentous day. She begins to retrace the steps she took last August, which feels like a trillion eons and centuries ago. Her heart beats quickly as she walks all around the church and into the yard itself, barren and dismal in the cold. Walking along the narrow path, she passes the squat white building, as well as the wading pool that's now bereft of water. It's so cold she can see her own breath, and she wipes her runny nose with her mittened hand.

And then at last, she comes to the statue. "*My* statue," she thinks. Mary is as beautiful as Emma remembers: her haunting, wise eyes; her tender mouth; her glowing, otherworldly hands. In Mary's presence, the sky seems silvery and smoky.

Literally jumping with joy, her feet rising of their own accord, Emma feels both intimidated and exhilarated. Back on earth, she curtsies as gracefully as she can, dipping and curving her body, then, standing upright, gathering her courage, presses her hands together in prayer position, and silently asks: *Did I make May sick? Or did God?*

She waits, but there's no response. She tries again. *Is May going to die? Do my parents hate me?*

No answer.

Mary's expression is utterly and bewilderingly closed to her. Emma, face raw from the cold, feels desperate. She presses her hands together so tightly they hurt.

Fat tears cloud her eyes, and she lets them drip onto her lips and chin. Why is Mary rejecting her? What has changed since last August, when Mary was so kind? Is it because Mary sees now that Emma truly *is* bad, that she has worked dark magic upon her sister, that her heart is black at its core, rendering her undeserving of kindness? Or is Mary simply fed up with every one of the crazy Rosens, the whole *meshugane* bad-Jew group of them?

Defeated, Emma hangs her head. She feels like a lost, abandoned puppy, all alone in the world, unable to fend for herself. Tears stinging her eyes, she heads quickly back along the path the way she came. But as she exits the churchyard onto Gun Hill Road, she sees someone heading toward her. A big man, red-faced, in a checked, flannel jacket and woolen watch cap.

"What are you doing?" her father shouts angrily, moving more quickly toward her, jangling his car keys in his hands, his voice hard like a fist, his mouth like a fire-breathing dragon's. The exposed tips of his ears are a hellish scarlet, and through his jacket Emma can see his chest heaving. He must have been heading to work, a very, very bad break for her.

"I just stepped inside the churchyard for one minute. I was on my way to Shelley's." She can hear how false and unconvincing her own voice sounds. Not only is she a bad witch and a bad Jew, she's a bad liar.

Roughly, he grabs her by her arm and begins dragging her along the street. "No child of mine sets foot inside a church!" he says. "No child of mine is that weak." His eyes are blazing, and he's beginning to hit her, slapping her face. At last, she has captured his attention. Blood rises in her throat. She hates him with all her heart. Despite herself, she begins to cry, to shriek with pain and rage. Tears scald the inside of her nose, her lips are flooded, and her face squeezes tight. She will never be able to stop weeping, as though the sole reason she exists is to weep, to be a human river.

Inside the elevator, he's still hitting her, punching her in the shoulder, his blue eyes squinting in anger, as if he can't bear to take in the whole sight of her. His mouth is curled in a sneer that exposes his teeth like an animal's. She *must* protest, must tell him that visiting the Virgin Mary is neither a crime nor a sin, and that anyway it doesn't matter, since Mary wouldn't talk to her. She will tell him that even Mary has grown sick of her.

But her shoulders and her face are burning, she's bitten her own tongue, and she's seeing glittering, flashing stars, the way characters do in cartoons. Her body is one giant bruise. Even her eyes smart. Words—precious, glorious words—have become lost to her. She cannot speak to defend herself. In his rage, he has stolen all her words.

Leo opens the apartment door and throws Emma inside. A part of him watches himself in horror, but at the moment it's a very small part. Mostly he sees and feels the cold white heat completely surrounding him, returned and as familiar as a second skin. He's shaking with rage, his pulse races, his heart ticks rapidly inside his chest. An image from one of his most persistent nightmares comes to him: his father with the stinging Cat O'Nine Tails, his own battered flesh. This enrages him more, and he begins to kick Emma as though she's a sack of garbage that's gotten in his way.

Annette has come rushing into the living room from the bathroom, where, on her hands and knees, she was scrubbing the bathtub. She stops short as she sees Leo, who, for no reason she can fathom, is beating Emma with a ferocity she hasn't witnessed in years, slapping her relentlessly across the face, punching her, even kicking her.

A rush of air rises in her throat. This brutal man, with this distorted, inflamed face, is her husband. How can he be the same man whose warm breath she inhales across her pillow like an elixir each night?

A rustling sound beside Annette; she looks up, and there is May, standing next to her, wearing one of her frothy nightgowns, her face pinched and tired, her pitiful, bunched-up hair sticking to her scalp. Her lazy eye seems to be careening about, with a fierce will of its own.

For a moment, Annette focuses all of her attention on May instead of on the cruel scene in front of her. She struggles to read May's expression, but it's inscrutable, like a pool of still water. Is she distraught and horrified by Leo's behavior, or is she glad to see her younger sister suffering so much, since she herself has been through such hell?

But then poor Emma, wailing and screaming, commands Annette's attention once again for the first time in a long time. Emma, whose skin is flushed and wet, breathes loudly and hoarsely, gasps for breath, like someone having an asthma attack. Annette grasps her hands so tightly together her knuckles whiten; she wants to rush over and hit and kick and punch and slap her own husband, to do to him the very things he's doing to their daughter.

One thing Annette does know is that this time, for the sake of both her daughters, she must stop him. He might forever injure her child, irreparably, forever, causing damage that nothing, not love, not time, not medicine, can ever undo. Once and for all, her own fears must crumble, like dead leaves at her feet. She must transform herself into a woman of strength, at least for this one desperate moment. She hears herself yell fiercely, "Leo, stop it! Now!"

Stunned, he immediately stops. He steps back, staring with surprise at his own hands. The cold white heat around him begins to evaporate. A tear streaks rapidly down his cheek, and this amazes him. He can't remember the last time he cried. A sharp tingling begins at the base of his neck and runs along his spine, then down his legs and directly into the soles of his feet. He feels as though his entire body, his entire being, has been asleep for a long, long time, and is finally coming back to life.

May, who's beginning to feel slightly dizzy, stifles a tremor in her hand. She has been terrified, she realizes. Although terrified of what—and why—she doesn't know. Why should she care what happens to the Emma, who has undoubtedly been lying to her about having given Marvin the letter. If she had her full strength back, she herself would beat the shit out of Emma. Yet, the truth is that at this moment she does care, doesn't want to see more of this, and she feels a momentary sense of reprieve—although reprieve from what? This she doesn't know, either.

Emma sniffles, wipes her eyes, curls her hands into fists, stamps her feet in a furious rhythm. Sweat pools beneath her arms, and she feels a tremor of rage throughout her body. She yearns to explain herself, to declare, once and for all, her innocence before her family, and before Mary, and God, too, if they exist. She tries to speak, but her jaw aches and her throat closes up. Words stream into her head, too many for her to make sense of. She opens her mouth again, collapses onto her knees, and howls like a dog. Where are her words? She opens her mouth again, and this time her throat releases. "I am not bad!" she shouts. The sound of her own voice, although loud and shrill, is nevertheless soothing and comforting: She has stolen her words back from her father and reclaimed them. She collapses once more, now sobbing with as much happiness as rage and sorrow.

32

On Valentine's Day, the entire Rosen family is having breakfast together, which is an occasion, and it is Leo who has insisted upon it. He quickly eats three slices of the thick, buttery *challah* French Toast Annette has prepared, then sips his coffee while watching the others eat. Annette, head down, not meeting his eyes, eats her food mechanically, almost as quickly as he; May takes a bite, but then begins to push it aimlessly around on her place. Once he might have yelled at her for wasting food, but not today. May's appetite has become, for him, a focal point. He notices her eating every day. He's become her coach, her champion. *Eat*, he wills her to do, like a Jewish mother, and this fact doesn't embarrass him.

As for Emma ... Leo has been aware of how unusually quiet she's been around him this last couple of weeks, not showing him any new poems, not laughing and flirting in his presence. She's been like this ever since the day he hit her—well, more than merely hit her, he acknowledges to himself—ever since the day he used his hands so savagely and *beat* her because of something that, in retrospect, he has to admit hardly deserved such unprecedented wrath. So what if Emma is curious about religion, and Catholics? They live surrounded by Catholics who speak of Church and God and Jesus Christ—why *wouldn't* she be curious and intrigued? Doesn't he want her to have a lively, inquisitive mind? In the end, she'll follow his path, no matter what means take her there, no matter what byways she ventures down. She's too smart, and too strong, not to come around to his way of thinking and viewing the world, no matter how seductive the drama of Catholic ritual may be for a girl her age.

She will always be *his*. She will always remember that it was he who recited Shakespeare, Poe, Shelley, and Keats to her when she was in diapers, he who taught her about the garrulous Ancient Mariner and the romantic highwayman who rides, rides, rides for the love of Bess, the landlord's black-eyed daughter. It is he who has been preparing her to grow strong and tough and resolute, to help her to survive in a world without God or gods; it is he who has loved her beyond reason since the day she was born.

He watches how purposefully Emma eats her meal, with no apparent self-consciousness, seeming to be relaxed once more in his presence. In her typically slow, deliberate manner, she drenches her French toast in syrup and butter, pausing to sprinkle cinnamon on the soft, egg-soaked bread, clearly savoring every bite. Sometimes in the past, her slowness at meals has driven him crazy, but not today. Today, he is tolerant and forgiving, made magnanimous by love.

Emma is acutely aware that her father is staring at her. She sees the quizzical arch of his dark eyebrows, the questioning look in his eyes. At this moment, it becomes too difficult for her, too painful, to hold onto her anger at him any longer. Withdrawing from him means living without his praise, without his endearments. Who else will ever whisper to her that her eyes are "bluer than the most beautiful sea on the planet," and that, "like Cleopatra's," her features are "proud and dazzling?" Living without his attention and adoration is unimaginable. Without those things, she is simply too lonely. Without them, she's a poem stillborn.

Of course, she's still afraid of him, still vigilant in his presence, and even, she has to admit, still somewhat angry. Nevertheless, she finds herself opening her eyes wide for him, trying to look as innocent and appealing as perky Lily when she won the heart of the puppeteer in the movie.

Contentment floods Leo as he watches Emma deliberately batting her eyelashes at him like a film ingénue. He and she will always have their special connection. Whatever else may happen, no matter how terrible, the two of them are bound together. And so today he intends to celebrate. Not just his connection with Emma, but the way his heart swells and pulses, the way it expands with love for his whole family. To his surprise, he includes his sisters, Brenda and Evie, who have been as damaged as he by their parents. Perhaps more so. He thinks about how devastated they would both be if Freddie were ever to fall as ill as May, and about how their love for that boy is as genuine and deep as his for his two daughters—and how that is worth something. Maybe it's worth enough that one day he'll be able to forgive them for their inability to come to his aid. Maybe one day he'll be able to help them to grow as he hopes he is growing. Or, perhaps he will never forgive them, never try to help them. Perhaps their actions, or lack of actions, are unforgivable. He has a lifetime ahead to figure it all out.

He has never before felt like this, never before wanted to celebrate Valentine's Day, even though like Christmas, it means good business for the store. But it's always struck him as a phony, *bourgeois*, totally commercial holiday. "My three Semitic beauties," he says, not trying to conceal his excitement, "I have something special for you."

Annette, across the table, finally looks up at him, squinting slightly. He appears blurry and out of focus, and she's having trouble making him out. Her instinct is to be suspicious of his seeming transformation, but perhaps she's resisting too much. Today he's a strong, glowing planet, drawing his three girls closer and closer to his orbit.

He rises from the table, heading quickly to his bedroom, where he's hidden their gifts in the back of the closet: three heart-shaped boxes of the most elegant and expensive chocolates from the store, which he'd ordered especially for today, each box adorned with shiny, curlicue bows and ribbons.

Returning to the kitchen with the chocolates, Leo pauses for a moment to marvel at how breathtakingly lovely the three females in his life are, assembled around the table like a painting by Diego Rivera, his favorite artist. Annette with the exotic, white streak racing through her dark hair; May, showing signs of improvement, temporary though they may be—today for instance there's real color in her cheeks, and her short hair shows off the sculptured lines of her face; and, feisty, blue eyed, poetic Emma, his special, baby girl.

"Happy Valentine's Day," he says softly, presenting his gifts with a flourish, and he promises himself now at the breakfast table that if either May or Emma express envy over the candy that the other has—not an unlikely scenario—he won't allow himself to get angry, won't allow himself to give in to the cold white heat that so often engulfs him. He will honor the promise he has made to himself, and to them.

Leo's heart jumps with pleasure as Emma immediately tears open her crimson box, reaches inside and grabs a large strawberry-shaped chocolate. She bites hard, gleefully smearing her rosebud mouth in the process.

Annette looks at him with an expression he can't quite read. Puzzlement laced with tenderness, perhaps. "Thank you," she says quietly. "I'll save it for later." With atypical, refined, movements, she places her box on the table, then runs her pinkie carefully along the white bow in its center, and stands and begins clearing the plates.

May stares at her box, and at him, then at Annette and Emma, and back at him. Will she blow up, shrieking about how Emma got the better box, about how "mistreated and neglected" she always is? Holding his breath, he's a suitor awaiting a lover's response.

"Daddy," she finally says, unusually playful, blowing out her cheeks and imitating Jackie Gleason, "you're the greatest!"

As he lets out an audible breath, Leo feels tears in his eyes. This, he realizes, is what he was waiting to hear. He will do anything to make May happy, and he promises himself that next year—and there *will* be a next year for her, and a year after that, and, eventually, she will outlive him and grow old, changing all the while, from angry young girl to ebullient young woman, and finally to a creature old, wise, and more content than he himself will likely ever be. She, and Emma, and Annette, are mysteries that he will never fully be able to solve.

He promises himself that he will do something special for all three of them, not just chocolates, but abundant bouquets of flowers, and overflowing, many-flavored, ice cream sundaes dotted with cherries and sprinkles at Jahn's Ice Cream Parlour on Fordham Road, and maybe a night out at the movies, the four of them all together, something they haven't done in ages ... Now that he thinks about it, something they haven't ever done.

~

By late afternoon, the weather has turned milder, and a fierce sun is blazing through the living room window, shining on the faded rug. Two pigeons nestle together on the windowsill, and through the closed window, Annette hears them cooing like lovebirds, which is surely appropriate on Valentine's Day. On the sofa, leaning her stiff back against the soft pillows, she's taking a break from cleaning floors for what feels like the millionth time this month, and trying for one moment of one day not to worry about May, who's been all alone in her room since breakfast, as she so often is these days, refusing any company.

How unlike Leo, Annette thinks, his giving them all Valentine's Day gifts this morning. Although not unlike the way he'd been back during their courtship, when he'd written all those love poems for her, and painstakingly drawn her portrait in pen-and-ink, capturing the swirls of her long, dark hair, and the rise of her collarbone, titling it, *Vision Of My Own True Love.*

Since she'd stood up to him on the day he blew up so ferociously at Emma, he's been behaving more and more like the man he was back then. Although they haven't discussed it, she can see how hard he's working to change, and she is truly grateful. There's a word for what he's doing, but what is it? *Mellowing,* she decides. Maybe this won't last long, this mellowing, this leaf turning over, this metamorphosis, since it's mostly May's terrible illness that is precipitating this change in him. She has no illusions that he's a brand new person. The legacy he carries from his own parents can't be erased overnight, may never be erased. And yet May's illness has stirred inside him what some would call "the fear of God." She prefers to call it *humanity.*

He's still Leo, of course, still volatile, but less so. No violence. And to some extent, a large extent, she has to admit, the volatility is part of his charm and appeal. She doesn't want him to become someone else; she wants him to remain her Leo, unpredictable and boyishly impulsive, charming one moment, didactic and obnoxious the next, passionately opinionated and obtuse. But she wants him not to be cruel. Never cruel. She wants him never to lay a hand on either of their children again. She wants him to love their daughters equally—and she will try to do the same. As he has favored Emma, she has long favored May. And for herself, she wants his respect, not just his love.

Does the transformation in Leo mean, too, that the specter of Cookie Coke will no longer haunt their marriage? She heard from Shelley's mother, Tessa Gould, whom she ran into the other day in the laundry room, who had run into·Cookie the week before at the beauty parlor, that Cookie has fallen in love and is going to be married.

Now, Annette slowly opens her box of chocolates, setting aside the glossy ribbon and bow as mementos of this day, of his transformation, of her family's happiness for at least one brief moment. The chocolates, blooming like rich brown flowers amidst a silver garden of foil, are seductive, and her lips work in anticipation of their taste. Since the onset of May's illness, Annette hasn't allowed herself sweets of any kind, not her favorite candies from Leo's store, not the chocolate *rugelahs* from the deli on Allerton Avenue that she loves. She's come to believe that indulging in any kind of pleasure— even culinary—will make May worse. Another irrational superstition—how could a sweet piece of Jewish pastry foster the growth of her daughter's cancer? Yet, the rational world has failed her, and superstition—although never religion—may be all she has to cling to.

The doorbell rings, startling her. Probably a Jehovah's Witness. They infiltrate the Projects, going door to door with pious, otherworldly expressions, hawking their Bible-based Watchtower Magazines. She never invites them in, and May's illness will not change that. She will never join their ranks, nor that of any organized religion on this planet, no matter what tragedies befall her loved ones. She and Leo are forever united on this front; it's one of the strongest foundations of their love. Rubbing her lower back, which aches on a regular basis these days, and sometimes foretells a mighty migraine to come, she walks slowly to the door.

Looking through the peephole, she's not sure who it is. A young boy with a serious, intense expression. Has he come to the wrong door? But then she recognizes him—Marvin Ludwig, Aaron and

Julia's son, the boy with whom May is obsessed. Is he collecting for Boy Scouts, or, has he really and truly appeared in order to visit May? *Marvin*, she wants to say, *this is too little, too late.*

"Mrs. Rosen," he says, in a surprisingly deep, almost adult voice, when she opens the door, "I'm here to see May." His smile reveals teeth that shine like a row of small stars.

"Of course. Come in." Her politeness is automatic, not felt. She continues to rub her throbbing lower back as she leads him into the living room, with small, unwelcoming footsteps. "Wait here."

She knocks, then opens May's door, forgetting once again to wait to be given permission to enter. *I'm playing a role*, Annette tells herself. *The mother of a normal girl whose suitor has come calling.* Like someone from an earlier century, not the mother of an angry girl with brain cancer in a twentieth-century Bronx housing project.

In her bed, May is sitting up, wearing a short, ruffled nightgown. She scowls at her mother in the doorway. "You have once again violated my sacred rule about knocking."

"You have a visitor," Annette says, not apologizing for barging in, trying to keep her voice, like a straight line, even and unrevealing, trying to shield May from a moment of too much happiness, a moment that will not last. "Marvin Ludwig."

She's almost hoping that May turns him away; what if, once he sees her, he grows scared? That would devastate May, and possibly be the final straw that breaks the Rosen family's back. Doom and Gloom, their legacy and destiny, will be spurred on by this blonde, religious young man, still really a child.

What will he do when he's in May's presence? Children are terrified of cancer, of illness—adults are too, for that matter. Not that May looks bad or frightening in any way these days. She's not her old self, true, perhaps a bit worn for a thirteen year old, but you would never guess the truth just by looking at her. It will probably be fine for Marvin to witness her as she is; it may be just what she needs, the best medicine. In any case, this moment is really out of her hands. Her daughter's life is her own to live—even if is a short one, and at this thought Annette feels a wave of trembling through her own body.

May too feels a wave of trembling through her whole body, but for a different reason: Marvin has come to her. She should have known that he would wait for today, the day meant for lovers. She refuses to reveal the extent of both her excitement and fear to her mother. "Give me ten minutes to ready myself," she commands, "and then send him in." She's proud of the way she sounds, like Kim Novak playing an imperious woman with a heart of gold that's about to be mined. Gratitude toward Emma floods her—she hadn't lied when she said she'd given Marvin the letter.

At her closet, without hesitation, May selects her above-the-knee, tangerine-colored, Empire-waist dress, the one she's been planning all along to wear for him, because it makes her double-A breasts look fuller, almost like 34-Bs, and also because it shows off her shapely calves and slim ankles.

Effortlessly, she slips the shapely dress over her head and stares at herself in the mirror on the wall between her bureau and Emma's. She clasps her hands behind her neck. What to do about her short, choppy hair, the hair that has been growing in so irritatingly slowly since she was shaved bald at the hospital? She wishes now that she had bought a wig, like one of the nurses had suggested. But there's a girl who lives in the Projects, Cheryl Feruge, who lost all her hair to Scarlet Fever and who now wears a shiny red wig that often sits lopsided on her head. The meanest kids call her Baldy and try to pull her wig off. May would rather take a chance on Marvin seeing her as she is than risk becoming another Cheryl.

At least her hair has grown long enough to hide the flap—she hopes. She's been trying to convince herself that she resembles Kim playing a young Frenchwoman with a darling, boyish, pixie haircut, mischievous, fiery, and classy all at once. In fact, her hair is just an unholy, unruly mess. But … two plastic, bow-shaped barrettes, one on each side, and it *is* a genuine pixie and she *is* a fiery French girl, and that's *The Truth With A Capital T*.

Pale pink lipstick applied as neatly as possible with a hand that still trembles. What about jewelry? Grandma Thelma's pearls? No, old-fashioned and bad luck, since she wore them on Halloween. Later, when Marvin has left, she will throw those pearls out. She never wants to see them again. Anyway, her exquisite swan neck needs no adornment. Finally, she slips her feet into her white, teardrop shoes with inward-curving heels, the shoes she wore to her sixth grade graduation.

Gently easing herself onto her bed, plumping her pillow up behind her, leaning against the headboard. Breathing deeply, she smoothes the vanilla-colored blanket. *Regally*, she tells herself, *sit regally*. Back straight, head so high she could balance a teacup on it, hands delicately folded in her lap, legs crossed in front of her, she's a royal princess, a Hollywood bombshell, and a French pixie rolled into one delicious, irresistible package.

Here he is, standing in the doorway, stepping inside, closing the door, standing over her bed, not seeming to mind having to step over Emma's dirty clothes on the floor, his blond hair lustrous and gleaming, his posture as perfect and regal as her own, one hand behind his back, obviously bearing a gift, like the nice Jewish boy she has always known him to be, despite his dalliance with the two-faced Bonita.

May marvels at Marvin's broad shoulders, his fine white shirt, his dungaree jeans with their perfectly measured, rolled-up cuffs. She sees how he will look as an adult, in his crisp, white doctor's coat, so self assured and wise. If she ever gets sick like this again—not that she will, but if she ever does—he alone will be the one to heal her.

He doesn't blink, doesn't register any surprise at how she looks. Her breath freezes in her mouth. He's standing so close she can see an endearing little mauve-colored pimple forming on his chin. Exhaling at last, she closes her eyes, savoring and memorizing his scent. Today he smells of bananas and vanilla, fruity and sweet, not unlike Cookie's perfume. She will remember and treasure this scent for the rest of her life, as if it's a butterfly to be preserved in a book.

And what of her own scent? If she can inhale his, he can surely inhale hers. Not that of a sick girl, she hopes. Not sour and old like the hospital. Maybe peaches and cream, sugar, spice and everything nice. Her stomach burns with excitement. And terror. *Let him find me beautiful*, she prays directly to God, who sometimes seems to hear her, and sometimes not. Let this be a time He does.

"These are for you," Marvin says. His eyes are luminous, and he hands her a box of Sweethearts, those tiny, pastel-colored, heart-shaped Valentine's Day candies, the ones her father orders for his store by the caseload at the beginning of February, with romantic mottos inked on them: *U Are Mine 4-Ever; Too Cute 2 Be 4-Gotten.*

She reaches out to accept his offering, willing her arm not to tremble, grateful that her fingernails are meticulously polished, a lovely tangerine color that, not coincidentally, matches this dress she knew she would one day soon be wearing in Marvin's presence. "Thank you," she whispers, her voice perfectly sexy and husky. God is listening to her. He is here, in this room with her. She is indeed one of His Chosen. Today — Valentine's Day — is a true Day of Awe.

Gently, she places Marvin's box beside her, hardly believing that she has received two marvelous gifts in one day. "I knew you'd come," she says.

"Listen, I'm sorry ..."

His words are halting, and he hangs his head, something May has never seen him do, and she feels a flutter of fear that he will leave.

"What I mean is ... I'm sorry about that other time ... in the laundry room." He raises his head, meets her gaze squarely.

She uncrosses, then re-crosses her legs, hoping he's observing the sliver of thigh she exposes. She's about to ask him *why, why* he fled from her in the laundry room, but before she can, he has joined her on the bed and is leaning over and kissing her with his full, banana-scented lips, and then it no longer matters why.

She removes her eyeglasses, and kisses him back as expertly and genuinely as she can. Their lips briefly flutter, then come to rest upon each other, finding what they need. Her heart clenches and then unclenches as he runs his fingers through her choppy hair, and she worries for an instant about what will happen if he touches the flap. But his fingers intuitively avoid that spot. This is the happiest moment of her life. She could die right now, and it would be okay. For one moment, in his arms, she thinks of Dawn, who's back in the hospital, and she wishes she could describe this happiness to her. She wishes she could assure Dawn that she too will one day know such bliss.

And at that very moment, Emma, just home from school, opens the bedroom door. She stands in the doorway, her heart stirred by the sight of May's awkward body gathered in Marvin's golden arms. They are kissing as passionately as Lily and the puppeteer in the movie, their bodies perfectly entwined, as if they will be together for eons and centuries to come, their love the stuff of poetry and dreams.

Very, very quietly, Emma closes the door, wanting to protect them from her mother, who, moments ago, when Emma had come home, was frenetically cleaning the kitchen floor on her hands and knees, and who would not be happy, were she to witness her sick daughter so uninhibited in a boy's arms.

But what should she do now? Where should she go? To Shelley's, she supposes, to offer comfort, since—and this was another big surprise—beautiful, black-eyed Shelley hadn't received a single Valentine's Day card at school, although Emma had gotten two, one from Bobby Gaglione and one from Lester Ryan, a boy she barely knows, whose father is a fireman, a fact that seems suddenly extremely interesting.

On her way outside, walking as softly as she can, Emma passes the kitchen and sees yet another astonishing sight: her mother, hair tousled, in one of her loose-fitting housedresses, leaning against the refrigerator door, eyes closed, not doing a thing, not cleaning the floor or putting away groceries or defrosting the refrigerator or washing dishes, but looking, for the first time that Emma can remember, at peace.

As soon as she's outside, Emma decides she really wants to be alone, not with Shelley or anyone else, in order to better savor this day of extraordinary surprises. Instead of going to Shelley's, she decides to take a walk along White Plains Road, not venturing too far, so she won't incur her father's wrath, should he find out. Despite his newfound calm, she doesn't fully trust him, and isn't sure she ever will.

It's about four o'clock, and the sun is starting to set. The air is cold and invigorating, and she blows her nose. For once she has remembered to bring her handkerchief, and isn't that another awe-inspiring thing? Her chest puffs out with pride-- she's growing up, not needing her mother to remind her to do every little thing.

As she walks through the Projects, a sharp ache floods her insides, and her excitement vanishes as suddenly as it arrived. Abruptly, let down and deflated, her body becomes too small a container for this unexpected sadness. *Double double toil and trouble,* she whispers, trying to comfort herself, and she hears in her head the words to a song that her mother sometimes sings in her off-key voice: *Que sera, sera, whatever will be, will be ...*

Where is her sadness coming from? Why can't she hold onto happiness when it strikes? Will she always be a girl whose moods flip flop from sunlit yellow to deep sea blue, whose yearning for the unknown flows through her veins, leaving her never full, never content?

She thinks of May upstairs in the arms of the boy she loves, and she wonders whether, like Poe's Annabel Lee, who resides for all eternity in "her sepulcher there by the sea," and who was loved deeply and madly by Poe, or at least by his *persona,* as Miss Harper has taught her to distinguish, May is a tragic heroine, surely destined to die young, despite the brave lies their parents speak ... And if May is doomed, isn't Emma, herself, also doomed? Doomed to be forever scorned and unloved by her own sister, who will never forgive Emma for having been born?

She feels her chest rising and falling with each breath she takes. Quickening her pace, she exits the Projects and crosses Gun Hill Road. Overcome by enormous sorrow, she yearns to know the future, to know that she and May and her parents will survive. She never wants to be completely alone, never wants to be completely unloved. She remembers the questions she had asked the Virgin Mary on the day Mary refused to speak to her, and, at last, she understands Mary's silence. Wasn't Mary — or whomever it is who speaks to her through Mary—trying to tell her, by not answering, that asking the questions is far more important than knowing the answers? But if that's true, then the world is a terribly dangerous place, more dangerous than she has previously imagined, filled with too many unknowns, too many unmarked twists and turns, too many cliffs to fall over and too many oceans in which to drown. How will she ever feel safe enough to grow up in such a world?

Emma holds her breath, waiting for the answer to her questions to come to her in the form of a bolt of lightning, or a booming, thunderous voice addressing her directly from the sky. But there is no lightning, no voice; instead, gradually, the sharp, unsettling ache she's feeling begins to fade, and taking its place is yet another astonishing thing, a glow that spreads and expands and feels like sunshine and moonlight and starlight swirling all around together inside her, like magical ingredients in a witch's brew.

Emma stands still on the corner of Gun Hill Road, staring up at the dusky wintertime sky, feeling as if a thousand lines of poetry have taken root in her heart. She ignores all the people passing by, treasuring this unexpected and wonderful feeling she has no name for. Despite the odds against it, she will survive—no, she will do even more than that—she will blossom and thrive. A word comes to her, one she's read in books but has never spoken aloud: She will *transcend.*

Something Emma doesn't know yet, of course, as she stands on the corner of Gun Hill Road, is that one afternoon, a little over a decade away, she'll be sitting at her very own desk in her very own apartment, not downtown in bohemian Greenwich Village, where she always had assumed she would live, but further uptown, in a more affordable neighborhood she'd barely heard of back then, in the very northern reaches of Manhattan. Since moving to this neighborhood, she frequently visits the nearby Cloisters, the uptown branch of the Met, looking for inspiration which never fails to come at the sight of the Medieval unicorn tapestries and the museum's lush, cultivated gardens.

On this particular winter afternoon, she will sit at her second-hand, wooden desk and she'll remember this long-ago, marvelous moment when she was a child in the Bronx.

Staring out her narrow window at a dusky, shadowy sky not so very different from the sky above her back then, she will begin to compose in her mind a poem about her sister, that brave, sometimes cruel, deeply troubled girl, gone these many years, a poem that is, at its heart, about the complex, mixed-up, sometimes daunting, sometimes exhilarating, natures of both love and faith.

As it happens, Emma's poem about May will be her first to appear in a magazine, and she will be very proud of it. Leo and Annette, now in their fifties, will also be very proud, so proud that they'll read it aloud to each other many times in their spacious, brightly lit, Upper West Side apartment, which is filled with photographs of both of their daughters—the apartment into which they moved a few years after May's death, shortly after Cookie Coke, living in New Jersey with her accountant husband, sent Leo and Annette a birth announcement of her twin sons, and shortly after Leo acknowledged to himself that he would never finish his novel, and shortly after one of the Sweets Brothers slept with the other's wife, and their opulent candy store closed its doors forever, allowing Leo to pay off his debts.

But, for the moment, ten-year-old Emma Rosen, who knows nothing of her future, stands still in the bracing air on the corner of Gun Hill Road, aware that she is experiencing something extraordinary, and she finds herself marveling, for the very first time, at all the things that are *right*, not wrong, with the Rosens.